WILLIA

NAP-TOWN'S DIRTY LITTLE SECRETS

ISBN 978-1-959450-81-8 (softcover)
ISBN 978-1-959450-82-5 (ebook)
Library of Congress Control Number: 2022922483

Printed in the United States of America.

Book Vine Press
2516 Highland Dr.
Palatine, IL 60067

To those who believed in doing what's right
Thanks

CHAPTER 1

Time—the only constant in our lives eventually runs out for one and all. It is elusive; we never know from one moment to the next when time has run its course. Time is like an hourglass that slowly trickles down into a lower chamber if left alone, unimpeded with constant velocity, eventually coming to an abrupt ending.

Juan Grajales' life was like that of the hourglass running the gamut. He looked at things for what they were, not as they appeared. Juan Grajales had a mind cluttered with thoughts of how to change the solitary survival mode he now lived. As a high school dropout with no hope for the future, no job, or even a prospect of one, had he been destined to wander aimlessly through this dirty, unforgiving city day after day, searching for that pot of gold at the end of an elusive rainbow?

After dropping out of school, his parents banned him from home after stealing a cherished diamond ring from his mother's jewelry box. It was not the first time Juan had taken things from their home, but the ring—that was the coup de grâce. It was the only remaining item of her mother's she revered. His parents were tired of helping Juan, who had trouble controlling his impulse. Stealing became the straw that broke the camel's back. They banned him from home until he proves he had learned his lesson. Juan became an outcast, another statistic, living in the backstreets and alleyways, surviving as best as he could, coping with his new role in life that was brought about by tough love. He wandered the back alleys of this large metropolis and searched miles of dirty trash bins and alleyways, looking for food or anything of value. As of now, it was his only means of survival. He wandered aimlessly throughout the dirty city, day in and day out, like countless derelicts who called this callous and unforgiving town home.

Winter was fast approaching; temperatures, dropping noticeably as it grew colder daily. Sleeping outdoors was a challenge, especially as the cold winds of winter slowly descended from the north. Juan was not fond of the outdoors and even less now that winter was on the doorstep. This part of the country could be brutally cold, something he was not prepared for, not now or ever.

One cold morning, while wandering through the alleyways, he chanced upon a most unlikely character, Al. Al and he crossed paths that cold and daunting morning, changing Juan's life.

Juan stepped from an alleyway and walked to the crosswalk before crossing the street. Al, standing alone on a deserted street corner near the liquor store, had just purchased a halt pint of Four Roses whiskey. Al started each morning with a stiff drink he liked, referred to as nectar of the Gods, just as Juan appeared on the corner. Juan noticed Al leaning against a light pole, holding in his left hand the half-pint bottle, still wrapped in a small brown paper bag. Al reached down with his right hand and removed the cap, raised the bottle to his lips, and took a drink of the golden liquid inside. Juan was standing near the crosswalk as Al removed the bottle from his lips.

Al looked over at Juan and asked, "Hey, buddy, care to join me for an early morning toast? You name it, and we'll toast to it."

At first, Juan refused Al's otter by turning away.

Al asked Juan a second time, "Hey, buddy, care to have a drink with me? it'll help warm you up, looks like you could use something to warm your insides. You look mighty cold."

Juan, realizing just how cold he was, thought this might not be such a bad idea-anything to help warm him up. The temptation was too great to pass up, so he accepted Al's offer.

After drinking from the bottle, he handed it back to Al. At that point, they struck up a conversation.

Al looked at Juan and asked, "What are you doing out so early this morning, roaming the streets?"

"I've got no money, been looking in the trash containers up and down the alleys for anything to sell and make enough money to buy something to eat."

"If you are strapped for cash, I could possibly help. That is, if You're interested.

"What is it you can do to help me earn a little cash?"

"Well, I worked for an organization which collects protection money from local merchants here on the south side. Is that something you would consider?"

Juan was hesitant at first, but after learning more, plus a couple extra swallows of Four Roses, decided to take Al up on his offer.

Al screwed the top back on the half-empty bottle and stuffed it inside his overcoat. Al then reached over, putting his arm on Juan's shoulder as they moseyed down the street to a local dive to meet Ivan Cohen, better known as Boss Man. Upon entering this damp, musty, smelly establishment, Juan followed Al to the rear of the bar, where they entered small dingy, dirty, smoke-filled office.

Juan was already having second thoughts as they entered Boss Man's office. Unsure if he would regret accepting Al's earlier offer, time would be the judge.

Al introduced Juan to Ivan, a short, tat, grubby-looking fellow with beady eyes and two days growth of facial hair, who was smoking a large Cuban cigar.

Boss Man looked up and saw Al and Juan standing in front of his desk and asked Al, "What do I owe this visit by you two so early in the morning?"

"Good morning, Boss Man. I've brought a potential trainee l met earlier. I've discussed the collection business with him, and he seemed interested."

"Good morning, young man. What's your name?"

"Juan."

"So, Juan, you think you would like a shot at working in the collection business?

After talking with Juan and listening to his answers, Ivan liked what he heard and Juan's seemingly calm demeanor. He decided to give him a shot collecting alongside Al starting that morning.

Juan was not quite sure of what he had gotten himself into, but he was committed after giving his word. Juan was not looking forward to spending the approaching winter outside, roaming the cold, dirty streets.

At least, this job allowed him to earn money and to afford to eat and a stay at a cheap hotel room. It was better than living outside on the cold, mean streets of Indy.

After his introduction to Ivan, Al and Juan walked outside and found a bench near the corner and sat down. Al once again went over the job description, which Juan was now committed and ready to embark upon. Al explained in detail what he and the organization expected. It was not the job Juan had anticipated, but hearing Al's spiel on collections, he, at least, was willing to give it a try. The job was better than scrounging around all winter, freezing his derriere off in those cold dark alleys and sleeping in beat-up old cardboard box he presently called home. After Juan's briefing to the good and bad side of [collectioning], he accepted the challenge and its consequences.

CHAPTER 2

After they finished their tête-à-tête, Al asked, "Would you like to go have breakfast?"

"Yes, I'm starving"

They got up from the bench and walked to a small restaurant nearby. Upon entering the restaurant, Al casually looked around, found a table in the corner to sit, and continued talking. After being seated, a waitress came to the table, carrying a fresh pot of hot coffee and two cups, then asked, "Would you fellows like coffee this morning?"

Al answered yes.

"And are you having breakfast?"

Again, Al answered yes. She set two cups on the table, filling both three-quarters full of hot coffee, then asked, "Would you like cream and sugar?"

"Neither, I like my java black," Al told the waitress. Juan looked at the waitress and said, "Bring me the sugar and cream."

Returning to the counter, she retrieved the sugar and creamer containers, then returned to the table, placing both containers in front of Juan. She removed an order pad from her apron pocket and the pencil stuck behind her ear, "Is this going to be one check or two?"

"One check," Al said. Al and Juan proceeded to give their orders. She scribbled the orders down and returned behind the counter, handing the order to the cook. She returned to finish cleaning the counter, and filling the salt and pepper shakers while waiting for Al's and Juan's orders to come up.

Meanwhile, Al and Juan talked about what had transpired earlier in Ivan's office. Juan was still apprehensive about the job but accepted the fact it was better than being jobless and homeless.

The job at least allowed him to earn money and, eventually, could lead to something better down the road, who knows? The job Al described was concerning to Juan. It would change a lifetime of values taught him growing up. He was not a mean-spirited person by any means, but he was now heading in an entirely different direction after accepting Ivan's offer. New rules and values would be forthcoming once he started work. He had to be heartless, merciless, and at times, downright cruel; which had not been part of his DNA. He thought to himself, If Al's capable of doing such reprehensible deeds, why not me? After all, it's just a job.

Breakfast finally arrived. Juan wasted no time digging in. It was his first hot meal in three days, and there was no time to savor the moment. Al continued his briefing as Juan ate. Al explained what he could expect from different merchants as they went about their collecting.

Al told him, "Don't worry. I'll teach you the ropes before you wander off and start collecting on your own."

Juan asked Al several germane questions while eating breakfast. Al answered his queries to the best of his ability, explaining in depth the ins and outs of the job and what was expected of him. It seemed overwhelming at the moment, but Juan was bright, perceptive. He would learn to accept whatever circumstances came with the territory and deal with them accordingly.

Being a newbie to this line of work, it would take time for Juan to become as efficient and confident as Al. After breakfast, Al settled the bill with the waitress and exited the restaurant. It was time Al initiated Juan to the collecting business.

The first place they went to was a local pawnshop not far from the restaurant. Entering the pawnshop, Juan noticed the proprietor was busy and did not acknowledge their presence. They walked to the counter and stopped. They made an intimidating-looking pair as they stood waiting to get the proprietors attention. Finally, he looked up and saw the two standing in front of the counter. This was not what the proprietor had in mind when he came to work that day, being intimidated by these two.

Al reached into his overcoat and removed a small ledger, turning the pages until he found the notes for the pawnshop owner's account.

Al then looked at the proprietor and told him, "My associate and I are here to collect your weekly dues. Do you have the envelope?"

The owner balked as always at paying but reluctantly decided not to rock the boat that morning as he handed over the large envelope that he placed under the counter earlier. Al handed the envelope to Juan while he wrote a note in his ledger. After the transaction, Al and Juan walked out the door without any further provocation.

Once outside again, Al turned to Juan and asked, "Have any questions about what just transpired inside the pawnshop?"

"No, not at all. It went down like clockwork. If that's all there is to this collection business, I am ready to jump in and get my feet wet," Juan replied.

"Not all businesses are that easy. Sometimes we cause a scene and, on occasions, have to rearrange the business. I infrequently raise havoc until the proprietor pleads to stop and ponies up. When property is destroyed, the proprietor understands, without it, he's unable to continue business. Basically, it's the only source of income the owner has and tries everything in his arsenal to protect his investment.

You must be prepared mentally and physically each time you enter a business. It's a new experience each and every time. Nothing stays the same. Occasionally, you'll catch an owner reluctant in paying because he's short on cash or disgruntled in paying. Things in this business change constantly. You'll learn to take the good with the bad, but you'll do fine.

"Be ready for anything-from owners trying to buy you off to threatening to call the cops. Sometimes they resort to violence themselves, pulling out their own personal weapons from under the counter, ready to end it right there. You have to be on guard to make it in this business. If an owner gets to you, and Ivan finds out, what happens next is not a pretty sight. You must be committed," Al told Juan.

With his first taste at collecting, Juan thought it was not such a bad choice after all. He and Al left the pawnshop and continued down the street. It was not long before they entered another client's store. Walking in, the clerk was busy with a customer. They browsed around until he finished. Once the customer made his purchase and left the store, Al approached the clerk and asked, "Is the owner around?"

"No, he is out. Will not be back for several hours. Is there something I can help you with?" the clerk asked.

"Did the owner by any chance leave an envelope with you?"

"Yes, what's the name on the envelope?"

"Boss Man."

"Yes, he left it on his desk in the back."

"I'm here to pick it up"

"Okay, I'll get it. Give me a minute."

The clerk walked to the office where he retrieved the envelope, returned to the front, and handed it to Al.

Al looked at the envelope, and when he was satisfied, put it in his overcoat pocket, turned once again to Juan. "Think we are done here. It's time to move," he said.

This completed their morning rounds, and as they were leaving, Al explained to Juan, "Occasionally, it's convenient for an owner to leave the envelope with whoever's in charge rather than waiting around to pay their dues themselves. We, as collectors, are not permitted to open and check the contents if the envelope is sealed. Only Boss Man has privilege to open the sealed packet. Sporadically he finds a note or an empty envelope, at which time, he'll direct the collector what to do next time he visits the store, making sure the proprietor pays up."

Juan was impressed at how the merchants cooperated with Al, and captivated at how smooth Al ran his side of the collection business.

Finishing the morning's collection, Al told Juan, "It's time to break for lunch."

It was none too soon for Juan, who was getting hungry. They were near the five-and-dime Al frequented on occasions for lunch.

They walked down the street and entered the five-and-dime, then went to the lunch counter, where they found two stools, and sat down.

A waitress came over. She leaned over the counter and said, "Hi, sweetie, long time no see. What can I do for you this morning?"

Al told her, "That's a loaded question? Ha ha. I'll have a chicken salad sandwich and a large Coke."

She giggled, as she turned to Juan, asking him the same question.

"A grilled cheese sandwich and a hot cup of coffee with cream and sugar."

Reaching behind her, where the cups were stacked, she picked up a coffee cup, then proceeded to the coffee pot sitting on the coffee warmer, filling the cup with freshly brewed coffee. With cup in hand, walked back to the counter and placed the hot cup of coffee in front of Juan. She turned again; this time removing a large glass from the back counter, filling it with ice and fountain Coke. Setting it on the counter in front of Al, she asked if there was anything else they needed.

Al replied, "No, not right now, but if I think of something, I'll let you know."

Al and Juan sat back discussing the morning's activities and how lucky they were at not having to confront or threaten anyone for late or nonpayment of dues. It had turned out to be a rather routine day so far. Al hoped it would stay that way, but knew their next stop would be a hassle. It always had been.

Juan, like Al, detested violence; but in this profession, violence was part of doing business.

Al told Juan, "I rarely resort to violence but do when necessary. I try to avoid it at all cost, but sometimes it's unavoidable."

CHAPTER 3

After lunch and leaving the five-and-dime, Al decided to let Juan try his hand at collecting. As they made their way down the street, a block or so south, they entered a laundry business owned and operated by an oriental named Wong. Mr. Wong had been a problem lately and was confrontational when paying his dues. Mr. Wong, standing behind the counter, was busily darning a small hole in a customer's jacket as they entered. Looking up at hearing the bell ring as the door opened, Mr. Wong saw Juan out of the corner of his eye, making eye contact with Al. Al could tell by the look in Mr. Wong's eyes this was not going to be an easy pickup, especially for Juan since he was the one doing the pickup.

As the two collectors approached Mr. Wong, Juan caught the attention of Mr. Wong by looking him straight in the eyes and said,

"Mr. Wong. I'm here to pick up the weekly dues."

Mr. Wong immediately began ranting and raving, "Why I give up hard-earned money, for what? I work hard for money. I tired giving away for what you call protection. Who needs your protection, anyway? You tell Boss Man I finish giving money 'cause I not need protection. Only protection I need is from Boss Man."

Al stepped in, trying to persuade Mr. Wong to do what was right and hand over his envelope. Again, Mr. Wong bristled and defended his accusations, "You go back, tell Big Man stick protection up his ass. I refuse give him any more money." Juan looked at Mr. Wong and told him in no uncertain terms, "I think you're making a big mistake, Mr. Wong. Next time we comeback, it will not be a social visit, understand?"

"Get out my laundry."

Leaving the laundry, Al stopped outside, removed his accounting log from his jacket pocket, and made an entry on what had just transpired inside the laundry with Mr. Wong. This had been Juan's first encounter with a dissatisfied and unhappy client. Juan understood the next visit with Mr. Wong would take persuading, not small talk. What happens next time would not be pleasant for Mr. Wong.

Al and Juan finished their day collecting without further incidents.

Returning to the bar, Al and Juan walked into Ivan's office where Al handed their daily take to Boss Man. Al removed his log book and read out loud to Boss Man what Mr. Wong told him and Juan to tell Boss Man.

Mr. Wong said, "Tell Boss Man, I done paying. He take his protection, shove up his ass. I no pay"

After hearing Mr. Wong's statement, Boss Man replied, "When you two revisit Mr. Wong's laundry tomorrow, make sure you don't leave empty-handed, understood? Do what you have to. Bring back the money Mr. Wong owes. Don't make me look bad. It not only reflects on me but shows the local businesses I'm not capable of con trolling my accounts. If we let this slide, others may revolt against paying. It is imperative this situation be nipped in the bud, capisce? You know what I expect of you tomorrow. I'm sure you two are capable of handling such a minor infraction. Now get out of here and do what I hired you to do."

CHAPTER 4

Leaving Ivan's office, returning to the street, Al and Juan decided on having an early dinner. Al told Juan he knew a local diner on Al's way to Al's hotel. They could stop there and have dinner before calling it a day.

Al looked over at Juan and asked, "By the way, do you have a place to sleep in tonight?"

"No, I've been sleeping in a large cardboard box filled with old newspapers I've collected to keep me warm at night. I sleep there when I don't have money for a room. It's not the best accommodations but suffices until I can get back on my feet."

"I'll tell you what, after dinner, follow me to the hotel where I bunk down occasionally. I'm sure they have an extra room. I stay there it I'm running late or my wife and family are out of town. You will be more comfortable there than in your cardboard box. Plus, with a hot bath and a good night's sleep, you'll be ready to start work in earnest tomorrow."

"I appreciate your offer and accept, was Juan's reply.

After dinner, they headed straight to the hotel, which was a couple of blocks south of the circle. Juan felt a sigh of relief as they entered the sleazy small hotel. It was not the Ritz, but an upgrade from the alleys he lived in. Walking into the hotel, the clerk on duty recognized Al.

"Good evening, Al."

Good evening, Sidney. I need an extra room for the evening."

The hotel clerk looked down at the chart on the counter for an available room, then back at Al and told him, "You're in luck. I just happen to have an empty room on the same floor as yours. It's down the hall. Nothing special but clean."

"Fine, Sidney, I don't know how long my friend will be needing it, but II let you know."

"It's his as long as he needs it."

"Thanks, Sidney."

The clerk reached over, pulled a key off the keyboard on the wall behind the counter, and handed Juan the key.

"Room 7, second floor, first room on your left."

Al thanked Sidney, and they quickly headed up to the second floor by way of the stairs. Reaching the second floor, Al pointed to number 7 and said, "That's your room. Mine is down the hallway on the right. If you need anything, let me know."

Juan watched as Al walked down the hall toward his room. Juan inserted the key in the lock and opened the door. First thing that hit Juan as he opened the door was a slight musty smell emanating from the small room, indicating the room had not been used lately. The room smelled of mold and mildew, but the last thing he was going to do was complain, at least, not tonight. It was semiwarm, not like the cold, uncomfortable cardboard box he normally bedded down in. Entering the room, he closed the door. The first thing he did was remove his coat, shirt, and pants. Then made a beeline to the bath- room where he took a well-deserved hot bath.

It had been several days since his last bath, and could not believe how good it felt. He didn't want to leave the tub, but as the water began cooling off, he decided it was time to get out, dry off, and get ready for bed. Once out of the tub, he looked in the mirror on the wall and hardly recognized the person staring back. Living on the streets had not been kind to him. In his travels up and down the alleyways, he had acquired a small comb with several teeth missing. but still useful as he run it through his wet long hair. Looking at his reflection in the mirror, he saw that his hair was much longer than usual. He was definitely in need of a haircut. He would get it cut later, but for now he was relishing in the moment. After bathing, combing his hair, brushing his teeth with his fingers, he proceeded into the small room, quickly crawling into bed. He found the sheets clean, musty, but soft against his body. It did not take long until he was sound asleep.

The next morning, around 6:00 a.m., a knock on his door woke him. He crawled out of bed and opened the door. To his surprise, Al pushed the door open, walked in, sat down, and told Juan, "Its time you get up and get dressed. We need to eat breakfast before we start.

Work.

"It l take me a minute to get ready." Juan walked into the bathroom, took care of business, splashed water on his face. He reentered the room and hurriedly dressed. It was not long until they were walking down the stairs, back through the small lobby, and outside.

Upon reaching the restaurant, which was nearby, they walked in, sat down at the counter, and ordered two cups of coffee and breakfast. As they sat at the counter talking, Al explained in detail what he expected today from Juan.

"You'll be collecting again today. I want to see how well you handle yourself in different situations you encounter. I need to know if you are capable handling the job Ivan hired you to do. I need to see how you're going to handle the irate Mr. Wong. I will be observing your style as you apply pressure on him to pay up."

Al knew this morning would be a huge challenge tor Juan. Was he calm and collected as he appears and ready to face adversity he found himself involved in? He showed little regard at what Al said earlier about facing Mr. Wong. Yesterday had been a teaser. What Juan would soon face with Mr. Wong today would become highly volatile.

Al mentioned to Juan, "Since Mr. Wong is behind in his dues, he needs to be taught a lesson. You are elected to perform that task. Are you up to it?"

"Only one way to know. Lead the way."

As Al and Juan finished their breakfast, they got up from the counter walked over to the cash register where Al paid the tab. Their first stop was Mr. Wong's laundry. Juan's job that morning was convincing Mr. Wong to pay his dues or suffer the consequences.

Entering the laundry, they saw Mr. Wong was busy placing a large load of laundry into one of the huge washing machines near the rear of the shop. After stuffing laundry inside the large industrial washing machine, he finally closed the door, locking it. Once the door was secured, he flipped a switch on the side of the machine turning it on. As he did, he looked over his shoulder; that's when he saw the two standing in front of the counter, waiting. He was frightened, intimidated, and infuriated all at the same time at seeing them.

Mr. Wong's first thought as he stared at them was what they were going to do to him for refusing to pony up his dues yesterday.

Once Mr. Wong and Juan locked eyes, Juan did not hesitate in sliding behind the counter, then proceeded to where Mr. Wong stood. Juan looked at him with a frightening stare. With somewhat of an authoritative voice, he asked, "Do you have the envelope for Boss Man, or are you going to be as problematic as yesterday?"

Mr. Wong did not wince and stood his ground, telling Juan once again in no uncertain terms, "I no pay more money to Boss Man for protection. I done paying."

Juan quickly changed his demeanor. Without warning, he gave Mr. Wong a hard backhand across the face, then with a closed fist, he punched him once in the face and, for good measure, a hard punch to the gut. Mr. Wong immediately bent over from the pain, his mouth now bleeding, his left eye beginning to close, and his gut pained from Juan's fist being thrust into it.

He fought back with words to no avail. Juan again punched Mr. Wong in his face and gut. It was evident after the last series of punches Mr. Wong had reached his tolerance for pain. The hurt he suffered at the hands of Juan was over the top. Mr. Wong, who had dropped on his knees on the floor, was having difficulty breathing. His nose felt like it was broken. A front tooth had been knocked out. A rib or two were cracked or possibly broken. It was difficult for Mr. Wong to tell the difference. Juan, standing over Mr. Wong and looking down at the pitiful shape lying on the floor in a somewhat fetal position, stopped his vicious attack. Mr. Wong, no match for these two thugs, had not raised his hand in anger. It would have been futile, possibly causing him more pain and suffering.

Juan had taken care of business, while Al was busy removing the freshly washed clothes from another machine near the front of the store scattering them onto the dirty floor. The clothes hanging on racks, which were cleaned and pressed, were removed and strewn throughout. The floor now littered with cleaned, pressed clothes, and the hanging racks along with other items essential in the laundry business were destroyed or damaged while Juan took care of Mr. Wong.

Mr. Wong, lying on the floor in excruciating pain, could hear the destruction up front, but unable to stop it. He looked up at Juan through his swollen eyes, tears running down his cheeks and holding his ribs with both arms, softly and almost inaudibly told Juan, "Stop. I pay up."

Mr. Wong eventually relented, giving in to Juan and Al's request. Juan stopped his attack immediately, reached down, and helped Mr. Wong off the floor. With Juan's help, Mr. Wong slowly walked into his small office, removed a paper sack from the top drawer of his desk, and counted out the monies owed to Boss Man. He stuffed the cash in an envelope, sealed it, wrote Boss Man's name on the front, handing it to Juan. Juan took the envelope with the money inside, telling Mr. Wong, "Next time, you'll not be so lucky."

They left the laundry and proceeded down the street, heading to the next business on Al's route. As they walked, Al told Juan, "I'm impressed with the way you handled Mr. Wong. It was textbook perfect [known as a score in the collection business]. I think you're going to be an asset to the organization."

CHAPTER 5

Juan, satisfied with his first encounter strong-arming a reluctant client, found it was not as hard as he imagined when accepting Ivan's offer. With his first attempt at collecting. Juan felt he was some- what of a natural and didn't realize how good he was until Mr. Wong handed him the envelope. At the end of the second day, they returned to the bar. When they entered Ivan's office, they presented him with Mr. Wong's envelope along with several others. Al explained to Ivan how Juan handled Mr. Wong and how relentless he went about business until Mr. Wong relented, handing over the envelope to Juan.

"Don't think our Mr. Wong will be any trouble after our visit this morning," Al told Ivan.

*****

Juan and Al continued working together, collecting dues for a second week. When the second week ended and they turned in the dues collected, Al asked Juan to leave, telling him, "I have something I need to talk to Boss Man about."

Juan vacated the office and left Al alone with Boss Man.

Once Juan was gone, he said to Ivan, "I Think Juan is ready for his own collection route. I don't know what else I can do to help him. He's able in taking care of business with a calm but forceful demeanor. Those whom he has had dealings with for the past week understand who he is and respect his power and control. Thanks, Al, for your assessment of Juan. It's helpful in my decision as to the where I can best utilize Juan going forward."

Ivan then asked Al to leave and send Juan back in. "I need to talk to Juan alone," he said.

Al left Boss Man's office and approached the table where Juan and Tony sat talking. Tony Dipalito worn many hats during the time He's worked for Ivan. After a near fatal accident, was no longer able in performing certain duties, Ivan assigned him as personal security inside the bar near Ivan's office. When Al told Juan, Ivan wants to see you.

Juan, puzzled at what was so important Ivan had requested him to return to the office, got up from the table and proceeded to Ivan's office. As Juan entered, he was told to come in and shut the door. Ivan looked up and told Juan, "Sit down. I have a proposition for you.

Juan sat on the couch when Ivan asked, "Would you be interested in being my personal bodyguard-driver? It's a full-time job, requiring you to be on call twenty-four seven. The bennies are well worth the extra time and effort."

Juan, taken aback at Ivan's offer, sat on the couch in awe. With his mind racing, trying to get a handle on what Ivan just said and giving it serious thought, he could not think of a single reason not to accept his offer. Juan told Ivan, "After thinking about what you've said, I can think of no reason for not accepting your generous offer. It sounds too good to pass up, and yes, I appreciate and accept."

"Good. Now that you've accepted my offer, your new position will require you to follow a new, stricter, and demanding code of conduct and behavior. As my personal bodyguard-driver, you will be required to know how to act and handle yourself when in my presence at all times, understand?

Yes."

"Okay. Next, I need to know, Do you have a valid driver's license?"

"Yes, it's valid through November of next year."

"Good. Since you've accepted my offer, you'll need a new set of threads." At that point, Ivan opened his safe, removed five hundred dollars, which he handed to Juan, and told him, "Go to a men's store. Buy yourself a couple of new suits, new shoes, and several everyday outfits.

Juan accepted the five hundred dollars, thanking Ivan again as he left the office. The first thing he needed to do was find a men's store and purchase a complete new wardrobe. He told Al and Tony he had an errand to run. He immediately left the bar and walked to the circle downtown, where he found a high-end men's store. He had never seen so many fine-looking clothes, so took his time searching for the perfect items to wear for his new gig. With the help of a salesman, he was able to buy two suits, several dress shirts, three pairs of everyday slacks, two pairs of shoes, and a new winter coat, plus accessories.

Before leaving, he told the store manager, "You can discard my old clothes. I no longer have a need for them."

"No problem, sir, I'll discard them as soon as you leave."

Wearing a new pair of slacks, a new shirt, and a new pair of shoes with the winter coat proudly hung over his left arm and with the remainder of the clothes in a large shopping bag, he walked briskly back to the hotel. When Juan entered the hotel, the desk clerk on duty looked up from behind the desk and was surprised at seeing him dressed in his new duds.

Juan asked for his key, which the clerk quickly retrieved from the keyboard, and handed it to him. Juan picked up his packages from off the counter and headed toward the stairs. Back in his room, he carefully hanged his new suits and shirts in the closet, placing the rest in the small chest of drawers in the room. After putting away his purchases, he went back downstairs to return his key and headed back to the office where Ivan was waiting for his return. When Juan entered Ivan's office, Ivan was surprised at how good Juan cleaned up. He was impressed with Juan's choice of clothing and his new look.

Ivan reached in his desk, removing a key ring with a set of keys to his Cadillac, handing them to Juan, who placed them in his pocket.

Ivan then told him, "Part of your new position is sitting in the bar area with Tony until I call you. You can do whatever you want inside the bar as long as it is between the front door and my office. That's yours and Tony's domain. Make sure whoever enters the bar does not get past you two without getting my approval first. You or Tony find out who's wanting to see me and what business they have to conduct with me. Absolutely, I repeat, absolutely no one is allowed inside my office without being frisked and approved by me first, understood?"

"Yes, Boss Man."

After Ivan instructed Juan on his new position, he then asked, "Is there anything you do not understand or have a question about what I told you so far? If you understand the guidelines I've given you, then get out of here and go to work."

"I understand the rules, and yes, I'm ready to go to work."

Ivan smiled at Juan, knowing he still had a lot to learn, but what better time than now to begin the program. With Tony's assistance and guidance, it would not take Juan long to grasp the totality of his new position within the association. With those two sitting between the entrance and office, anyone trying to reach Ivan's office without authority or approval would be in a world of hurt.

CHAPTER 6

Ivan's selection of Juan as his personal bodyguard was because of Juan's no-nonsense approach to work and work ethics shown by his past accomplishments, especially the laundry incident. Ivan saw the potential and knew he was the type needed in this business. Juan showed he was not afraid to tackle any job given him and finish it with positive results. Ivan needed somebody fearless like Juan, some- one whom he could count on when push came to shove, someone with no fear or remorse, someone he could trust to carry out his orders without blinking or complaining. Juan had shown those qualities and more. Ivan had been in business long enough to see these rare qualities Juan possessed. He was young enough to teach and learn yet old enough to carry out any unexpected encounters as they presented their ugly heads.

Ivan's last bodyguard-driver had been injured in a confrontation and no longer carry out the duties associated with being Ivan's driver. It was Ivan's lucky day when Juan appeared out of nowhere that morning with Al. Credit had to be given to Al's quick thinking after meeting Juan on that cold and wintery morning and asking, "Care for a drink?"

The job Ivan offered Juan carried a lot of respect and power within the organization. Juan would soon learn just how important his new position really was. Juan's position was second only to Boss Man's. He was on his way to becoming a reputable member of the association. Those associates around him would soon sit up and take notice as he becomes a force to be reckoned with. Most of Ivan's employees would have killed for this position, yet Juan was handed it on a silver platter, not realizing that when he accepted the position, many members of the organization would be resentful of the power and respect he now commanded. Being the new guy on the block, he would come under scrutiny from all sides.

Al had been with the group several years and, still, just a col- lector. He had had his eye on advancement within the organization, but nothing had come of it. Learning of Juan's promotion, Al would become one of Juan's adversaries to watch out for. Al would make Juan's job a living hell any chance he had. Al could be very vindictive; Juan was about to find out just how cruel and spiteful Al could be.

Juan, with the help of Tony, began learning the ways of new his job. Tony was to be his mentor, teaching Juan all the facets of his new position. Tony had been around a long time and wanted nothing more than to sit around taking care of his tiny corner of the business. He had no ambition or desire in climbing higher up the ladder inside the organization. Being a bodyguard-driver meant he would have less time with family, less free time for himself, and was not willing to give that up. He had taught several bodyguard-drivers prior to Juan and knew exactly what Ivan's expectation were.

Tony's job was teach Juan all aspects of his new job and how to carry out orders requested by Boss Man, completing each request in manner conducive to its mission. The position not only required protecting Boss Man around the office but around the clock. He was at Ivan's beck and call, day or night, twenty-four seven. His main concern was keeping a watchful eye out for trouble, making sure Boss Man was safe and never in harm's way.

No matter what came up, he was not to take any threat or situation lightly. Take care of business first, ask questions later. Take each happenstance seriously, act immediately, no ifs and buts. Ivan did not take his security lightly; he expected to be protected in any inescapable circumstance he found himself involved in. He expected his bodyguard-driver to protect him from any form of violence, including murder it necessary. Juan was Ivan's go-to man and was to react instantly to any situation in the blink of an eye, without hesitation or reluctance.

Tony would instruct Juan in the many aspects of security, including the use of weapons, self-defense, offensive- and defensive-driving techniques. Each area of expertise would be covered in due time. At present, Juan needed to learn the basics to begin with. It was a huge commitment on Juan's part learning each area and becoming proficient in each segment from the ground up. Ivan had the ability to see in Juan something special. That's why he chose him over the others. There was a lot to learn, but Juan was gifted, committed to weathering the storm-one he was about to face just over the horizon.

CHAPTER 7

Juan, promoted after only a couple of weeks with the organization, had a hard row to hoe within the association. Many felt more qualified and voiced their displeasure, while others held back their reservations.

The following morning. Juan opened the door to the hallway to leave, saw Al out of the corner of his eye walking toward him. Juan finished locking the door and turned to face Al. As their eyes met, Juan could tell Al was upset and felt the tension as they met.

Al spoke first. "What the hell did you say to Ivan? How were you able to convince him to promote you so quickly? Did you kiss his ass? What gives? Why did Ivan suddenly select you over so many others who were more qualified and deserving of the position, including me?"

"Maybe, Al, it was your version on how I handled Mr. Wong after I beat the hell out of him, d'ya think?"

It was a tense moment standing in the hallway face to face. Al knew nothing would be settled this morning, so he quickly changed the subject.

Al then asked Juan, "Are you having breakfast before going to work? If so, why don't we walk over to the café and have breakfast together?"

At that moment, Juan felt the tension ease somewhat.

"Sure, don't know why not. Well get through this thing together. As far as I'm concerned, nothing's changed between you and I. I still owe everything to you for what you did that morning we met. You were a godsend. Trust me, I'll do what I can to help you anyway I can within the organization. That's a promise."

After a short conversation in the hallway, which seemed to be fruitful, they proceeded down the hallway to the stairwell, into the small lobby, and out the door, heading for breakfast as they had each morning Since Juan joined the organization.

Juan thought having breakfast with Al would lessen the tension that had been festering between them. Sitting in the café, Al immediately brought up Ivan's choice for his new driver.-security job. After discussing it at length, both agreed it had been Ivan's decision, his alone, after all, he was the boss.

Juan recapped Ivan's choice to Al in a way he hoped Al under Stood, ending with, "That's the way things happen sometimes, Al. We'll never know the real reason. You'll have to accept Ivan's judgment and move on. Life does not stop because of a promotion.

Al related to Juan that Ivan had always run a successful business, and up to now, no one ever questioned his decisions. But since this latest promotion, there was a lot of discontent among the rank and file after they found out. Al continued, "I've worked tor Ivan several years, and I've never seen him promote someone as unqualified as you to number two. The ones waiting for this slot were shocked at seeing him promote the newest hire to that position. It doesn't make sense to us his reasoning for doing this. Understand our position?

"Yes, I see your point, Al, but it was Ivan's decision, and he apparently felt he made the right choice. I feel bad for you and the others. But it was not my doing and everyone working tor Ivan has to live with his choice."

Juan's promotion weighed heavily on Al's mind as they parted ways that morning. A knew he had no recourse in the matter, so he needed to drop the subject. It had been Ivan's decision; he had to abide by it or move on. It would not gain him brownie points with either Juan or Ivan by pressing the issue. Certain problems had to wait and be addressed later as things settled down.

Later that day, as other coworkers learned of Juan's advancement, they, too, were disappointed at the newbie being selected. Passed over once again, along with Al, they had to suck it up it they wanted to stay working tor the organization. Life was not always fair. They had to abide by Ivan's decision or move along.

Al, as he started off alone collecting that morning, began thinking to himself, *With Juan close to the helm, maybe it is not such a bad thing after all, knowing how Juan felt about me being instrumental in finding him and introducing him to Ivan. If I play my cards right, I can talk to Juan about related jobs within the association as they open up. Maybe, I now have a better chance of landing one. I can go through Juan to talk to Ivan on my behalf and help me move up within the organization. I've had my eyes on several jobs in the past. When they became available, I asked Ivan, but for some reason, he never showed interest promoting me. With Juan's help, I stand a better chance in landing one, time would tell.*

Upon leaving the restaurant that morning, Al was back to working alone and collecting as he had for the past several years. Meanwhile, Juan headed to the garage to pick up the car and headed over to picked up Ivan. As he approached the garage, Juan thanked his lucky stars at not having to pound the streets this morning collecting. It was much too cold and miserable to be out walking the streets all day. He was thankful to Al for finding him as he aimlessly wandered the cold streets looking for scraps to eat or things to sell. It was not the kind of life he envisioned.

It was the beginning of a new day for Juan, excited about his promotion and indebted to Al for giving him this opportunity and fulfilling a dream. Juan had something exciting and something new to look forward to every day-a good job.

As he entered the garage, he spotted the red Caddy; he could not wait to get in and start her up and begin his new occupation. He opened the heavy door of the Caddy, crawled behind the wheel, and closed the door. With the key in hand, he inserted it into the ignition, turned the key, and suddenly the car came alive. The hum of the powerful V-eight engine was sweet music to his ears. Juan slowly backed the car out of its assigned parking space toward the entrance, turning onto the street, heading north to pick up Ivan.

Ivan lived in an exclusive gated community about twenty-minute drive from downtown. It did not take long for the car's heater to warm the inside of the car. It certainly felt good inside the warm car, not like walking the cold streets.

Burr, he thought.

Upon reaching the community where Ivan lived with his family, he slowed, turning on his turn signal as he made a left turn into the entrance. Driving up to the gate, stopped the car, rolled down the window as the guard came out of the guard shack, and asked him whom he was there to see.

He told the guard, "Tm Juan Grajales. I'm here to pick up Mr. Ivan Cohen."

The guard checked the roster for his name, upon finding it, raised the gate arm, and Juan drove through the opened gate, arriving at Ivan's house at precisely 8:00 a.m. While Juan was pulling into Ivan's circular driveway, Ivan was walking out his front door. Juan stopped the car, quickly jumped out, and opened the right rear door. Once Ivan was inside and comfortably seated, Juan shut the door, walked back to the driver's side, slid back into the driver's seat, closing the door.

"Good morning, Boss Man," Juan said.

Ivan acknowledged, but nothing more.

It was a quiet ride across town with minimal traffic. Timing the traffic lights as he drove, they reached the bar in short order. As they approached the entrance to the bar, Juan stopped alongside the curb, got out, and opened the door tor Ivan. Ivan exited without a word and walked inside the bar, never looking back. Juan got back in the car, drove back to the garage, and parked the car in the same parking space he took it from earlier. After parking the car, Juan walked back to the bar. As he entered the dark and musty-smelling bar, spotted.

Tony sitting at the table. Tony smiled at Juan and motioned him over.

As Juan reached the table, Tony said, "Good morning. Juan, how was your trip over to Ivan's this morning?"

"Everything was copacetic. I kept a watchful eye out, in case we were followed, but saw nothing."

"Glad you kept close tabs on that. It is important you keep a close watch on your surroundings while driving with or without Ivan. As I have told you, you can never be too careful or cautious in this business."

Tony was glad at having Juan around not only as backup but to teach and talk with while keeping an eye out for anything going on in or near the bar. Tony enjoyed teaching newbies the right and wrong way in looking after Ivan. The stressful demands Ivan placed on subordinates closest to him were almost over the top.

Tony enjoyed the one-on-one sessions, teaching what he knew of the other side of the business. Having worked years for Ivan, Tony knew every quirky thing Ivan had in his arsenal, plus enjoyed relating them to the newbies. First on Tony's agenda this morning was make sure Juan understood the importance of Ivan's strict dress code. With his new assignment came certain stringent protocols associated with his advancement.

CHAPTER 8

Juan's character and demeanor showed in his wiliness to take care of business without prompting. He displayed to Ivan and others his ability to change like a chameleon from a ruffian in street clothes to a Dapper Dan in his new threads. His persona was a plus in appeasing Ivan's sometimes quirky demeanor. Last, but not least, Juan's allegiance to Ivan and Al showed in that first couple of weeks he worked.

Ivan wanted his top employees not only to look smart but act accordingly, as if they were the upper crust, yet fearless and relentless in any situation they were involved. Ivan, a man of means, expected respect from all his employees and accomplished this, in part, by the company he surrounded himself with. Juan was off to a good start by his actions, which he displayed during his short association with the organization.

Tony's List of dos and don'ts for Juan this morning was how to properly carry and shoot his personal sidearm, using it to its full potential in any self-defense setting he found himself involved. Juan, having never owned or discharged a weapon, had to be taught the basics prior to carrying his weapon. Tony made sure both Juan and his weapon were prepared when called into play.

Juan joined Tony at the table. Tony slowly reached inside his jacket and removed his weapon from the shoulder holster he was wearing. With his weapon in hand, began explaining the basic rules pertaining to cleaning, carrying, and firing a weapon.

Tony stressed to Juan that "safety is the most important aspect of carrying a firearm."

As he continued his lesson, he slowly removed the dip from his gun's grip handle and placed the fully loaded clip on the table. With the weapon in his left hand, Tony pulled back the slide mechanism with his right hand, extracting the shell inside the chamber. He then handed the weapon to Juan and asked him to inspect the chamber to make sure it was clear.

Juan examined the chamber, telling Tony, "I see no round visible inside the chamber"

This meant the weapon was secure.

Tony continued, "Take a good look at the weapon. The safety is located near the trigger. Always keep it in the locked position when not in use. When cleaning or working on your weapon, make sure it's never loaded. That's how most accidents occur if this rule is not followed. Now that you've checked the weapon thoroughly, I'll proceed to dismantle it. Remember, safety is paramount when handling your weapon. When finished with dismantling the weapon for cleaning or replacing a part, simply reverse the procedure. It should fit together just as smoothly.

"Once your weapon has been reassembled, you are ready to reinsert the clip back into the grip handle, but never pull the slide back until you are ready to use it. And always leave the safety on until the weapon is ready to use. A most important rule to remember is, never draw your weapon unless you intend on using it. The next day or two, we'll take a ride out to the firing range and let you get the feel of firing your weapon while you work on your target practice at the same time. That's the only way you'll learn to shoot accurately and correctly.

"Next on my list is being vigilant when certain activities around you occur without becoming distracted. There are times you'll need to be fully focused and in total control of your surroundings. You must not become distracted by nonissues with situations you find yourself involved. This is critical. You must be totally focused on the status quo and nothing else. Little things, which are distracting, could spell disaster not only for you to Ivan. We don't want that to happen. I'm giving you a list of things to do, and I expect you to learn each item thoroughly, backward and forward in the next few weeks. Do you have any questions?"

"Yes, does Ivan have you do this for all his newbies or personal security people?"

"No, only the ones he surrounds himself providing him protection. Now that you're aware of your agenda for the next few weeks. Remember what I've shown you here this morning and memorize the list frontward and backward. By this time next month, you'll be ready to take on any given situation you're faced with, without hesitation. Now let's talk about why Ivan chose you.

"First, he was highly impressed with your handling of Mr. Wong at the laundry. He saw the potential and liked what he saw. You earned his trust and admiration immediately by the way you handled that situation. He wanted to reward you for your no-non- sense approach in carrying out assignments given you. Plus, it met his high standards of allegiance you showed without being coerced by Al. If you work this methodically in the future, you'll reap the paybacks many times over.

"Few in the organization are given a chance like he gave you, even after years working for him. Ivan felt there was something special about you, that you were different, a notch above the others. Your acceptance of a task without question is not found in most people he hires. You showed him from the beginning you had what it takes and up to any assignment without question. Even when he offered you this position, you did not question him or his reason behind his action. He likes those who do not question his authority and are willing to do whatever it takes to get the job done. That's what he saw in you. Let's go into Ivan's office and find out what's on his agenda for you today."

They walked back to Ivan's office, finding him busy with collections from the previous day. Ivan looked up as they entered and told them, "Have a seat. I'll be with you shortly. I have a few things left to do. Make yourselves comfortable until I finish.

Ivan completed his count from yesterday's collections. He put the receipts along with the daily dues in a large bag. Rising from his desk, he walked over to the safe, opened it, and placed the bag inside. Afterward, he closed the safe door, locked it, then returned to his chair behind the desk and sat back down. Looking over at Juan and Tony, he told them, "I need you two to split up this morning. Tony, you're to go out and check on the collectors. Make sure they are doing their job and not pussyfooting around. They have a job. That's what they get paid for. Make sure they are working. If not, I want to know."

"Right, Boss Man, is that all? If there's nothing else, I'm ready to rock 'n' roll, Tony told Ivan.

"Then get out of here, hit the streets, and keep those collectors in line. If you find one of them sluffing off, jerk them back into line, and let me know who it is so I can have a talk with them later.

Tony got up and headed out for his morning vigilance; Juan stayed behind to learn what Ivan had in store for him.

"Juan, you stick around this morning. Keep your eyes open. When I'm finished here, I want you to drive me out to the breeders' farm north of town. I need to check on a breeder horse I'm interested in purchasing. That's if have time after visiting a couple of other associates this morning"

It came as a complete surprised to Juan learning Ivan was not only interested in breeder horses but owned a substantial horse farm outside Lexington, Kentucky. Juan was interested in seeing the breeder farm Ivan referred to. He had never seen a real farm, especially one used specifically for breeding purposes.

It was not long after Tony left the office, Ivan told Juan, "Get the car. I'll meet you out front in five minutes. I'll be ready by the time you get back. If not, sit in the car until I come out."

Juan left the office, walked through the bar out the door, and headed to the garage located in the next block. He soon returned to the bar with the car, parking it alongside the curb where he waited for Ivan's arrival. As he sat in the car, he kept his eyes peeled for any- thing of interest or out of the ordinary. Soon, the bartender appeared at the door, motioning Juan to come back inside. Once inside, the bartender said, "Ivan's waiting to meet someone before leaving.

Juan sat down at the table and began playing cards while he waited for Ivan. It was not long until a gentleman entered the bar, heading toward the back where Juan sat. As he approached, Juan stood up and asked, "Can I help you?"

"Yeah, I'm Shorty I've come here to meet Ivan. We have some business to discuss."

"Wait here. I'll let Mr. Cohen know you're here."

Juan walked to the office and knocked on the door. He heard Ivan ask "who is it?"

"Juan."

"Yes, come in, Juan."

Juan opened the door, peeked in, and told Ivan, "A man by the name of Shorty is here to see you, said he had some sort of business to discuss with you. Is it okay to send him in?"

"Yes, I'm expecting him. Give me a couple of minutes, so I can find the information I need before allowing him in."

Juan walked back into the bar and told Shorty, "Have a seat. Mr. Cohen will be with you shortly"

Shorty sat down at another table and waited. When Ivan finally came to the door, he motioned Shorty to come in. Juan got up and approached Shorty."

"Before you enter Mr. Cohen's office, I fist have to frisk you. Raise your hands above your head."

Shorty reluctantly raised his hands while Juan checked his person. Finding a gun holstered inside his coat on the left side, Juan told Shorty, "You'll need to remove your gun, then hand it to me. Mr.

Cohen does not allow guns in his office."

Shorty slowly reached inside his coat, removed the revolver and handed it to Juan, butt first. Juan took the gun and laid it on the table where Shorty stood. Shorty immediately turned away from.

Juan and walked toward the office where he was greeted by Ivan.

Juan sat back down and continued playing cards until he heard the office door open behind him. Turning around, he saw Shorty walking back to the table where he sat. Juan reached over to the table next to him, picked up the gun with the barrel first, stood up, and handed the gun to Shorty on his way out. After Shorty left Ivan, he called Juan into his office.

"I'm ready. Go back outside and get the car warmed up. I'll be there in a couple of minutes."

Juan walked from the office, through the bar, to where Boss Man's car was parked, while, Ivan waited until the car had been sufficiently warmed up before leaving. Before long Ivan appeared in the doorway, closing the door behind him, and walked outside. Juan immediately jumped out of the car and hurried around the back to the other side and opened the back door. Once Ivan was inside and seated, Juan shut the door, walked back around to the driver's side, crawled in, and closed the door.

Ivan said, "My first stop will be the Silver Dollar Saloon. Head north. I have a meeting with my old friend Big Sid, whom I need to talk to, so step on it. After that, if it is not too late, we will drive out to the farm."

Juan delivered Boss Man to the Silver Dollar Saloon in under fifteen minutes, which was good timing in a city with so much morning traffic. Reaching the saloon, Juan stopped in front of the Silver.

Dollar Saloon's entrance, Ivan got out and hurried inside while Juan parked the car.

This was Juan's first visit to the Silver Dollar Saloon. He was surprised to see how large it was inside. It was nothing like the place Ivan ran on the south side. Juan found a table not far from Big Sid's office and sat down, his back against a wall and a bird's eye view of the entire place. He did not wait long until Boss Man exited Big Sid's office after only fifteen minutes. Juan quickly got up, walked back outside, retrieved the car, and drove it back to where Ivan waited patiently.

Ivan got back in the car and told Juan, "Let's drive back down-town. There's a restaurant near the circle where I want to go for lunch."

Juan drove to one of Ivan's favorite restaurants called the Sportsman's. Entering the Sportsman's, Ivan found a small table near the rear of the restaurant, again sitting with their backs against the wall. That way keeping an eye out for any unwanted interruptions or intrusions while having lunch.

After lunch, it was back to the car; this time, Juan drove Ivan to the west end of town down by an old, abandoned railroad yard. Here Ivan was to meet Big Jimmy, a local bar owner, to discuss an upcoming trip to New Orleans. It was to finalize their annual R&R trip for a local group of Ivan's associates. The group consisted of restaurant owners, small-time gamblers, collectors, hit men, loan sharks, your typical run-of-the-mill small-time wannabes. This was their way of keeping in contact with one another, also find out what the word was on the streets.

They met twice a year in New Orleans for a semiannual vacation, giving them time to settle and air their differences. A get-a-way trip to catch up on the latest gossip and enjoying the fruits of their labor. Usually, after a day or two in New Orleans, a small group got together and drove down to Grand Isle, where a couple of chartered fishing boats waited their arrival for an all-day fishing trip out in the Gulf of Mexico.

Boss Man, after meeting with Big Jimmy at the railroad yard, told Juan, "I'm finished here. Take me back to the office. I have work to do before leaving for the day. Don't have time today for a trip to the breeders' farm. We'll make it another day."

CHAPTER 9

Juan returned Ivan to the bar, dropping him off in front, waited until he was safely inside before returning the car to the parking garage. On his return to the bar, Juan found Tony sitting at the table, looking over the notes he compiled earlier while checking on the collectors.

Juan sat down across from Tony. "How were things out on the street today?" he asked.

"Hey, Juan, everyone on the streets were firing on all eight cylinders. The ones I talked to had had no run-ins so far with the owners. Overall, I would say the streets were relatively safe, ha ha. That's what they pay for. I saw Al as I made my rounds. He's the only one I found who was still slightly irritated, not at his route but at you. Everything else appeared copacetic."

Juan pleased at Tony's assessment of the collectors. Doing their jobs made his and everyone else's job at the office easier when things ran smoothly.

Tony, hearing his name called, quickly got up from the table, placed his notepad in his jacket pocket, then hurried back to Ivan's office.

After entering the office, Ivan asked him, "Do you have your follow-up notes on the collectors?"

"Yes, I do."

Tony reached into his jacket and removed the notepad, handing over his notes on his morning activity to Boss Man. Tony told Ivan,

"The collectors are doing a bang-up job. You should be pleased."

Ivan looked over his notes, noticing the entry concerning Al.

He looked up at Tony and asked, "What's this entry about Al? Sounds like he's still disgruntled."

"Yes, I had a long talk with him this morning. He said he was still irritated and was reluctant in discussing what was gnawing at him. He's not the same Al we knew and respected before you hired Juan."

"Did he, by any chance, say anything derogatory about me or his new boss, Juan?"

"No, I found him distant with the very mention of Juan's name. I think after Juan's promotion, he's become discouraged. He's disappointed losing the promotion. Other than Al being upset at Juan, he's basically civil and okay with everything else."

"Tony, I don't want Al's attitude to continue festering. It can only lead to bigger problems among the rank and file. It's not beneficial to the overall health and well-being of the organization. His contempt for Juan needs to cease, and if it continues, I may have to replace him.

"Would you and Juan talk to Al when he comes in this evening? He needs to be straightened out before it spills over into something more unmanageable. If you two cannot make him understand what he's doing by carrying this chip on his shoulder, send him to me. I'll straighten his ass out, or he is out of here. One way or the other, his antagonism toward Juan has to be quelled before he does something stupid. Do we understand each other?"

"Yes, Boss Man, Juan and I will talk to him this evening before he leaves."

Ivan was not one to mince words. He was going to put an end to this problem posthaste, sooner rather than later. Tony left Ivan's office to discuss with Juan what Ivan wanted them to do when Al arrived later that afternoon. They were to recommend he stop this petty resentment toward Juan, but if he continues, Ivan had only one option left, fire his sorry ass.

Al worked for Ivan several years, and had become his top collector. Al believed he merited the position more than anyone in the association but passed over once again. It had been a difficult pill for him to swallow. Al saw Juan, a newbie, basically walked in off the streets and handed the job he himself worked so hard for, suddenly disappeared. He had a hard time accepting Juan as his new boss Taking orders from this kid, still green behind the ears, did not bode well with him.

Al, was not thinking rationally or clearly, had to realize it was Ivan's choice he had been passed over. It was a matter of bad timing in this case. Al was not aware of Ivan's ulterior motive behind this latest promotion. Ivan was looking ahead for when he decides to retire; he needed someone to take over and run the business. Juan just happened to come along at the right time. Ivan felt the job required someone younger, eager, and capable of running the business after his retirement. He believed strongly in Juan's capabilities—that they were in line with what the business required. Ivan was not getting any younger and did not have the drive or spunk he had when he was younger. When it came time for him to retire and hand the reins over to someone else, his first thought was Juan. With his help and guidance, Juan should be ready in taking over and running the organization when that time came.

If Al wanted to continue working, he'd better just bite his lip, swallow his pride, and move past this bump in the road. He needed to suck it up and take one day at a time. Tomorrow is another day, no telling what it may bring. Who knows, could be Al's lucky day?

Tony and Juan had to put a stop to Al's volatile and explosive attitude lately; the sooner, the better. They must reason with him, pointing out what his emotional anguish was doing not only to himself but the organization overall.

As Al arrived with his day's receipts and before he went back to the office, Al was asked to stop by the table when he finished with Ivan. Al looked over at Juan with loathing and, without saying a word, passed by without acknowledging the request. Later, walking out of Ivan's office grudgingly, he stopped by where Tony and Juan sat waiting patiently.

Al asked Juan, 'What is it that you want to talk to me about?"

"Do you have a few minutes to spare? Tony and I would like to talk man to man with you."

"Yeah, what's it about?"

Tony said, "Sit down, Al. Boss Man wants you to put an end to this hostility you have for Juan. He wants you to back off, stop whatever it is you are resentful about, and move past it. He said if you plan to continue working, you need to straighten up your act and drop this animosity against Juan immediately."

Juan interjected at that point, asking, "Why are you upset with me? I've done nothing to offend you as far as I know, have I? I had nothing to do with the promotion. That was Ivan's decision, his alone."

"My displeasure at being passed over as Ivan's personal assistant, a job I've strived for years. It doesn't seem right a newbie like yourself be given that job after such a short time on the job. I've worked years for that position. It don't make sense." Was Al's response.

"Al, Boss Man thinks you are getting a bit too old to continue walking the streets collecting. Maybe you need a less stressful position, lessening the pressure you are under. Boss Man asked us to look around and find something else you'd be interested. A less demanding position, giving you more time for yourself and your family. If that's an option and you agree, Juan and I will look around. We'll find you a new position within the organization and, hopefully, ending this discontent you have toward Juan."

For the moment, it seemed to ease the tension between Al and Juan. It was a tall order for Tony and Juan to put on the table and pledged to Al.

Juan mentioned to Al, "I'll talk to Ivan. See what avenues are open within the organization that would be suitable. Ivan is interested in promoting you to a less arduous position, if that's agreeable. Ivan, as you know, finds it hard to acquire good collectors. Most of the new hires find collecting difficult work, and soon move on."

Al unenthusiastically agreed to a new position within the organization if one came available.

"Yeah, talk to Boss Man. See what you all come up with since my chances of becoming his right-hand man will never come to fruition."

Juan and Tony decided to leave it there. Al had accepted their proposition; it was up to them to follow through with their end of the bargain. Al was still not happy with his situation, but was some-what satisfied with the offer presented him. He would not rock the boat until he heard back from Juan.

As the meeting ended, Al got up to leave and thanked both Juan and Tony for their input in finding him a new niche. Shaking their hands, he left to find a restaurant and have a nice, quiet dinner and contemplate on what had just transpired before heading home to his family.

Sitting at the table after Al's exit, Tony looked over at Juan and said, "There's very few openings within the organization that Al qualifies for. Only one comes to mind. Ivan can always use an extra body in the muscle group—the group used specifically by Ivan in dealing with large organizations indebted to the association through the loan-sharking business, owned and operated by the association. The work was something Al was all too familiar with working as a collector, mainly attitude and violence.

They would run it by Ivan, see what his thoughts were in relocating Al to that group. Al, accustomed to doing dirty work as a collector, should fit in perfectly. The group was a small, highly motivated muscle group of individuals, consisting of ex-cons, hit men hired by Ivan to take care of his second-biggest income producer within the organization. Hopefully, Al would be up to working within that group and not working alone as he had for so many years on the streets. The only drawback was he would be on call 24/7. They did not know if that would appeal to Al, but it was worth following up on.

After Al left, Ivan came to the door, asking both Tony and Juan to come to his office. He was interested in hearing what was discussed between them and Al.

They walked back to Ivan's office, and once inside, Ivan told them, "Please have seat. What did you two decide about putting a damper on the situation with Al? Were you able to recommend a suitable substitute job, and if so, what's the job and what was his reaction?"

Juan answered, "Our thought was move Al from street collections to your highly motivated muscle group dealing with the hard-liners."

Ivan gave it some thought and said, "I do need good, dependable people in that sector. Go ahead, run it by Al, and see if he's interested. I want your feedback about Al's feelings on leaving collections and hooking up with the muscle group. It would be a challenge to Al, working with others, and not solo. Do you think he's capable working with others after working many so years as a lone wolf?"

"I'm sure it'll take some adjustment and time, but he seems flexible enough. Maybe it'll work," Tony told Ivan.

Ending on that note, Ivan told Juan, "Go get the car. I'm ready to leave. I'll meet you out front."

CHAPTER 10

Juan headed out to pick up the car, and as he passed by Tony, he told him, "See you tomorrow."

"You betcha."

Juan was informed by Ivan he wanted him to drive over to a couple of his usual haunts to take care of some unfinished business before he retired for the evening. When Juan returned with the car, Ivan motioned to Juan where to stop the car along the curb. Juan stopped where Ivan indicated and exited the car, proceeded to the other side opened the door as Ivan emerged from the bar.

Ivan looked at Juan before getting in the car, "I need you to drive me over to the Silver Dollar Saloon. I have someone waiting there for me, and step on it."

"Yes, sir."

Juan closed the door once Ivan was inside and seated. He raced off down the street as fast as possible through the crowded streets of this sinful city to the Silver Dollar Saloon. Upon their arrival, Juan dropped off Ivan in front before parking the car in the side parking lot. Walking back to the saloon, Juan entered and spotted a small two-top table near a wall with an unobstructed view and sat down.

A waitress stopped by his table and said, "Good evening, sir. Can I get you something to drink from the bar?"

"No, thanks. On second thought, I'll have a Coke," he replied.

The waitress took his order as he sat observing the coming and going inside the establishment. Suddenly he noticed three shady-looking characters entering the saloon. He stayed totally focused on the three as he waited for Ivan. He learned quickly they were regulars and not the threat he imagined them to be.

The waitress returned with his Coke and asked, "Would there be anything else?"

"No, that's all, thanks."

It was not long until Ivan returned, found Juan sitting at the table, and told him, "I'm ready. Fetch the car. I'll be waiting out front."

Ivan, again safely back in the car, told Juan, "I'm ready for you to take me home."

Ivan arrived home, but before exiting the car, he told Juan, "Meet me early in the morning. The rest of the group has finalized our semi-yearly trip to New Orleans. I'd like to get an early start in the morning. You need to have the car checked out, then top it off with gas. You'll need to pack a suitcase. We'll be away for several days. Meet me here no later than eight o'clock sharp."

This came as a complete surprise to Juan, never having been out of Indianapolis, let alone the state. After dropping Ivan off, he drove back to the city and parked the car. It was getting late, and he was hungry. He found a restaurant nearby where he ate dinner before going to the hotel. Once inside his room at the hotel, he had to decide what to pack for the trip to New Orleans.

Juan had thought earlier about visiting Al and continuing the discussion Tony and he had after Al left. But that had to be put on hold until his return from New Orleans.

The following morning, Juan was up earlier than usual. He began by taking a hot bath, shaving, brushing his teeth, combing his hair, then dressing. He then packed a few things in an overnight bag and took the car to a service station nearby that opened early. Stopping by the station had the attendant check the oil, water, transmission fluid, tire pressure, and top off the tank before picking up Ivan at eight. The attendant checked all the fluid levels and topped the gas tank. Juan paid the bill and was soon on his way to pick up Ivan.

When Juan stopped at the main gate, the guard on duty poked his head out the door, asked his name, then picked up his log-in sheet, exited the guard shack, walked to the back of the car, and logged in the license plate number before allowing him to enter. Juan drove up to the front of Ivan's home where he noticed two suitcases sitting on the front stoop. He stopped the car, exiting, then proceeded up the steps where he picked up the two suitcases and placed them in the trunk. About that time, the housekeeper appeared at the door and invited Juan inside. Juan walked back up the steps, where he entered the house, and saw Ivan sitting at the kitchen table having breakfast.

"Come in, Juan. Sit down while I'm having my breakfast. By the way, have you had breakfast yet?"

"No, I didn't have time after having the car checked out this morning and driving here."

"Good, have a seat."

Ivan told the cook nearby in the kitchen, "Fix Juan something special for breakfast. We have a long drive ahead of us. He's going to need plenty of nourishment."

It was not long until the cook brought Juan a large plate of eggs, ham, biscuits, jelly, and coffee; placed it in front of him; and asked, "Would there be anything else, sir?"

"No, I think this will last me the rest of the day. Thanks."

When they finished with breakfast, Ivan pushed his chair back from the table, stood up, walked into the hallway where he put on a sports jacket. Then he picked up his overcoat, placed it over his left arm, reached over, grabbed his oversized briefcase on the table near him with his right hand, and said, "I'm ready."

Leaving the house, they proceeded down the steps to the car when Ivan looked at Juan and questioned, "Are we ready?"

"Yes, as ready as I can tell."

Ivan set his briefcase on the back seat before getting in and placed his overcoat over on the back passenger seat. Then shed his jacket and, finally, crawled into the back seat.

Once inside, he told Juan, "I'm ready, let's get started."

Ivan made himself as comfortable as possible as they left the confines of the community where he lived for the long trip south. Once underway, Ivan was nestled comfortably in his seat. Then reaching, opened his briefcase looking through the many papers inside, studying each one carefully. Before long they were leaving Indiana, heading into Kentucky. Ivan asked Juan to stop at the next restaurant they came to; he had to take a leak and his morning constitution.

It was not long until Juan spotted a restaurant; he slowed the car, pulled off the highway, stopping near the front entrance. Ivan quickly vanished inside. Juan parked and locked the car before going inside. He found a table near the restroom and sat down. Soon, Ivan opened the door to the restroom, still drying his hands and face with a wet paper towel. He saw Juan and joined him at the table.

A waitress slowly wandered over and asked, "Can I get you gentlemen something to drink?"

"Two coffees, one black, one with sugar and cream," Juan answered.

Ivan opened a menu, looked at Juan, and asked, "Would you like to order lunch while we're here? We still have a long drive ahead of us, and since we're here, we might as well eat."

"Yes, a club sandwich and piece of that fresh apple pie on the counter sounds great."

The waitress returned with their coffee. Ivan ordered a meatloaf special with mashed potatoes, mixed veggies, and a salad for himself and a club sandwich for Juan, plus a piece of fresh apple pie. After eating, Juan decided he had better go to the restroom before leaving. He too washed his face and hands before leaving.

Returning to the car, Juan told Ivan, "I'll have to stop and gas up the car before driving any further. We only have a quarter of a tank remaining and many miles to go."

"Stop anytime. Here's a hundred dollars."

Juan took the money and put it in his pocket. A half hour later, Juan stopped and filled the car as they were passing through Western Tennessee. With the car's gas tank once again full, it was possible to finish the trip to New Orleans without stopping again. It was later that evening when they arrived in downtown New Orleans.

Ivan gave Juan directions on how to get to the Roosevelt Hotel, when suddenly it appeared just ahead on Canal Street. Juan pulled along the curbside in front of the hotel. Ivan got out and told the doorman who he was and that he had reservations.

"Yes, Mr. Cohen, we've been expecting you. Welcome to New Orleans."

Juan, in the meantime, had opened the trunk and was starting to remove the luggage when a bellhop appeared out of nowhere, "Excuse me, sir, but may I take care of the luggage?"

Juan did not know what to say or do, so he sidestepped out of the bellhop's way. Juan learned quickly his only job was to take care of Ivan, nothing else unless otherwise told.

Inside the hotel, Ivan registered in at the front desk, afterward followed the bellhop up to his suite. Juan was unsure of what arrangements Ivan had made for him. All he could do was follow Ivan and the bellhop and wait. Reaching Ivan's suite, he told the bellhop to drop off his luggage and take the remaining bag across the hallway and drop it off. The rooms were not joined but near enough if Ivan needed him. Juan settled in his room after the long and exhausting drive but did take time out to admire his accommodations. It was nothing like the fleabag hotel room he occupied back in Naptown.

The next morning, Juan's phone rang. It was Ivan asking Juan over to help with a list of things he had to present at the meeting that morning. Juan hurriedly got dressed, ran across the hall where he found Ivan up, clean-shaven, and ready for the day. Juan still had to take a bath, shave, and change before leaving. He learned quickly that morning to be ready on a moment's notice whenever Ivan called. Once Ivan and Juan finished with a question-and-answer session, Juan told Ivan he would finish getting ready and meet him in the dining room in ten minutes.

"I'll wait this time, but I want you up and ready to go by 6:00 sharp every morning from here on in. Is that understood?" Ivan reiterated to Juan.

"Yes, sorry about this morning. Guess I was tired as we did not arrive until late last night."

"Don't let it happen again. Do I make myself clear?"

CHAPTER 11

Ivan turned away from Juan as he slowly began walking down the hallway toward the elevator. Pushing the call button, waited a few seconds before the elevator arrived and the door opened. Standing alone in the elevator was one of his business associates from Indy. On the way down, they talked about the upcoming meeting scheduled that morning and what had happened in their lives since the last conference six months prior. As the elevator descended on its way to the lobby, they agreed to meet for lunch before leaving if time permitted. Soon, the elevator reached the main floor; the doors opened. They shook hands and went their separate ways.

It did not take Juan long after returning to his room to change and rush down downstairs where Ivan was waiting on him. Entering the dining room, Juan quickly spotted Ivan looking over the menu. Ivan looked up and saw Juan enter the dining room. He motioned him over where he was seated. As Juan approached the table, Ivan pointed to a chair and told him, "Sit down, Juan. I've not yet ordered. Would you care for a cup of coffee before ordering our breakfast?"

"Yes, a hot cup of coffee sounds good."

Ivan, glancing around the room, spotted two more associates from Indianapolis sitting on the other side of the dining facility. Ivan thought it strange that he only had seen a couple of associates from the group so far, who are attending the eight o'clock meeting. As he and Juan sat having breakfast, more and more associates began showing up. Ivan was happy to see so many now in the dining room; it meant the meeting that morning would be well-attended.

The morning meeting had an assortment of business issues running the gambit of legal and illegal enterprises in and around Naptown. The group assembled were businessmen with attitudes, believing themselves to be upstanding citizens in the community, doing a job helping out their fellow Hoosiers cope with pressure and stress of everyday life. Most were smooth-talking con men with attitude, not at all what they pigeonholed themselves to be, in fact, just the opposite. But business was business.

Juan noticed Shorty as he walked toward the table where he and Ivan sat. He stopped at the table and said to Ivan, "I see you made it. I wondered if you were coming down this year after hearing your pressing problems back in Indy."

"Good morning, Shorty, and what problems are you talking about?"

"The rumor one of your collectors is spreading around town. That of being railroaded in favor of a recent hire of yours, the newbie."

"Are we talking about Al? Is he the one you've heard was spreading the rumors?"

"Yes."

"I thought that matter was settled, and he had moved on."

"Oh, then why is he still spreading the rumor?"

"This is news to me, but you can bet your bottom dollar I will get to the bottom of it when I return. You can take that to the bank."

"Enjoy your stay. By the way, is the fellow sitting with you that same person from the bar back in Indy, and is he the newbie Al is referring to?"

"Yes, I'm sorry. I did not introduce you two. Shorty, this is Juan. Juan, Shorty."

"Oh yeah, I remember him now. He's the one who had me remove my pistol before allowing me into your office."

"One and the same," Ivan said.

Before leaving, Shorty told Ivan he would catch up to him later.

"Thanks for the tip about Al. I'll look into the matter when I return. See ya later."

"Oh, by the way, are we still going fishing later this week?"

"You betcha. Wouldn't miss it for the world."

"Okay, later."

After breakfast, Ivan and Juan went back upstairs to finish getting ready for the meeting in the conference room at 8:00 a.m. It was seven thirty when they finished breakfast. Ivan still had a half hour to look over his notes before heading back downstairs to the conference room by eight. As Ivan was leaving for the meeting, he stopped by Juan's and told him, "Why don't you take the next couple of hours off. Do whatever you want, but meet me in the lobby by eleven o'clock sharp."

After Ivan left, Juan decided he would walk the downtown district and explore the sights and sounds of New Orleans while Ivan attended his meeting.

Once inside the conference room, Ivan looked around and spotted Shorty sitting by himself. Ivan headed over to question Shorty again about the rumor Al was again spreading around town about Juan. Reaching Shorty's table, Ivan asked, "Are you expecting anyone else?"

"No, have a seat. I was hoping you would join me."

Sitting down, Ivan turned to Shorty and said, "I'd like you to tell me more about the rumor you heard back in Indy."

"One of my boys spoke to Al about a week ago. That's when Al told him about being passed over for the driver-bodyguard position, and he was determined to get even with the newbie. He told my boy he would do whatever it takes to even the score to have him terminated. My boy was adamant what Al's intentions were."

Ivan expressed his appreciation to Shorty and said, "I'm not happy hearing the rumor. It could cause me a lot of problems among the rank and file as you know. I need to get this shit straightened out pronto. And when I return, you can bet your bottom dollar on that. By the way, Shorty, how have you been, and how's your health? See, when you came to see me last time, you told me you were not doing as well as you had been doing. What's the problem?"

"Thanks for asking. I had a problem with my back, but since then, I've seen a specialist and had it corrected. Plus, I've been exceptionally busy lately, not a lot of free time. We need to get together more often after we get back, like old times, ha ha. I have a few things in the works I need your advice about too. I'll call when I get back. Maybe we can get together over lunch and talk."

"Sounds like a winner."

Ivan told Shorty, "We need to discuss several issues that's come to my attention."

A voice suddenly came over the PA system, calling the meeting to order. Once all the preliminary speeches were given, it was time for

Big Sid's address to the group. He earned a big round of applause as he stepped up to the podium.

The main speaker was Big Sid, who owned and operated the Silver Dollar Saloon, one of his many investments. He was revered by the group as one of the most successful businessmen in Indianapolis. He had a way about himself that everyone who knew him liked him and enjoyed being in his company. He could quell major problems just by being verbal. His demeanor was uncanny, not rough and tough like some in the audience. He ran his businesses like a fine-running Bugatti. Everyone here had the highest respect for Big Sid who had earned their trust through his kindness, his generosity, and most of all, his fortitude. He was the type of person everyone gravitated to when in his presence. That was why at the convention Big Sid was always selected as the main speaker. He told them what they wanted to hear and what was expected of them as businesspeople operating in Indy. He had no problems browbeating a fellow businessman about a problem causing locals to have a negative image of the group. Big Sid handled most problems associated with the group in a way as to not cause conflict within the organizations or upset locals; he was the man.

Before ending that day's meeting, Big Sid brought up the rumor circulating around town about a disgruntled employee. He mentioned only that one of the organizations was having trouble with one of its own. He made the point that this type of behavior was not acceptable and had to cease. If not stopped, it could possibly cause dissension throughout the rank and file, causing more problems.

Ivan knew the insinuation by Big Sid was aimed directly at him and his association. He was not a happy camper as Big Sid uttered the accusation at the end of the meeting. He would do whatever was necessary to quell the rumor upon his return. He'd get to the bottom of the problem Al was initiating not only inside his association but, apparently, in other associations. Al overstepped his boundary this time and had to answer personally to Ivan for his misdeeds. This was something he did not need and did not appreciate from his employees. Ivan swore to put an end to it one way or other; Al's number was up.

CHAPTER 12

After the meeting adjourned, Ivan wanted to have a word with Big Sid before leaving. He wanted to reassure Big Sid the problem with Al would be nipped in the bud once he returned to Indy. Big Sid was getting ready to leave the stage when Ivan approached him.

"Excuse me, Big Sid, but can you spare a few minutes?"

"Yes, Ivan. You know I always have time for you. What's up?"

"I want to assure you the situation you referred to back in Indianapolis will be taken care once I return. I just wanted you to know."

"I know it will be and appreciate your candidness in telling me. You know as well as anyone what this situation with Al could do to us and to the organizations if this rumor continues. It is something we don't need hanging over our heads. It only leads to more contempt and dissension among our ranks. It's something we can do without."

"I know. I had no idea it had gone this far. I had Juan and Tony talk to him before. We are trying to relocate Al within the association, but as you know, it's hard sometimes because of one's exposure and experience," Ivan explained to Big Sid.

"As long as you take care of the problem, that's all I ask. Just don't let this problem fester too long. It's a ticking time bomb. You need to suppress it now. No good can come of this if it continues, and you know this as well as anyone. You need to put a damper on it before it spills over into the rest of the organizations."

"I understand. I'll have it under control once I return to Indy. I assure you, one way or other."

Ivan's conversation with Big Sid ended when Big Sid changed the subject and asked Ivan, "Are you ready for our fishing trip tomorrow off Grand Isle?"

"Are you serious? You bet, I am. I've been ready since our last trip, ha ha."

"I think we need to look at the sign-up sheet we left at the entrance to the conference room earlier. It'll give us an idea how many are interested in going fishing tomorrow. Once we know how many, we will make reservations with the concierge tonight. Do you remember how many people they allowed last year per boat?" Big Sid questioned Ivan.

"If memory serves me correctly, it was five, but don't quote me. We had ten sign-ups, and we're told we needed two charter boats, remember? said Ivan.

"Yes, vaguely. I'm not sure all those who went last time want to go again. Some may stay in town this year and party."

"Yeah, ha ha. If memory serves me correctly, a couple of the fellows were hung over from the night before and did not enjoy the trip because of getting seasick, remember?" asked Ivan.

"Yes, especially Romero, who cussed the whole time we were out. Remember, he tried to bribe the captain in returning to shore early but to no avail."

"Yes, the captain told Romero, 'You paid for an all-day fishing trip, and you can forget about returning until I decide it's time.'"

"Ha ha, you're right. He had to spend most of the trip inside the cabin, puking, ha ha."

"If we get seven or eight sign-ups this year, it should be enough to warrant chartering two boats again. Will cost each of us more money, but not that much more."

"Okay, let's check the sign-up sheet before everyone leaves. That way, I can make a final announcement, letting those remaining in the hall know about the trip, and if interested, they need to sign-up as soon as possible," was Big Sid's reply.

They walked over to where the sign-up sheet lay on the table. Big Sid picked up the list and counted nine names. Big Sid, along with Ivan, returned to the conference room where Big Sid once again returned to the stage. Turning the mic back on and made the announcement about the fishing trip scheduled the next day.

"Those who signed up will be notified later this evening as to when and where they should gather tomorrow for the trip. Also, I would like to remind those remaining in the conference room, if interested, you can still sign up."

After the announcement, Big Sid turned the mic off and left the stage in order to finish his conversation with Ivan.

"If no one else comes forward to sign up, looks like we have a total of nine and we will need at least two charter boats. I suggest you find the concierge and make arrangements for two charters and transportation for tomorrow morning. Do you have time to do that this morning?"

"Yes, nine people, two charters, and transportation. Should be no problem for the concierge to handle."

Yeah, this time have him get two smaller transporter vans since there are only nine of us. If we take the larger bus like last year, it was too big and noisy. Two smaller transporter vans would be the answer, what do you think?"

"Sounds good to me," replied Ivan.

"Okay, Ivan, take care of the booking. I will see to it personally those who signed-up are in the lobby and ready by six thirty sharp tomorrow morning. I've got to go. I have other business to tend to. See you tomorrow bright and early."

Ivan turned and headed over to the concierge's office to set up scheduling for two smaller vans and two charter boats. After making the arrangements with the concierge, he handed him a list of names of those who signed up for the trip.

"Here's a list of names and room numbers of those going tomorrow. I need you to make nine copies of the itinerary and deliver a copy of the itinerary to each person on the list sometime this evening. Can you do that for me?"

"Would be my pleasure, Mr. Cohen."

Ivan left the concierge's office and headed to the lobby to find Juan. Ivan had previously made arrangements earlier to have lunch with Shorty and Jimmy the Turk, one of Ivan's competitors in theloan sharking business, out on Lake Pontchartrain. It had become a tradition for the three of them, taking one afternoon away from the hotel and having lunch on the lake. A few years back, while looking for some place different, they discovered Landry's Seafood Restaurant on Lake Pontchartrain. It had become one of the highlights of the trip for Jimmy the Turk.

It was impossible to get fresh crawfish bread in Indy, a staple at Landry's. For starters, they always started with a large order of New Orleans's crawfish bread along with three dozen freshly harvested oysters on the half shell, and for the main entrée, each ordered something different. When their lunch arrived, they tried a little of each entrée. It was a day out with the boys, so to speak, which had become a ritual for these three.

As the three met in the lobby that afternoon, Juan led them to the waiting car, then drove out to Lake Pontchartrain for their afternoon indulgence.

After lunch, Ivan had Juan drive them down along the Mississippi River waterfront in order to take in the sights and sounds before returning to the hotel. Once back at the hotel, they said their goodbyes and split up, going their separate ways.

The next morning, Ivan called Juan to see if he wanted to join him in the dining room for breakfast before he left on his fishing trip. It was to be a long day for Ivan, and he needed to eat something before starting the trip down to Grand Isle.

"Yes, I'll be ready in five. Meet you in the hall."

After breakfast, Ivan was ready for the trip to Grand Isle and the big day on the water. Since Ivan would be out of town for the entire day, he told Juan, "Enjoy yourself but be back at the hotel no later than six. We should be back by then, and I'll want dinner."

"Have a great trip. I'll see you at six," Juan told Ivan. Juan, having the day off, decided he would take a walk down to the wharf, have lunch later on the General Lee, which was moored dockside on the river. New Orleans was known for its fine cuisine, and he wanted to taste as much of it as he could before leaving. He made a small itinerary, a list of the things to do and see on this free day in the city. There was no lack of things that captured one's interest and imagination in New Orleans—antique shops, famous restaurants, Bourbon Street, Canal Street, trolley cars, downtown parks, famous hotels, the list was endless. He had no problem finding things of interest before and after lunch while Ivan was away.

The group going fishing assembled in the lobby by six, then continued outside where they boarded the two small vans. It would take time to drive down to Grand Isle, the southernmost part of the state of

Louisiana. Once settled comfortably in the vans, the vans began the drive south. Sitting in the vans, they talked about the upcoming fishing trip, making bets who would catch the biggest fish, the most fish, and the first to get seasick. Once out of town heading south, the scenery changed as they entered the marshes, no homes, few buildings, fishing boats along canals running alongside the road, birds, plus a few snakes and alligators. A few trailers were spotted twisted like a corkscrew, resting high off the ground between telephone poles, which was to protect the trailers from flooding, but useless in a hurricane.

The destruction to the trailers left behind from the previous hurricane had a devastating effect on the low-lying swamp lands and peninsula. Most buildings had been swept away by the latest hurricane with only telltale signs of buildings that once were. Concrete foundations dotting the area was a reminder of the devastating force of hurricanes.

Small shacks popped up along the roadside next to the marshlands advertising airboat rides while others sold cooked blue crabs and cold beer. It was a totally different lifestyle from anything back in Indy.

Arriving at Grand Isle at eight thirty, they saw moored at the dock were the two charter boats awaiting their arrival. The captains of the *Reel Screamer (One and Two)* had stocked their boats with everything needed for a fun-filled day of fishing in the gulf. As the vans stopped and the doors opened, they were escorted to one of the two boats. After boarding, the captains welcomed them aboard and told them, "Enjoy the morning cruise. In less than an hour, we should be in the middle grounds fishing."

After everyone was aboard, the captains gave their spiels on what they could expect. Starting their engines, the deckhands began untying the lines from the cleats on the dock and, afterward, slowly the boats left the dock in a southwestern direction, heading out to the middle grounds, where they would fish for grouper and red snapper along with other varieties of fishes found in the gulf.

Once they reached the middle grounds, fishing gears were placed securely in rod holders, bait was put on each hook, and the lines were dropped overboard and into the water. Each fisherman was given a seat by the pole he was to fish with. It did not take long until the reels began zinging as the line began singing from off the reels. They spent the rest of the morning and part of the afternoon fishing. There had been no problem catching fish where the boats stopped and were drifting; the spot was a gold mine. A successful day fishing was had by all. Several hours later, hot, tired, and worn-out from fishing, along with too much drinking, and sun, they were ready to head back to shore. All that fishing, bobbing up and down all day, this way and that way, sideways in the choppy waters of the gulf was a bit too much for a few of the landlubbers. They were more than happy when the captains announced it was time to reel-um in and return to dock.

Back on dry land, they recovered quickly from the motion of the boat and soon reestablish their land legs. The trip had been a success. It had been the highlight of the trip for some and would be remembered for years to come. They each caught their limit of grouper and redfish and had their catch cleaned and filleted by the deckhand on the way back in. After the fish was filleted and packaged in dry ice, it was ready to be shipped to Indy.

Exiting the boat, each carried their own Styrofoam boxes filled with their catch, which they later placed on the luggage rack atop the minivans. After everything were tied down and secured, they crawled back into the vans and headed north to New Orleans.

Ivan, who arrived back in New Orleans a little earlier than expected, found Juan in his room watching TV, awaiting his arrival. They talked about how each had spent their day: Ivan, his fishing trip; and Juan, what he saw on his outing in and around New Orleans. Before leaving Juan's room, Ivan told him to have the car ready to leave by six the following morning; they would be heading back north. Ivan then turned away from Juan, leaving to cross the hall and to his suite, where he showered and got ready for dinner.

The next morning, before leaving New Orleans, Ivan and Juan met for an early breakfast, as Ivan had finished eating and ready to leave when he spotted Big Sid on the other side of the dining room. After Ivan finished breakfast, walked over to where Big Sid and his party sat and said, "I'm heading back to Indianapolis this morning but want to thank all of you for a great time we've shared together. Especially like to express to Big Sid, I found the meeting very informative, and the fishing trip invigorating. I'm already looking forward to our next conference and getaway, ha ha."

Ivan shook hands with all four men sitting around the table, turned, and walked back to where Juan waited. Leaving the dining room, finding Juan near the door to the dining room. He motioned for him to start heading toward the lobby and outside, where the valet had parked the car. The doorman had the porter place the luggage in the trunk and told Ivan he was good to go. Ivan took out a five-dollar bill, giving it to the porter, and a ten-spot to the doorman, who thanked him and wished him a safe trip. Once Ivan was inside the car and comfortably seated, Juan started the car and drove away from the hotel for the long trip to Indy.

CHAPTER 13

It was getting late when they arrived back in Indianapolis. Ivan had Juan drive him to the bar before taking him home. He wanted to contact Al and confront him about the accusations he was still spreading. He called Al at the hotel where he told the desk clerk in no uncertain terms to have Al call him as soon as possible.

Al called minutes later. "Hi, Boss Man, got your message to call. What's up?"

"Get your sorry ass down to the bar. You and I need to talk," Ivan blurted-out.

Al showed up at the bar twenty minutes later. As he walked in, he saw several people sitting around the bar talking and drinking. He did not stop but proceeded straight to the office, where Ivan and Juan sat waiting for him. When he entered the office, he immediately realized something was off. He knew right away Ivan was not a happy camper.

Ivan in no uncertain terms told Al, "Sit your sorry ass down. I have something to say to you and don't interrupt or say a word until I'm finished. While away, I was informed you were spreading rumors again about Juan and the organization. What do you have to say about the allegation? I want your side of the story before I decide on what to do to correct the problem."

"I…I…I guess, I'm still upset being passed over for promotion and couldn't help shoot off my big mouth," Al stammered.

"Go on."

"I…I…felt I had been f——d over and was venting my frustrations. I said things I regret. If I could retract what I said, I would.

Since you and Juan were going out of town, I felt rejected and excluded. So I voiced my feeling in the only way I knew how."

"What do you think I should do about this state of affairs I find myself in because of you?"

"I know I've tarnished the organization, and I will do whatever is needed in correcting this injustice I've placed on the organization and you personally. You have been good to me over the years and hate what I've done staining both our reputations. Any form of reprimand or retribution you deem necessary, I'll accept and abide by without question or reprisal."

"Good. Do you have anything to say to Juan? If so, tell him now and never let me hear another f——g word from your chops about him or the organization. Is that clear?"

"Y-y-yes, Boss Man."

"Since this is your first blunder working for me, I'm going to suspend your pay for a week, but expect you to continue working and doing collections. Hopefully, this will give you time to think of the damage you've caused with your recklessness and misguided temper tantrums lately. At the end of the week, I want you, Juan, and Tony to sit down and talk about what you have done. Later, I'll meet with them and get their honest assessment of you. At which time, I'll determine whether I'm keeping you around or not. Is that clear?"

"Y…e…s, Boss Man."

"I expect you at work on time tomorrow morning. I better not hear of you bad-mouthing the organization or sluffing off on the job. Is that understood?"

"Y…e…s, Boss Man."

"Now get out of here. I'm tired and need to go home."

Al left Ivan and Juan sitting in the office. Before leaving for the night, Ivan told Juan, "After you and Tony talk about what Al's done and what we need to do with him, your conclusion will carry a lot of weigh on my decision concerning his future with the organization. Now take me home."

The next morning, Ivan called Juan and Tony into his office. He explained to Tony what was said to Al the evening before.

Tony said, "I'll keep close scrutiny on Al for the remainder of the week, making sure he walks the straight and narrow."

Juan expressed to Ivan, "I'm sure with what you told Al last night, the fear of God had been deeply instilled, and permanent dismissal if he hiccups."

Then Tony spoke up and told Ivan, "Juan and I will ride him like shit on stink. He knows there's no next time, that he would be finished and banned from the organization."

When Al showed up the next evening to turn in his collections and passed by the table Juan and Tony sat at, heard Juan say "Hey, Al, stop on your way out. Tony and I want to have a word with you."

When Al left Boss Man's office, he stopped by the table, pulled out a chair, and sat down. Tony and Juan talked to him for over an hour explaining what to expect the next time he overstepped his bounds. Al clearly understood the consequences and promised not to bad-mouth Juan or the organization again.

Al told Juan and Tony, "I've learned my lesson the hard way. I never intend to be chastised like this again. Twice is enough."

After Juan and Tony finished their admonishment, Al left the bar with his tail between his legs, like a dog who had been scolded. Al had been thoroughly disciplined not only by his boss but also his peers. He was ashamed of his actuations against Juan and the hurt it had caused Ivan and the association. After Al left, Ivan called Juan and Tony again into his office, asking Juan what he and Tony said to Al.

Juan explained in detail what they told Al. Ivan, who was now aware of the admonishment the two had given Al. Ivan felt the warning to be reasonable. Only time will tell. It was now a game of wait and see. Al was well aware of the consequences now in the event he repeated his actions. Ivan thanked Juan and Tony for their loyalty and told Juan, "It's time you drive me home."

Juan and Tony left the office, walked outside, and parted ways for the night. Juan walked to the garage, picked up the car, and drove back to the bar to pick up Ivan outside on the sidewalk, waiting as he arrived. Juan stopped the car; Ivan opened the back door and got in. Arriving at Ivan's home, Juan pulled into the circular driveway, dropped him off, along with his luggage.

Before leaving, Ivan told Juan, "I expect to see you in the morning at six, and don't be late."

Juan drove back to town to the garage where he parked the car. He walked back to the hotel after a long and arduous day. Dead tired, he was ready to catch a few winks before returning to work in just a few short hours. After a long and exhausting trip; he was ready for some well-deserved rest.

When Juan arrived at the hotel, picked up his key from the desk clerk, then proceeded upstairs. As he walked down the hallway, noticed a door to Al's unit was slightly ajar and the light was still on. Al had left the door open, in case Juan wanted to talk. But Juan was too tired, opened his door and entered his room instead. Al got up from his chair, closing his door after hearing Juan come in. Juan was too tired; the only thing he wanted was crawl into bed and sleep.

CHAPTER 14

The next morning, as the alarm clock sounded, Juan reached over turning it off, slowly crawled out of bed, and made his way to the bathroom, took a leak, then a well-deserved bath. Finished his bath, crawled from the tub, dried off, shaved, brushed his teeth, and lastly, combed his hair. Afterward, he went back into the bedroom and dressed for the day. After getting dressed, left the hotel to get the car and pick up Ivan.

Driving into the circular driveway, Juan saw Ivan waiting for him on the large front porch. Juan stopped the car, raced around, and opened the door for him.

Once inside the car, Ivan told Juan, "Drive me over to the horse farm this morning before taking me to the office. I've been informed I have a major problem with a breeder horse I purchased recently. I need to find out what happened before going downtown."

Arriving at the breeders' horse farm on the outskirts of town, Juan noticed several men milling around the stables. One of the men waiting was the foreman awaiting Ivan's arrival.

Juan stopped the car next to where Ivan's horse was boarded. Ivan exited the car and walked to where the foreman stood and talked to him briefly. The foreman then escorted Ivan inside stall number 8, where his horse was boarded. A short time later, Ivan and the foreman reappeared, closing the stall door behind them as they exited. In the meantime, another fellow appeared on the scene and introduced to Ivan. As the three men stood talking outside the stall, Ivan suddenly became upset and began shouting loudly, shaking his finger in the face of the individual who just arrived. It was not long until their conversation ended and Ivan returned to the car.

He told Juan, "Drive downtown to the bar."

As they drove toward downtown Indy, Ivan told Juan what happened earlier at the farm.

"The new breeder I purchased prior to the trip to New Orleans died sometime last night. Something happened overnight causing the horse's death, and I have to find out what."

Upon reaching the bar, Juan dropped Ivan off and drove back to the garage to parked the car.

As Juan entered the bar, Tony was sitting at the table waiting for him. As soon as Juan sat down across the table from Tony, Tony asked Juan, "Why is Boss Man in such a bad mood this morning? He hardly spoke to me as he walked by."

"I drove him out to the breeders' farm earlier after being informed a horse he recently purchased had been found dead inside its stall. Apparently, one of the farm workers entered the stall to check on the horse and found it dead."

"Really?"

"Yeah, he told me he'll be busy the rest of the morning finding out why his horse suddenly died."

About that time, Ivan called both Juan and Tony to his office. As they entered, they could tell Boss Man was upset and highly distraught over his prized breeder horse's passing. He told them sit.

"I have something I wanted to talk to you about. I expect possible trouble between the breeders' association and me. The breeders' association had not been pleased with my purchase of the horse in the first place. They frowned on it from the beginning. The horse sold to me should never have been approved as I later learned. The farm that owned the horse was in dire straits and needed money and offered it to me at a reasonable price, so I purchased it. I really had no interest in owning a breeder but purchased it on a whim. I was thinking it could possibly increase my bottom line and overall income down the road.

"Since I am an outsider, I am excluded in their eyes from making such a purchase. The word on the streets was I had not conformed to their by-laws when I purchased the horse. I'm assuming they are showing their dissatisfaction by killing my horse, teaching me a lesson not to infringe on their territory.

"After learning of my horse's death, I'm assuming some worker at the farm or someone inside their organization slipped the horse poison or, possibly a tranquilizer, putting it down. Since the horse has not been insured, I stand to lose a ton of money, but I'm not going down without a fight to get to the bottom of this. I'm determined to learn what happened, and hopefully, be reimbursed by the breeders' association even if I have to sue. At this time, I'm holding them totally responsible until I learn differently.

"I may need the muscle group in case this blows up in my face. We need to prepare for an all-out altercation with the breeders' association. In any case, there could be some sort of retaliation anytime, anywhere until the matter is settled.

"The breeders' association is not the squeaky-clean organization most in the business think it to be. There is the possibility of aggression by them. We need to put this situation on the front burner once I began my inquiry as to why my horse died so suddenly.

"I'm going to need a lot of backup when I start bucking the breeders' association. I've heard from the foreman this morning they are a very vindictive group. I want you two to inform the muscle group of a possible encounter and for them to be vigilant as they go about their daily routines and duties. Now get out of here. Get the word on the streets to our groups within the association to be extremely alert until this matter is settled."

Juan and Tony left Ivan's office and began calling, setting up a meeting with those in charge of the different aspects of the organization. After everyone had been informed and put on notice to be available, if and when, all hell breaks loose in the coming days or weeks.

Ivan had a large contingency, between twenty and twenty-five, working for him at any given time. They were all abled-body men willing and able to take care of their part inside the association. Juan and Tony worked the streets and phones for the better part of the morning, spreading the word. By noon, they had contacted most of Boss Man's muscle group and the people working the streets. Those whom they were not able to contact would be informed later. With the word out on the streets, they informed Ivan that mostly everyone had been notified and were ready to rumble at a moment's notice when called to arms.

Ivan looked up at Juan, and said, "I think it's time for lunch. Get the car and meet me out front in five minutes."

Juan was sitting in the car when Ivan exited the bar. Ivan quickly crawled into the back seat.

He told Juan, "Drive me back to the farm first before we go to lunch. I need to talk to Anthony Stefano (the Bull), the CEO running the farm. I need to learn firsthand what happened. That is, if he knows or is willing to discuss it with me. I want you to warn me at the first sign of trouble while I'm inside with him."

"You got it, Boss Man."

Arriving out front of Tony Stefano's office, Ivan had Juan stop the car. Ivan exited, walked to the entrance of the office, opened the door and entered.

While Juan sat in the car waiting on Ivan's return, he was approached by a security guard who walked up to the driver's side of the car, bent down, looked through the window, and asked Juan, "Who are you, and what is your business at the farm?"

"I'm Ivan Cohen's personal driver. He's inside talking to Tony Stefano while I wait," Juan replied.

The security guard told Juan in no uncertain terms, "I need you to step out of the vehicle and follow me inside."

Juan opened the door, stepped out of the car, and followed him inside the lobby, where he was searched.

As the security frisked Juan, he felt the gun under Juan's jacket and told him, "You need to remove your gun from the shoulder holster, hand it to me butt first, then have a seat over there. You need to stay seated until your Mr. Cohen returns."

The guard took his gun, leaving Juan seated in the lobby. Juan unexpectedly heard loud shouting coming from one of the offices down the hallway. It sounded like Ivan was arguing with Tony the Bull. The arguing continued for several minutes when suddenly Ivan appeared in the hallway, slamming the door behind him as he left the Bull's office. Ivan headed back down the hallway to where Juan was seated, who immediately stood up in order to escort Ivan from the building. Outside, they walked to where the car was parked without uttering a word. Ivan crawled into the back seat and told Juan,"Drive me back to the stables. I need to talk again to the foreman."

The security guard who was standing outside when Juan and Ivan came out handed Juan back his piece.

Back at the stables, Ivan got out of the car, walked over, and asked one of the hired hands, "Do you know where the foreman is? If so, get hold of him. I need to talk to him."

The worker picked up a phone hanging on the side of the barn and made a quick phone call to the foreman Jimmy Kapos. When Jimmy arrived, Ivan took him by the arm leading him to the other end of the stables, where they could talk in private. He wanted to find out if Jimmy knew any more about what caused the death of his horse. After a brief exchange, Boss Man and Jimmy walked back to where Juan waited. At that point, Ivan and Jimmy shook hands. Jimmy turned and walked back toward the bunkhouse to his office.

Ivan had settled down after his conversation with Jimmy, but upset with the situation at the breeder's farm, especially with Tony the Bull.

Ivan looked at Juan and said, "I think it is time we find a place to have a late lunch. What d'ya you think?"

"Sounds good, Boss Man."

Juan started driving toward the city where they stopped at the Italian Villa. Once inside, Ivan spotted Butch (the owner) tending the bar. Butch looked up, saw Ivan as he entered, and hollered to him, "Ivan Cohen, you old snake in the grass. Is that really you?"

Ivan hollered back, "You old fart, what are you doing working behind the bar?"

Ivan walked over to the bar where Butch was, reached over the bar, and shook his hand.

"Good to see you, Butch. How you doing these days?"

"Fine, Ivan. And how are you? It has been a while since I've seen you.

"Yes, too long. I was on my way back into town when I told my driver I wanted to come by see my old friend and have lunch. My driver Juan has not seen your place, plus I wanted to see you and reminisce about the good old days, ha...Have you had lunch yet, Butch?"

"No, as a matter of fact, I too am hungry."

"Then find someone to tend bar and let's have lunch."

"Okay, I'll be right back. Find a table, and I'll come back and join you."

Ivan and Juan found a table nearby and sat down waiting for Butch's return. After they were seated, a waitress came over, asking if they would like something to drink from the bar.

"Not from the bar," Ivan said, "I'll have a cup of coffee black."

She turned to Juan. "What would you like?"

"I'll have a cup of coffee, but with cream and sugar."

The waitress left to fill their drink order. It was not long before Butch came out of the kitchen and went over to the table where Ivan and Juan sat.

"It's sure good to see you, Ivan. You are looking fit as a fiddle these days."

"Thanks, Butch, but don't feel like that. I've had a rough day so far."

"What's the matter?"

"I'm having a problem with the breeders' association about a horse I purchased recently. For some unknown reason, it died at their farm last night. I've just left the farm after confronting the Bull, who was tight-lipped and noncommittal, telling me he knows nothing about the incident. But the foreman, on the other hand, was a bit more informative about finding the dead horse. He said he was awakened earlier after being informed of the horse's passing by one of the farmhands. He told the foreman about finding the horse unresponsive, not breathing, and had no idea what happened since seeing him only a couple of hours before. The horse died so suddenly I can only speculate someone gave him something, putting him down. We will not know for sure until I have an autopsy performed, then I should know the reason for the horse's demise.

"I told you I talked to the Bull, but indicated to me it was nothing they did caused the horses death. I'm not one hundred percent sure he was telling me the truth. I intend to do battle with him if I find out my horse died from an overdose or poisoned. Only time will tell."

"Sorry to hear you are having trouble with the breeders. I know for a fact they are a dangerous group to deal with. I've heard war stories about how ruthless they can be. I've also heard rumors of corruption within the association. It's been corrupted as far back as I can remember.

My advice to you is, be careful dealing with them. Don't overstep your bounds. It could mean real trouble."

"I'm sorry I became involved with them. I'll watch my back. You can bet your sweet ass on that. Enough about my problems. How are you doing, Butch? Do you still run the cigar store and the bookie joint in the back?"

Yeah, still have the cigar store, and the bookie joint is holding its own."

"How has business overall been lately, making any money?"

"Oh, you know, some days it's good, and other days not so good, but that's another story for another day, ha. But I have more good days than bad days most of the time. Glad the players are not that smart. The ball is in my court, if you get my drift," said Butch.

"I know exactly what you are saying. My days are like that too," replied Ivan.

"Good. How are your different enterprises doing since branching out into so many different ones, must keep you on your toes?"

"Yes, running the collection business, the loan company, the restaurant, and the farm in Lexington. They keep me humping. Like everything else, business could be better, but overall, I can't complain."

"Have you thought about opening any new businesses?" Butch inquired.

"No...ha, my wife says enough is enough. She doesn't see me as it is. I don't need another excuse keeping me away, ha ha. I would be chastised by her more, if you know what I mean?"

"I understand. I'm in the same boat, ha ha."

"Ready for lunch?" Butch asked.

"Yes, it's been a taxing morning, and I'm starved." Butch motioned the waitress to come back to the table and take their order.

After lunch, Butch said to Ivan, "We need to meet again soon and have dinner with the wives like old times. The wives always enjoy each other's company when we got together for dinner and a movie afterward. I'll be in touch. Let's plan going out for dinner and taking in a movie like old times." Butch left it at that.

"Thanks for lunch, Butch. I must be going, need to get back, and see what is going on the south end of town." Ivan told Butch before leaving, "Keep in touch."

Ivan and Juan left the restaurant and headed back to the bar.

Tony met Ivan at the front door as he entered and told him, "A couple of officers from the breeders' farm are waiting for you in your office."

Meanwhile, Juan was returning the car to the garage.

Ivan, hearing that two officers from the breeders' association were in his office, asked Tony, "Did you check them for weapons before allowing them in?"

"Yeah, I patted them down but found nothing, so told them to go into the office and wait, you would be back soon."

Juan, returning from parking the car, saw Ivan had visitors.

He asked Tony, "Who is in the office with Boss Man?"

"Two men from the breeders' association."

Juan joined Tony at the table. They could hear them talking, but it was not loud enough to hear what was being said. After ten minutes or so, the two walked out with Ivan following behind them.

Ivan was saying, "Let the Bull know I'm returning to the farm once the results come back from the vets."

They never acknowledged Ivan and kept walking to the front and out the door. Ivan walked over and stood by the table where Tony and Juan were seated.

Then he said, "Those bastards think I'm going to take this lying down. They have another thought coming. It's not over until the fat lady sings, and she's not entered the building yet."

Juan fetch the car.

"I want to go over to the vet's where they took my horse. I need to talk to the vet and find out if there is any news as to the cause of death. If he has any new information, I'll decide at that time what my option is with the breeders."

Juan drove Ivan to the vets where his horse had been taken for the autopsy. Arriving at the vet's, the vet was in the process of doing a complete postmortem examination on the horse's carcass.

As Ivan entered the lab, the vet looked up, saw Ivan, and told him, "Please come in."

Ivan walked to where the vet was working. The vet began describing to Ivan what he was doing, and the tests he had performed to this point.

"The tests I've run so far all look normal, looks like a natural death. I've not been able to find anything suspicious. The death was not caused by injections of drugs or poison. I'm one hundred percent sure of that. When I finish, I'll give you a complete rundown in the report of each of my test findings."

This was not at all what Ivan expected to hear from the vet. He was at a lost as to what to think or say. It did not make sense—a horse this young and appeared in excellent health, yet die of natural causes? It did not compute, but he would wait for the final report before revisiting the breeders' association to either confront the Bull or apologize.

CHAPTER 15

Back at the office, Ivan was confronted with yet another problem. One of his larger loan accounts had again slipped through the cracks. He had to get the account back on track before it got completely out of control, causing more problems at the loan company.

Ivan called Tony and Juan to his office where he explained to them about this latest wrinkle at the loan company.

"The commercial loan business, as you both know, is the most lucrative business I have. The loan company has invested large amounts of money keeping a certain company solvent. For some reason, the trucking company continues to be delinquent in paying back their loan, and I need to give them a visit and straighten things out ASAP.

"So what I want you to do is inform the muscle group we will take a ride out there this evening for a visit. I need to get the owner's attention and hasten him into paying his debt. He needs to be reminded he did not sign up for a free ride when given the loan. The loan company has bent over backward in the past trying to help this trucking company keep its head above the water line. But for some reason, the owner is once again dragging his feet. The time has come he face the harsh reality of either paying the piper or paying the price. That's why I'm calling on the muscle group to help me deliver that message."

Later that evening, the muscle group gathered outside the trucking company's gates, awaiting Ivan's arrival. When Ivan arrived, motioned as he passed by them to follow his lead into the compound.

The trucks had been skillfully parked along the loading docks, loaded, ready to roll for the late evenings' and early mornings' deliveries. Juan maneuvered the vehicle around the lot until he reached a ramp leading to the loading dock. Here he was told by Ivan to stop the car. Ivan exited the vehicle and walked up the ramp onto the loading dock.

As he did, he passed by a lone security guard who acknowledged his presence but said nothing. Ivan headed straight through the warehouse to the owner's office. When Ivan burst into the office unannounced, the owner looked up from his desk and immediately froze when he saw Ivan.

Ivan looked straight into the owner's eyes without blinking and said, "I'm here to collect in full the debt you owe my loan company. I'm not leaving until I get it or your trucks will not be leaving the docks tonight or tomorrow. Do I make myself clear?"

"Y-y-yes, I-I-Iv-Ivan, but I don't have that kind of cash lying around the office right now to give you. I've been in dire straits lately, more monies going out than coming in. I'm sure you can understand my situation? I've been trying to keep my business afloat from going belly-up. I promise when I get the extra cash, I'll pay up."

"Sounds like a personal problem to me. My problem is with you, and the money you owe me. I'm going to tell you one more time, I'm here to collect, and I'm not leaving until I have what I came for. Is that clear? Are you going to make this easy or difficult?"

"Like I told you Ivan, I don't have that kind of cash lying around, give me a couple of days, and I will come up with the money somehow and pay my debt."

"That's not what I wanted to hear. Guess you'll have to be taught a lesson. When you owe money, it's your responsibility to make good on that debt, understood?"

"Uh…uh…yeah, I guess. I've messed up again, didn't I?"

Ivan, without responding to his last comment, turned, walked out of the office, and returned to the loading dock. Standing alone on the dock, Ivan motioned to the muscle group awaiting his order. He raised his arms and shouted, "Okay, get busy. Let's do some rearranging and teach this leech a lesson on taking care of his obligations."

The muscle group climbed out of their cars and onto the loading dock where they commenced busting locks on the semitrailers' doors. Once the locks were removed, opened the large doors on the trailers and began destroying the contents stored inside. Part of the group went inside the warehouse where they started destroying the merchandise that were stored in boxes and stacked on pallets. Using crowbars, ripped off the metal bands securing the boxes stacked on the pallets. As the metal bands were removed, the boxes and contents fell on the floor and spilled all over the warehouse floor.

The owner, hearing the commotion of the wrecking crew Ivan had brought along, came out of his office and into the warehouse. He saw what was happening, the devastation and havoc inside the warehouse, plus the merchandise inside the trailers lying all over the docks. After seeing the damage, he began begging Ivan to stop.

Ivan's response was, "Only when you pay up, asshole, will I stop, but not until."

"Okay, okay, let me go back in the office and see what I can do before you do any more damage to the merchandise and trucks."

"I'm not willing to wait much longer. What do you have in mind to stop my crew from destroying the rest of your property? Whatever it is, you better make it good. Tell me and tell me quick."

"Okay, just give me a minute to go to my office and see how much cash I have in the safe and my checking account. I'm sure I can come up with most, if not all of it, tonight."

At hearing that, Ivan raised his hands once again and the devastation ceased.

"Okay, boys, stop what you're doing until this asshole returns with my money; if he does not satisfy me with his offer you can go back to work."

The owner reluctantly returned to the office and went directly to his safe, opened it, removed all the cash inside. Then took his checkbook and wrote out a check, not the full amount he owed, but a figure he hoped would suffice until he could get to the bank the following morning. He was counting on the bank to float him a loan to pay the balance of his debt to Ivan.

Taking what money in the safe plus the check he unenthusiastically wrote, walked slowly back to the loading dock where Ivan waited patiently along with his group. The owner nervously handed over the cash and check to Ivan, then said, "I…will…have…the rest of your money by tomorrow morning, hand deliver it to your office by 10:00 a.m."

Ivan took what money he had, glanced at the check, satisfied with the amounts, told his men they could return to their cars; were finished for the night. Ivan looked the owner straight in the eye, told him in no uncertain terms if he was a no-show by 10:00 a.m. the following morning, he would return and finish what he started. Ivan turned and walked down the ramp to his car and left the trucking company grounds along with his entourage following close behind.

As the owner looked around at the carnage and damage, he wondered to himself if it was possible to recoup part of the damaged merchandise, which had been strewn about the dock and warehouse. The loading dock and warehouse was a total disaster. Somehow, he had to get his men back to work tonight and clean this mess up. He had to salvage as much of the merchandise as possible if his trucks were to be on the road in just a few hours delivering what little cargo was salvageable. He had to recover as much merchandise as possible in order to keep his losses to a bare minimum.

Back inside his office, he called his foreman, telling him, "I need you to contact as many dock workers and drivers as possible tonight to get their asses back to work pronto. I had a visit from Ivan tonight. His group left this place in shambles. We need it cleaned up before sending the trucks out for their delivery run later tonight. Do I make myself clear?"

"Yeah, boss, I'll round up as many as I can and have them meet at the warehouse as soon as they can get ready and drive over there. We'll get the place cleaned up and have as many trucks as possible reloaded for tonight's deliveries."

CHAPTER 16

Meanwhile, Ivan headed back to his office to drop off what monies had collected from the trucking company owner before going home. With the money securely locked up safely in the safe, left the office, closing the door behind him. He walked through the bar to his waiting car, and told Juan, "I'm ready but have one more place to go before you take me home. Drive over to the vet's office. I want to see if he has any new information concerning the death of my horse."

Arriving a short time later at the vet's, Ivan walked inside the waiting room where the vet's secretary was still working. She looked up and saw Ivan come in. She told him the clinic was closed.

Ivan said, "Is it possible to see the vet? Is he was still around?"

"I'm sorry, Mr. Cohen, but the doctor has gone for the evening. He will not return until tomorrow morning."

"Would you have him call me when he comes to work in the morning? I really need to talk to him."

"Okay, leave me your phone number, and I'll have him call first thing when he arrives."

"Thanks."

Ivan turned around heading toward the door when he suddenly stopped, turning around facing the secretary, told her, "Make sure you tell the doctor to call. It's important."

"I promise as soon as he comes in."

"Thank you again."

Ivan proceeded out the building and back to the car where he informed Juan, "You can now take me home.

The next morning, as Ivan arrived at work and before he sat down, the phone on his desk rang; it was the doctor from the veterinary hospital.

"Good morning, Mr. Cohen, this is Dr. Ted at the veterinary hospital. I heard you came by to see me late last evening?"

"Yes, Ted, I dropped by to see if you had any news for me about my horse."

"I've finished the examination. My findings for what caused the death of the animal was not by some lethal injection or foreign substances but presumptive pulmonary failure."

"What…what does pulmonary failure mean, Doc?"

"It means your horse suffered from some sort of lung failure. It's rare, but not that uncommon in racehorses. I'm sending you a copy of the report this morning, detailing the entire exam. It should ease your mind knowing the horse did not die because of some deliberate overdose or injection."

"Thanks, Doc. I appreciate your due diligence in finding the root cause of the horse's demise."

Hanging the phone up, Ivan called Tony and Juan into his office. As they entered Ivan's office, they were told to take a seat.

"I've just talked to the veterinarian who has informed me my horse died of something called pulmonary lung condition. A rare genetic condition, but not uncommon in racehorses. I wanted you two to know his findings, and this matter is no longer a concern to the organization. I wanted to let you know before you heard it from some other source.

"I need to contact the breeders' association and apologize for insinuating they had something to do with the horse's death. I'm glad it did not involve them, me being new to this game and all. There had been a lot of innuendos flying around about their organization, plus I had my doubts as to the real cause of death. Now that's it's been confirmed, hope you too understood my concern over the incident."

"Sure, we understand. It's only natural you thought what you did concerning this matter."

Returning to their table, Tony and Juan were relieved the problem was over between the breeders' association and their organization. They were glad it had not escalated to a higher and more volatile situation. It could have erupted in an all-out disaster between the two groups.

The muscle group and other entities inside the association were informed to stand down and were no longer on call, that the hostile confrontation with the breeders' association had been quashed by the vet's findings.

However, the muscle group was still on call concerning the problem with the trucking company. Ivan had not heard from the owner as yet this morning. Ten o'clock was the time the owner promised Ivan he would be in to pay off his debt. But, ten o'clock was still a half hour away.

As Juan and Tony sat at the table playing cards, when the owner of the trucking company walked in. You could tell by his mannerisms he was not a happy camper, but had an obligation and had stepped up to the plate. He was stopped and frisked before allowed access to the office. After being patted down, with no weapon found on his person, he was allowed to proceed to Ivan's office, closing the door behind him as he entered. It was not long after the door opened that the trucking company owner departed. He walked back through the bar and out the front door, never looking back.

Ivan called Tony and Juan to his office for the second time that morning. He explained to them another crisis had been averted; the debt owed by the trucking company had been satisfied. Another sigh of relief was felt between Tony and Juan. Two really nasty problems had been quashed in less than two hours that morning. Everyone in the organization could now relax and take a deep breath.

CHAPTER 17

Not long after the trucking company owner left, Al came barging into the bar wanting to see Boss Man about a problem collecting from one of his more difficult accounts. He walked briskly past Juan and Tony without acknowledgment to either of them into Ivan's office, where he explained the trouble he was having with the shoe store owner. The store owner had always been full of excuses when it came time to collect. But this time, Al was forced to confront the owner who threatened him if he did not leave. Out of nowhere, the shop owner retrieved his gun from under the counter, pointed it at Al, and told him if he did not get out he was going to shoot him.

He asked Ivan, "Is it possible to borrow Juan or Tony, return to the shoe store, and try knocking some sense in the store owner?"

"Yes, why don't you ask Juan, but don't you two go overboard doing something stupid you'll regret? Understand what I'm saying?"

"Yes, Boss Man, I need to teach this son of a bitch a lesson he'll not soon forget."

"Go ask Juan if he is willing to help straighten out the situation at the shoe store but be careful and not overdo it."

"Yeah, Boss Man, I hear you loud and clear."

Al left the office and stopped by where Tony and Juan were seated. He joined them at the table explaining to them what Boss Man and he had discussed in the office.

"Juan, Boss Man said to ask you if you would assist me this morning in suppressing the problem I have with the owner of the shoe store. You remember him I'm sure. I think he would listen to you."

"Sure, I'll do what I can. Are you ready to go?"

They were out the door in a flash heading in the direction of the shoe store to take care of business.

When they entered the shoe store, the owner looked up to see Al and Juan. Quickly he reached under the counter, retrieving his gun. He looked at both of them straight in the eye and said, "I'm done paying protection money. Get the hell out of my store before I start shooting. Do I make myself clear?"

Al tried once again talking to him but to no avail. He would have none of it. Al told him he had marching orders from Boss Man, and he was not leaving until the dues had been collected. Juan took up the slack, proceeding slowly up to the owner and telling him to stop. "Put the gun down because we are not leaving until you pay."

The owner raised his weapon and fired one round, hitting Al in the left shoulder. In the meantime, Juan jumped over the counter and begun wrestling the weapon from the store owner. Luckily for Al he received only a superficial wound to his shoulder, and he told Juan not to worry since the bullet did not penetrate but just nicked his shoulder, that he was fine.

Once the initial conflict was quashed, Juan told the shoe store owner to get the money or they would disassemble his store before leaving.

The owner said, "I don't have the money and cannot pay."

Juan raised his hand with the gun smacking him upside the head with the butt end of his own pistol, then across the forehead before the owner dropped to the floor, holding his hands over his bleeding face. Once the owner was on the floor, Juan stood over him pointing the gun directly between his eyes, telling him one more time, "Now get us the f——g money."

The owner glared up at Juan and told him, "You go to hell."

At that, Juan walked over to the front door locking it, then placed a Closed sign in the front window. Juan walked back over to where Al was nursing his flesh wound and asked, "How are you doing? Sure, you are okay?"

"Yeah, I've had worse nicks while shaving, ha ha."

"Okay, let me get this son of a bitch back to his office and see if I can knock some sense into him."

Juan went behind the counter, grabbed the owner, and dragged him back to the office. Once inside the office, Juan sat the owner down in a chair and asked again for payment; again the owner refused. Juan then smacked him again with his open hand and told him, "We're not leaving without that payment."

The owner looked back at Juan and said nothing. Juan turned toward the door walking back to where Al stood near the door and handed him the gun.

Juan told Al, "Keep an eye on the owner. I'm going out front and rearrange the store."

Juan left the office closing the door, leaving Al and the owner alone inside. A short time later, Juan came back to the office where Al was watching the owner while Juan took care of business. Juan once again asked the owner about payment, but he was as defiant as ever.

Juan looked at the owner and said, "This is not over. We'll be back tomorrow. You have the money ready. If not, we will not be leaving until we have the money or you are in the hospital, capisce, old man?"

Leaving the shoe owner with that warning, they turned and walked out of the store. Bleeding and in terrible pain, the owner was as rebellious and defiant as ever when they departed from the store. Back on the street, Al and Juan shook their heads and talked about how tenacious the owner was. He was as hard a case as Al had encountered in all his years of collecting.

When they returned to the office to talk to Boss Man and get feedback as to what to do about the owner of the shoe store.

Boss Man told them, "Don't come back tomorrow without the Money."

With that, they left the office and returned to where Tony sat at the table to discuss what strategy to use against the store owner the following day, as they once again confront him. Juan wanted to go tomorrow to finish what he started. This did not upset Al in the least. He needed Juan's assistance. Al's left shoulder was giving him a bit of discomfort and was not looking forward to manhandling the shoe store owner in his condition.

It was agreed; Juan would rough up the owner to the point he was no longer capable of running the business.

The next morning, Al and Juan left the bar to meet with the owner of the shoe store. As they approached the shoe store, observed two police cars parked in front. The owner called the police after arriving at work and asked for their protection. It was contingent on Juan and Al returning. Instead of continuing toward the shoe store, they quickly ducked beside a building to discuss their options.

If the police stayed around the neighborhood, it would be impossible to complete their mission. Boss Man was not going to be happy if they returned without the dues, but sometimes things happened. This situation had to be put on the back burner until a later date. When they returned to the bar, they explained to Boss Man the quandary they ran into at the shoe store that morning.

Ivan told them, "No, you did the right thing. We will wait until a more favorable time. Do not worry, we'll eventually get our money."

Leaving the office, Juan told Al, "Are you up to working the rest of the day with that shoulder?"

"Yes, it is a bit stiff but will not be a problem."

"Good. Get out of here, go finish your collections. I'll see you later."

Al left Juan and Tony, sitting at the table discussing the situation he and Al had encountered that morning at the shoe store.

Tony told Juan, "Yeah, the owner of that store has always been a problem. It's never been easy for Al collecting from him. He is a rare bird, making it next to impossible to deal with once he makes up his mind."

Around noontime, Ivan called Juan into the office.

"Go get the car, bring it around front. It's time for lunch. After lunch, I have a few things to take care. Tell Tony we'll be out of the office the most part of the afternoon," Ivan informed Juan.

Juan drove Ivan to lunch at one of the oldest but nicest restaurants in town. It was called the Steer-Ins on Meridian Street, and already it was packed when they arrived. But they had nothing to worry about since Ivan knew the owner. It had never been a problem getting a table there. Ivan got out of the car, entered the establishment, and quickly ushered to a table near the rear of the restaurant, where he always sat. As soon as Juan entered, he was escorted back to where Ivan sat waiting. Juan sat across from Ivan, looking around the establishment and taking in all the lavish furnishings inside. Juan was impressed not only with the service but with the décor; it was magnificent. Most restaurants he visited with Ivan were your typical run-of-the-mill, nothing fancy, nothing like this place.

After lunch, Ivan had Juan head west of town to meet with his financial advisor concerning his portfolio and what changes, if any, should be made to it since the economy had improved recently. Ivan sat in the plush office of his advisor while Juan sat alone in the lobby.

Juan thought to himself, *I could become accustomed to Ivan's lifestyle. Someday, if I'm lucky, I too will be living in the lifestyle Ivan's exposed me to since working for him.*

Juan had become more and more enthralled with his surroundings lately—from the beautiful restaurants, horse farms, vacations; things he never knew existed before coming to work for Ivan. He had Al to thank for this success and lifestyle he now enjoyed.

Juan swore to himself. "Someday, I'll repay Al in some small way for his help in landing this job."

When Ivan was finished talking with his financial advisor, came out of the office telling Juan, "I'm ready to head back downtown."

*****

It was spring 1973. Another winter had passed, and time for the ninety-ninth running of the Kentucky Derby at Churchill Downs in Louisville, Kentucky. It was time Ivan met up with Shorty. Shorty was his go-to man when placing bets on anything from horses, baseball, hockey to who was to win the next presidential election. Shorty was a small-time bookie whom Ivan trusted explicitly for any bet placed with him.

The cigar store Shorty owned was a front for illegal gambling and was located in downtown Indy, just off the circle.

As Juan stopped the car along the curb, Ivan told him to wait he would return soon. Ivan exited the car and entered the cigar store, where he found Shorty. Ivan placed a bet on Secretariat to win the Kentucky Derby coming up on May 5, which was only a week away. Ivan received inside information from one of the stable hands at the breeders' farm that Secretariat was the favorite in this year's race. Since Secretariat was favored to win, Ivan placed a small amount of money on her to win. Because of the odds, Secretariat would not pay much if she won. He looked over the remaining list of horses running and made a couple more bets with Shorty. Ivan placed a bet on Sham too (place), hedging his bet with a bit more money, and his heaviest bet was on Forego, placing several hundred for the horse to (show).

After placing his bets with Shorty, Ivan walked out of the cigar store, and hopped back in the car. Juan drove him to the office. It was getting late when they arrived at the bar, Ivan got out, heading inside to his office. He still had work to complete before going home for the evening. Since he had been gone all afternoon, there was bookwork and collection money to count and put away.

After he finished counting the day's take and entering each amount into a daily logbook, placed both money and logbook in the large safe. With the day's work finished and loose ends tied up, it was time for Juan to take him home to see his wife and two children. That night, his youngest daughter was celebrating a birthday, and he was expected home for her surprise birthday party.

CHAPTER 18

Sometime during the night after the bar closed and everyone one had vacated the building, someone threw a Molotov cocktail through the glass window of the bar. The firebomb started a raging fire inside, and by the time the fire department arrived, the building was completely engulfed in flames. The firefighters found themselves at a disadvantage from the get-go, fighting a losing battle in putting the fire out and saving the old building. The structure itself was old; the wood inside was dry and burned quickly. The firefighters fought the fire several hours before bringing it under control. Once the fire was under control, the only area inside the burned-out building that was still basically intact was Ivan's office. Luckily for him it was located at the very back of the building.

Ivan was notified by the police that the building that housed the bar had been destroyed by fire, which firefighters were unable to contain since the fire had spread throughout much of the building prior to their arrival.

The police told Ivan, "The full extent of the damage would not be known until the fire marshal and fire investigator inspected the charred remains of the building."

After being informed of the fire, Ivan immediately called the hotel where Juan lived and told the desk clerk on duty to inform Juan to pick him up as soon as possible there had been a fire at the bar. Ivan hung the phone up, proceeded to get dressed in order to be ready upon Juan arrived.

About three-quarters of an hour later, Juan pulled up in front of Ivan's home. Ivan opened the front door and quickly walked down the front steps into the car as Juan held the door open. They rushed downtown as fast as possible to the bar without breaking the speed limit. When Ivan arrived and saw the destruction, he started asking around for the cause of the fire, but no one knew. Devastated at what he saw, he vowed he would get to the bottom of it and do whatever in rectifying the problem.

Who did this? Ivan wondered as he looked at the smoldering pile of rubble. It was a complete mystery to Ivan. Ivan had made a few enemies in the past; any one of them could have had a vendetta against him, but who? He would sort those thoughts out in his mind later; this was not the time or place. Once he learned the origin of the fire, he would take appropriate action at that time. It seemed surreal to him standing there looking at the devastation, vowing to find the responsible party if found to be arson. In that case, the responsible party would pay and pay dearly once the truth was known. He now understood and felt what shop owners felt when he destroyed their livelihoods from time to time; the feeling he felt inside was sickening.

The first thing he had to do was get in touch with the different groups in the organization and decide what to do in the meantime while trying to holding the organization together.

He told Juan, "I need you to get hold of Tony. Have him contact the head of each group in the organization and meet him at the Silver Dollar Saloon at noon."

Juan walked down the street where he found a pay phone to call Tony. After reaching Tony, he briefed him on what occurred and that Ivan wanted him to contact the head of each group for a special meeting to be held at the Silver Dollar Saloon. Juan also told Tony to try contacting later those whom he could not reach.

He walked back to the burned-out bar and found Ivan looking at the devastation surrounding him.

Juan approached Ivan and told him, "I've contacted Tony, explained the situation and what he needed to do."

Ivan thanked Juan. "I'm proud of you for being so understanding and businesslike this morning as the organization faces such a monumental crisis. I don't know what I would have done without your assistance this morning. I'm ready to find the source or culprit on who did this. If it's found to be arson, I'm going to burn some one's ass. Anyway, have you heard any rumors of anyone upset or wanting to retaliate about anything I or the organization has done recently?"

Juan answered Ivan, telling him, "Ah, no. Everything seemed calm around town at the moment. The two exceptions that come to mind is the trucking company and the shoe store incident. I know the trucking company owner was pissed at you for destroying some of his merchandise, and his workers annoyed and angry at being called back to clean up the mess you caused. If I were a betting man, I'd say it was the trucking company."

"I think I'll have you drive me over there sometime this afternoon after the meeting at the Silver Dollar and confront the owner. I need to find out his take on this matter. Maybe it wasn't him, but perhaps one or more of his union workers? I have to find out as soon as possible and put a stop to this tit for tat going on."

"Good idea," said Juan.

"Since we can do nothing else here, let's have breakfast and mull it over and try to make sense out of this mess."

"Where would you like to go?" asked Juan.

"Let's walk down the block to that little restaurant you, Tony, and Al go to on occasions. I have often thought about stopping there myself, but never gotten around to it."

As they walked down the street and approached the restaurant, Ivan took a quick look through the large picture window. He was looking inside, making sure none of his adversaries were inside; that was all he needed to top off his morning. Seeing none, he and Juan entered spotting an empty table where they could sit with their backs against the wall and a clear view of the entry; Ivan was taking no chances.

After being seated, a waitress came over and asked, "Coffee?" "Yes, two coffees, one black and one with cream and sugar," Ivan told the waitress.

Soon she returned with a fresh pot of coffee and two cups. Placing the cups on the table, she poured hot coffee in the two cups, and asked, "Are you having breakfast? If so, do you know what you want or do you need to look at our menu?

"Yes, to both questions. We are having breakfast, and yes, we need two menus."

Returning with menus, she placed them on the corner of the table. Ivan picked up a menu and looked it over. He quickly decided what he was having for breakfast and motioned for the waitress.

She returned to the table and asked, "Are you ready to order, and what are you having this morning?"

"I'll have two eggs over easy, two sausage patties, wheat toast with butter and jelly on the side" was Ivan's answer.

"And, you handsome, what's your pleasure this morning?"

"I'll have the short stack of pancakes, with lots of maple syrup and butter."

The restaurant was not busy, and able to be served rather quickly. It was not long until the waitress arrived carrying their food on a large tray. She placed the tray on a corner of the table removing the plates, placing their orders in front of them.

Before leaving, she said, "If you needed anything else, let me know."

Ivan thanked her as she turned and walked away to finish filling the salt and pepper shakers she was working on when they entered.

Sitting there having breakfast, Ivan turned and looked at Juan, and out of the blue, he asked him, "Juan, would you be interested or consider becoming my partner and help me run the business?"

Juan was taken aback and utterly surprised by the proposition Ivan just offered him. He sat speechless for a minute or two, letting the thought sink in and contemplating on how to answer such a question.

He finally looked up at Ivan and said, "Oh…I…I am not ready for that. But yes, even though I'm new at this. I'll need your guidance and assistance in the everyday aspects of the business until I learn more."

"I see no problem in you handling certain aspects of the business to start. You seem to be a very capable young man. No matter what I've asked of you so far, you've done it first rate with no questions asked. That's what I like about you. You've seen me and know how I operate. I think with a little push and prodding along with some experience under your belt, you should be able to take over the entire operation in no time. So do you want to give it a try?"

"You bet, yeah. Ivan, I'll do you proud."

"Okay, I'll tell the group this afternoon while we are gathered at the Silver Dollar. You and I are going to be business partners. I'm offering you 49 percent of the business up front. I still want to maintain control of the business until I fully retire in a year or so. I'll make it official this afternoon. It will come as a complete shock and surprise to the group, but they will have to get over it and move on."

"I appreciate the confidence you have in me, and I won't let you down," Juan told Ivan.

"I expect a lot from you. It's not going to be easy, but I think you are capable of handling the job or I would not have asked you. This afternoon after the meeting, I need you to think of a couple dependable drivers, then go out and purchase a car for yourself. You know most of the group, and when you decided on the drivers, let me know. We'll discuss them later. I'm sure we have individuals within the organization willing to step up to the plate and take the added responsibility." That was Ivan's final thought on the subject.

"Let me give it some thought. I'm sure there are two people on payroll who qualify. I'll get back to you with my recommendations when I make my decision."

"We have a lot on our plates this afternoon—first, the meeting at the Silver Dollar Saloon, the trip to the trucking company, buying yourself a new car, and adding two new drivers. I'm giving you a lot to do, but we need to get on the ball and have these tasks behind us so we can move on. I hope you are ready for the responsibility I'm placing on you." Ivan told Juan.

"I'm sure with your help and guidance I'll manage," Juan replied.

CHAPTER 19

At noon, Ivan arrived upstairs in the Silver Dollar Saloon's banquet room set aside for his hastily announced meeting. He was glad to see someone from each group show up. Tony had done an outstanding job getting a representative from each group. Ivan shook hands with a few of the organization's heads as he passed among them and made his way to the podium.

Ivan called the meeting to order. "First thing on the agenda this afternoon is…I don't know if everyone's aware of the situation downtown concerning a fire at the bar?"

A large moaning sound came from those assembled.

"Sounds like most of you've been informed by the sound of your response." Ivan told them in no uncertain terms, "I'm going to get to the bottom of this, and when I find out who's responsible, I'll take appropriate action. But at this time, I have no idea what happened. In time, I'm sure I'll learn what caused the fire and if it was a case of arson. They will be held accountable and pay the price."

After explaining what he knew about the fire, he told them he would keep them updated and informed of the evolving developments and circumstances, and in the meantime, maintain the status quo going forward.

Before continuing with his other big announcement, he asked, "Does anyone here have additional information they would like to share at this time? Also, if anyone has heard of a rumor or hate campaign against me or the organization, let me know after the meeting." Before adjourning the meeting, Ivan told those gathered, "I have one more item that I need to share with you. I want you to know, I've decided to take Juan in as my business partner. I know some of you will question my reasoning behind this announcement and wonder why I'm doing it at this time. I have been looking for someone of Juan's caliber for some time. Luckily, he showed up when he did. I'm ready to lighten my workload and need someone like Juan to take over the helm when I officially retire. He has been my confidant, driver-security man for the last few months, and I've come to respect and rely heavily on him. I've known most of you much longer than Juan, but in my mind, he's the most capable and qualified in carrying on the business if anything happens to me. I would like to have each and every one's approval of my decision. After today, he'll be your new boss, and what he says is final, no different than if I told you. Above all, don't underestimate him. Are there any questions? If none, the is meeting adjourned."

The group milled around the room discussing the bombshell Ivan dropped concerning the fire and appointment of Juan as his new partner. The appointment of Juan was the major topic, overshadowing the fire. It came as a complete shock to the rank and file, as it had to Juan earlier.

How would the rank and file overall accept Juan?

Would he be able to gain the confidence and respect of the organization being a newbie?

Of all the employees inside the association, why had Ivan considered him to be his partner after such a short time?

Ivan's appointment of Juan was not to be questioned but accepted. Ivan's choice to take Juan in as a partner was his idea and his alone and no one else's.

It was up to Juan to take the bull by the horns and run with it. No matter what, he was now the man in charge.

As the bombshell about Ivan's new partner slowly sank in, the majority of the group accepted Ivan's decision. Maybe Ivan knew what he was doing, and they had no recourse but to accept his choice. Thinking back, it occurred to them, Ivan, on several occasions had mentioned the organization needed new blood and ideas. Ivan, working the organization alone for many years, maybe saw the handwriting on the wall, that the times were changing and he was not getting any younger. The organization needed change in order to keep up with times. If Ivan had that much faith in Juan, they, too, should show the same conviction by trusting Boss Man's decision without question. As the meeting broke up, different groups assembled and congratulated Juan on his new partnership with Ivan.

After the meeting, it was time to get back to work; and for Juan and Ivan, it was a new and exciting chapter in their lives and the organization as well. Ivan and Juan walked down the stairs, through the saloon and out to the car. Ivan, drained from so much going on, needed to rest and collect his thoughts. It had been a turbulent and tempestuous day so far. There was a lot Ivan and Juan had to contemplate and accomplish in the next few days, weeks, and months.

Ivan had several pressing issues to follow up on in the coming days. First and foremost, he had to notify the local bank and horse farm in Lexington, Kentucky, of Juan's appointment. His attorney had to be informed to draw up necessary papers awarding Juan 49 percent of the organization, then look for a building to house their new office. Ivan owned a large commercial building downtown. If a real estate company could not find him a suitable building, he would look into using it and remodel it to suit their needs. The most difficult thing going forward was preparing Juan to run the day-to-day operation.

Dropping Ivan off at his home, Juan drove to the garage and park the car, then hustled back to the hotel to start on a list of names for security-drivers for Ivan and himself. It was his first official duty since becoming a partner. It was a difficult decision for Juan, but had to be completed, and the sooner the better. As he sat in his room considering his short list of names, decided on two individuals he thought best suited the position and highly qualified for the job (in his opinion). The two names were names Ivan mentioned in the past as two of his best and most trusted associates over the years.

Knowing that Ivan previously mentioned their names showed he had confidence in the two. Juan was sure Ivan would be pleased with his choices. Upon reaching a decision and satisfied with the results, he laid down to rest. As he did, he wrapped his mind around the events that occurred earlier, not only the fire but to him personally. It did not take long after closing his eyes he fell asleep and slept throughout the night, never getting up to undress.

The next morning, Juan was up early. He took a hot bath, shaved, dressed, and ready to pick up Ivan when he called. The desk clerk called

Juan's room around 6:30 a.m. and relayed the message "A Mr. Cohen called and told me to tell you he was ready to be picked up."

Ivan, having had one of the worst days of his life the prior day, not up to his usual self that morning and was running late when he called Juan at the hotel.

As soon as Juan was informed Ivan was ready, he left the hotel. Upon reaching the garage, he found the Cadillac with all four tires flattened. During the night, someone punctured the outside walls of all four tires rendering the car useless. Hurrying back to the hotel, he called Ivan and told him of his dilemma.

"Okay, call a tire service. Have all four tires replaced. Once they have been replaced, call me."

Juan found a phone number for a tire company close by; he called the company and told them what had happened and he needed four new tires as soon as possible.

The tire company explained to Juan, "It will take at least an hour before we find four tires that size, then pick them up. I will call you as soon as we locate the tires and are on our way."

"Find those tires and get over here as fast as you can. I'll be waiting," Juan reiterated to the salesman.

Juan went back to his room, waiting to hear back from the tire company. An hour and fifteen minutes later, the phone rang at the front desk. The clerk answered.

"This is Elvis's tire company. Tell Mr. Juan Grajales someone's on their way to replace the tires on Mr. Cohen's car. You tell him the truck with the tires will be arriving within the next ten minutes."

The clerk immediately informed Juan, who hurried back down the stairs and out of the hotel, heading to the garage where he waited for the truck to arrive. Not long after, he heard the truck as it entered the garage. As the driver approached the area where the car was located, Juan waved to attract the driver's attention. The driver acknowledged and drove over to where Juan stood and stopped.

The driver got out of his truck to assess the situation, telling Juan, "It'll take me at least an hour to remove the tires from the rims and replace the new tires back on the rims, fill them with air and on the car."

Juan said, "I'll be back before you finish." He headed back to the hotel.

Back at the hotel, Juan called Ivan to let him know the time frame until he was able to drive out and pick him up. Neither Juan or Ivan was pleased with the status quo but had no choice until the tire problem was addressed.

As time approached for the car to be completed, Juan left the hotel and walked to the garage where he found the driver putting the last tire on the car. He walked back to the hotel, called Ivan to tell him he was on his way.

Before leaving the garage, out of the corner of his eye, Juan spotted an ice pick lying near the parapet walls encasing the outer aspect of the garage. He stopped the car, exited, and retrieved the ice pick. As he bent down and picked it up, thinking it could be the instrument used to puncture the tires. Without giving it any more thought, he threw the ice pick in the front floorboard and drove out to pick up Ivan.

Juan arrived two and a half hours late. Ivan was exiting the house and making his way down the stairs to meet Juan as he entered the driveway. When Juan stopped the car, Ivan climbed in the front seat; and as he did, he noticed the ice pick lying on the floorboard.

He immediately turned to Juan and asked, "Where did this come from?"

"Oh, I found it lying in the garage near the parapet wall a couple of spaces down from the car."

"This looks like the ice pick I use when I'm at the stables. I use it to hold notes I write when visiting the farm. I stick it on one of the four by fours near my stall. I use it when I write a note to the groomer or foreman, letting them know what I want when no one is around."

"Are you sure it's the same ice pick?"

"Yes. See the F on the name Franklin Ice Company logo is missing."

"Yes, so?"

"It was removed by me one day when I cut a sliver of wood off it to use as a toothpick to remove a piece of meat I had for lunch that stuck between my teeth. I would recognize that ice pick anywhere. And you said you found it in the garage along the parapet wall near the car?"

"Yes, a space or two from the caddy, along the parapet wall."

"Well, that tells me someone at the stables had something to do with flattening the tires and a good possibility that the same person had something to do with setting the fire at the bar."

"Makes sense, but how can we find out who's responsible for the events having occurred lately?" asked Juan.

"I'll do some snooping around. I'm sure I can weed out the person or persons at the stables who did these things or know who did. Let's head out there right now and see who's working."

After Ivan was seated, Juan closed the door, and they headed out the main gate, turning right onto the highway toward the breeders' stables. It was not long before they entered the lane leading to the farm. Juan was told to stop the car near the stables; that was when he bolted from the car before Juan came to a complete stop. Ivan hurriedly walked to the rear of the stables and stopped in front of the stall where his horse had been kept. He met one of the groomers exiting a stall nearby, who, when he saw Ivan, looked surprised.

The groomer's first words were "What brings you two out here today?"

"I'm looking for the foreman. Is he around?" Ivan asked.

"No, not this morning. He told me earlier he had some unfinished business out of town and would not be back for a couple of days."

"I would like to leave the foreman a note. As you know, I always leave it on the post in front of my stall."

"Yes, I remember."

He took out a pad and pencil from his jacket pocket and wrote a short note to the foreman to attach it to the post while the groomer looked on.

Ivan looked over at the groomer and asked casually, "Do you know where the ice pick is? I use it to post my notes. It's not on the post."

The groomer cowered and said, "Ah…don't know, ah…have no idea where it could be. Do you think maybe someone used it and forgot to return it?"

Ivan then asked the groomer, "Why don't you look around and see if you can find it before I leave."

"Yes, sir."

Before leaving, the groomer returned and told Ivan, "I've not found the ice pick, but I'll continue looking. I'm sure it is around here somewhere."

Ivan had enough of the groomer's ineptness at finding the ice pick, decided to leave and wait to hear from the foreman upon his return. Ivan was sure when the foreman learned he questioned the groomer about the missing ice pick, he would get in contact and try to rectify the incident. But if the foreman did not call, upon his next visit he'd mention to the foreman of the missing ice pick and if it had been located. If the foreman was vague about what happened to the ice pick, he would tell the foreman it was found in the garage next to the four flattened tires on his car. That should get a rise out of him or someone working at the stables.

Ivan was sure someone associated with the farm was aware of why his business had been torched and tires flattened on his car. It was just a matter of time before learning of the perpetrator/perpetrators. It stood to reason someone had a beef with him and sending him a message to be doubly cautious whom he associates with and to tread lightly.

For the life of him, Ivan had not a clue as to whom it might be. He stepped on more than a few toes over the years, but no clue as to anything serious enough to warrant this type of vandalism or reprisals.

Ivan vowed to Juan, "When I find who's responsible, I will not spare the rod. It's had a most devastating effect on my business. Someone's going to pay and pay big-time."

Juan drove Ivan back to the city where they located Tony, picked him up, then proceeded to the Sportsman's for a late lunch. When they arrived at the Sportsman's and seated, Ivan looked over at Juan and asked, "Have you decided yet on the two names I asked from you?"

"Yes."

Juan removed the list from his jacket pocket, handing it to Ivan.

Ivan opened up the note and saw two names. Looking them over, he seemed satisfied with Juan's choices. Since Tony was not aware what Ivan had asked Juan to do, Ivan looked over at Tony and said, "I've asked Juan for two names of trusted associates he would recommend for drivers-security now that he's no longer a driver and needs a driver himself. The two names are listed on the note he just handed me. I would like your opinion, Tony, if you think they are worthy and capable of handling the job."

Ivan handed the note to Tony; the two names were Johnny Leopold and Hank "the Irishman" O'Connor.

"What's your opinion of his choices?" Ivan asked Tony.

"They would be among my top picks, Boss Man. Both are reliable and honest. Both would be an asset if things get out of hand or become difficult. Both are street-smart, accept any job without question, also well-versed on the daily routine of the organization. Don't think Juan could have decided on a better pair."

"Now that's settled, let's have lunch before going back to the office. We still have a lot to accomplish before we finish today."

After lunch, the three of them headed to a local car dealership to pick out a car for Juan. After Juan decided on a car, Ivan took out his checkbook and wrote the car dealer a check.

Ivan, before leaving the dealership, looked over at Tony and told him, "Tony, you take my car back to the garage. We'll meet you at Leo's restaurant near the burned-out bar in a couple of hours."

Tony crawled behind the wheel of Ivan's Cadillac and drove it back to the garage. Ivan and Juan in the meantime left the dealership in Juan's new car, heading over to the bank to have Juan's name added to several accounts Ivan had at the bank. Finishing up at the bank, Juan drove to Leo's restaurant where they met up again with Tony.

While sitting in Leo's, their conversation turned to real estate and which real estate company they should talk to about a new storefront to run the business out of. During their conversation, Ivan remembered the building he owned and the possibility of it fitting their need. It was large enough for both Juan and him to have an office, plus, room for Tony and a receptionist to handle the phone calls and deliveries. They decided to go there first, look it over before contacting a real estate company.

After having coffee, Ivan, Juan, and Tony walked back to the burned-out building, which still had crime tape wrapped around the sidewalk and entrance. Police and firemen were milling around, making sure the hot spots had been that Ivan owned extinguished and no one came around to destroy evidence or pillage the place until a full arson investigation had been completed.

As they approached the burned-out building, a lone policeman appeared, stopping and asking them what business they had there. Ivan told him it had been his business that burned and wanted to go inside to retrieve a few things from his safe if possible. The policeman told him to wait. He had to have authorization before allowing anyone to enter the building. While waiting for approval, Ivan told Juan and Tony to go fetch Johnny and the Irishman and bring them back so they could start their new role as drivers.

It was not long until the policeman returned and told Ivan he could enter but not to touch or disturb anything inside except for personal items. Ivan entered and literally had to crawl through and over debris as he made his way to his office, located in the rear of the building. After reaching the partially burned-out office, he looked around; everything seemed to be fairly intact. No noticeable damage to the safe other than soot and debris caused by the use of fire hoses and dropped rubble from the ceiling. Walking over to the safe, he bent down and turned the combination; amazingly, it had not been damaged. Opening the safe, he removed its contents and stuffed them in a sack he brought along for that specific purpose. Looking around the small office and thinking of all the deals brokered and carried out from this tiny space over the years, he was saddened to leave those memories behind, but it was time to move on.

Once back outside, he found Juan, Tony, and the two new drivers sitting in their cars, waiting. Ivan crawled in his car, told his new driver Johnny Leopold, "I want you to drive over to this address so I can check on a building. I want to see if it is worth the time and effort to remodel and use for our new office."

Johnny started the car, drove Ivan over to check out the building that Ivan owned as a possible location for their new operations' headquarters. Behind Ivan came Juan, Tony, and his new driver, Hank "the Irishman" O'Connor in Juan's new car. Juan, now in his new role, a huge change in lifestyle; but in time, would become the norm not the exception. Ivan's new driver stopped in front of the building, where Ivan got out, followed by Juan and Tony. This was certainly going to be a huge change especially for Ivan and Juan. As they stood in the shadow of the building, standing on the sidewalk, Juan saw the potential immediately. It was long overdue. The organization had grown expeditiously over the years; moving into a new location was the next step in keeping up with the times.

CHAPTER 20

Arriving in front of the empty store, Johnny parked the car along the curb. Standing in front of the building, waiting on Ivan to retrieve the key picked up earlier at the burned-out bar. After Ivan found the key, he took it from his pocket and opened the door. Upon entering the building, they saw that it was larger and brighter inside than the dingy, smoked-filled small bar Ivan previously used for an office. Looking around inside the building and getting a good feel of the place, Juan envisioned several ideas as to what could be done to enhance its interior. Ivan also seemed excited about the possibilities of the new dig too. The first thing that entered Ivan's mind was finding a company to remodel the inside and outside to suit their needs.

Ivan looked over at Juan, asking him, "What do you think?"

"I can't believe you had this building all along and never utilized it. I think with a little help and luck, we can get it remodeled and turn it into an office anyone would be proud to work in."

"Then that's a yes?"

"Absolutely, unequivocally without question."

"You want to give it a shot yourself in getting it remodeled?"

"It would be my pleasure," Juan responded.

"If that be the case, we'll not need an architect or a decorator and use the extra monies we save for new furnishings and other things to get this place up and running."

"I appreciate the opportunity to remodel this space. I've often thought of participating in such a project growing up, but never had the chance to make my dream come to fruition. I've always had a feeling inside for changing most large spaces I've been in. I've often wished growing up I had had the ability to attend an architecture/ design school, always a desire of mine."

Without further ado, Ivan dropped the renovations and remodeling in Juan's hands.

He told him, "You are officially in charge of turning this empty building into a functioning business office. I'm going to give you one month to turn it into something we can be proud of. Do you think you can have it up running by then?"

"I'll make sure of it happening. With a little planning and help, I think I can turn this sow's ear into a silk purse. Now if you will excuse me, I need to get started."

Juan began by scoping out the building and getting a feel and sense of what had to be done to enhance the interior, bringing it up to his standards of what he envisioned as a workable business office.

Juan, under a time restraint, needed to come up with new ideas and innovations fast, letting his mind wander as he meandered throughout the large structure. The more he looked. the more possibilities he envisioned.

Having no formal training, letting his mind wander from pillar to post, Juan finally removed a pencil and pad from his coat pocket. He began sketching out plans and ideas for the remodelling. After spending hours of investigating every nook and cranny, Juan saw the possibilities were endless. Several hours later, had a design on paper to show Ivan. He was sure he would get Ivan's approval.

There were a few things Juan saw right away that captured his attention and imagination. One was the large room located toward the back of the building, a perfect place for two offices. It would not take much time in the scheme of things to get that space reconfigured and ready for occupancy. All it needed was a wall creating two rooms as opposed to the one large room as it was now. Once the wall was up, new electrical outlets and carpet installed, a chandelier hanged from the ceiling, painted, and office furniture furnished, voila, instant offices.

The open space in front would be used for a lobby and reception area. It needed more attention—wall coverings, paint, new carpet or large rugs on the wooden floor, a few well-selected pieces of modern furniture, pictures on the walls, a receptionist desk, comfortable chairs, and a nice large sofa with end tables and a coffee table.

For Tony, he would have his own personal area in a corner with an unencumbered view.

After giving much thought to the project, Juan thought it was time to leave. He was exhausted not only mentally but physically. He told Ivan he had written all his ideas down and asked Ivan if he would like to hear them before leaving?

Ivan said, "Yes, I'm very interested in what you have in mind for rehabbing this old building."

Juan read off the list of things to be accomplished in the next thirty days. Ivan listened intently to what Juan had in mind for the remodeling. After hearing what Juan wanted to do; he told Johnny Leopold he was ready to go home. It had been a long afternoon and was time to stop work and leave.

Before leaving, Ivan told Juan, "I'll meet you for breakfast at six thirty at Leo's restaurant down the street from the burned-out bar."

"I'll be there. I need to get an early start myself on this remodeling project. I have a lot to do, and I can't waste time if I expect to finish it within the time frame I have."

Juan told his driver, "I'm ready to go. Drive me back to the hotel. Afterward you can drop Tony off, then return the car to the garage.

Ivan told Johnny, "Let's get out of here. I want to go home." When they arrived home and before Ivan got out of the car, he told Johnny, "I expect you to be here no later than six o'clock sharp to pick me up, understood?"

"Yeah, Boss Man, I hear you. I'll be here at six sharp. You don't have to worry about that."

Meanwhile, Juan arrived at the hotel and told the Irishman, "Pick me up no later than 6:15 a.m.," repeating himself, "no later than 6:15 a.m. I'll be meeting Ivan for breakfast at Leo's, and don't intend being late. After breakfast, we'll drive to the new office building. I need to get an early start with the renovation project. Do you have a problem with anything I have told you so far?" "No, boss, no problem. See you at 6:15 a.m."

The next morning like clockwork, Ivan and Juan met at Leo's for breakfast before starting their day. They had a lot to discuss before and after breakfast. They talked about what each needed to accomplish that day going forward.

Ivan told Juan, "First thing I need you to do this morning is purchase a new desk, a comfortable office chair, two large file cabinets, and a four-foot-tall safe for my office. Also have the lights turned on, contact the gas company, get the gas turned back on. Go to the telephone company, put in a request for a new phone system and, if possible, have the service installed today. Once that's done, I need you to tell Tony to notify the different organizations of the new office. I want the collectors to start their drop-off this evening at the new location. The last thing, call a meeting with the different groups for this weekend. At that time, we'll inform them of the new changes. Think you can you handle all that today?"

"It will be something I can do but bear with me, in case I run into a snag, ha ha. That's a plateful, but I should be able to accomplish most of it if I keep my nose to the grindstone."

"Do you have any questions before I leave?"

"No, I'm going to head on to the office now and get started. I have a busy schedule and need to get started as early as possible. I'll have the desk and cabinets in your office sometime this afternoon. Don't know about the safe, but I'll have it delivered as soon as possible."

"That's fine. I have several things to do also before coming back this afternoon, so see you later."

"Take your time. See you when I see you, ha ha." Ivan and Johnny left Leo's, while Juan and the Irishman stood outside watching them as they drove away. Juan got in his car along with the Irishman. Juan had the Irishman drive him over to the new office building.

The Irishman parked the car in front of the building. Juan exited the car, proceeding to the front door where he opened the door and walked inside. He once again looked around the large room, making sure he had not forgotten anything on his to-do-list. As he began this exhilarating, arduous day recounting things to do and getting things back into perspective before jumping into the mix head first. He reached inside his jacket, removed a pencil and pad, and began jotting down those things Ivan mentioned at breakfast. After going over his list of things to do, he would start with the first thing on the list—get the electricity turned on.

He told the Irishman, "We have some running around to do, so let's head over to the electric company first."

It took most of the morning contacting the different utility companies getting them scheduled to come out today. He was lucky; the utility companies were all able in guaranteeing to have their services up and running by late afternoon. He spent most of the morning getting the utilities contacted and their word on finishing that part of Ivan's request.

In running the day's errands, Juan also ran across a contractor who guaranteed him he could install the inside wall separating the large room into two offices, remove the existing door, and install two new doors, before three thirty.

Juan told him, "It's got to be finished by three thirty. Are you willing to take on the task?"

"I'll have it done if I start now. I'll have my crew there in a half hour. As long as I don't run into any constructional problems, it should be completed by three thirty. If it's not finished by that time, it's free."

"Guess you know your business. We'll see you back at the building," Juan told the contractor as he was leaving.

Next, the Irishman drove him to a local office supply store where he purchased furniture for the two offices. Juan wanted the real feel of an office complex rather than some sleazy storefront for riff-raff to hang out. With so many ideas in his mind, he hoped he did not overstep his bounds with Ivan.

Juan left Tony in charge while he was shopping. He called Tony after contacting the utilities companies and after meeting with the contractor. Tony answered the pay phone on the corner when Juan called.

Juan told Tony, "I have a construction crew arriving there any time now. Let them in so they can get started on building the inter wall inside the large room in the back. They are transforming that space into two separate offices. I've explained we need not only electric outlets installed but telephone outlets. They can work in conjunction with the phone and electric company while they're there as to where to place the outlets for electricity and phone lines. I told the foreman I wanted plenty of light and phone outlets in each office. He said he had qualified people who could do that and would bring them along. The offices should be completed by the end of the day. Keep an eye on them. If they need anything or you can assist, give them a hand."

"Don't worry about the office. I'll keep close tabs on what's going on and let you know when you return if there's a problem."

The Irishman drove over to a local office supply store where Juan purchased the new furniture for both offices. He purchased two desks, two chairs, one safe, three file cabinets and had the solemn word of the store owner the items would be delivered that afternoon before 3:00 p.m. Ivan would have his office set up and ready to take care of business by day's end.

While looking for office furniture, etc., he found a store nearby where he purchased a receptionist desk and chair. And for Tony, the perfect table and chairs for the area he would utilize for his job.

For the lobby, he bought four overstuffed leather chairs, a leather couch, and several small end tables, coffee table, plus numerous pictures for the walls and two fake plants.

Juan had the Irishman drive around until he found the remaining items necessary in completing the furniture essentials for the offices and lobby.

After the utilities were turned on and his spending spree, he spent the rest of the afternoon with Tony and the Irishman receiving items that were being delivered. By two thirty, Ivan's office had been completed—painted, new rug installed, several pictures on the wall, desk and new file cabinets on the back wall in place, along with Ivan's new safe.

When Ivan entered the building that afternoon, he noticed the lights on, the gas furnace was running, and the phone company had installed a new phone system throughout the building. He was impressed at the job Juan did in such a short time. Ivan told him how much he appreciated his accomplishment on such short notice. Juan took Ivan back to show him his newly decorated office. Opening the door to his office, Ivan was astonished when he saw his new desk, a plush office chair, a four-foot safe along the wall, and two large file cabinets placed strategically along the wall, plus a beautiful carpet on the floor.

Admiring all of Juan's handiwork, Ivan turned to Johnny and sent him outside to the car to retrieve a bag that was in the trunk. Johnny returned handing the nondescript bag to Ivan. Ivan found the combination for the safe on his desk in a sealed envelope. After opening the envelope, he memorized the combination, then proceeded to open the safe. Once he had the safe opened, he reached over on his desk, retrieving the bag. He opened the bag and placed its contents inside the safe. One less thing Ivan now had to worry or fret over—the money; it was once again in a safe place.

It was late when Al came in with his daily collection.

When Al passed by Tony, Tony said, "Hi, Al, how you doing?"

"Fine, Tony."

"How you like your new dig?"

"Lot different than the old one, ha ha."

As Al passed by Juan's office, he saw Juan sitting behind his desk frantically trying to organize things around him. Poking his head in, he said, "Hi, boss. Wow! Are you moving on up or what?"

It caught Juan by surprise as he was in deep thought; looking up and seeing Al, he nodded. Al continued to Ivan's office, saw the way it had been set up, and respected the accomplished look. Ivan looked up and told Al to come in, then asked, "How's things on the streets?"

"Fine, Boss Man. Everything out there is as quiet as a church mouse. The owners I visited were more interested in talking about the fire than arguing or causing trouble. I've answered a million questions about the fire. Other than that, it was a quiet and peaceful day," he told Ivan as he handed over his collections, along with his daily log.

"Has Juan or Tony said anything to you about my new job yet?" Al asked.

"No, we've not had time to talk about your reassignment. I will stop and talk to them before leaving this evening. I'm interested too in knowing what they've decided. I'm sure when they have information for you, they will tell you."

"Thanks, Boss Man."

Ivan took the envelopes and ledger listing Al's daily activities. Before leaving Ivan's office, Al told Ivan, "No one has mentioned about hearing rumors of retaliation against the organization floating around on the streets."

This was good news after the last few days of chaos. Ivan was glad to hear everyone under his protection program was not using these latest mishaps to their advantage by avoiding paying their dues. He tried keeping his organization abreast of what he was doing so they understood what to expect if things started to flounder. He retained tight controls of the reins, and with Juan's help, he intended in keeping it that way.

Al's day now completed, left Ivan's office, walked over to where Tony sat, and asked, "Have you and Juan decided on what my new position might be, or is there a position opening up soon that you are waiting on to tell me about?"

Tony told Al, "We're still working on it, Al, but I'm meeting with Juan this evening, and we planned on making our decision then. After that, we will run it past Ivan for his approval."

Tony got up from his chair, pointing to Juan's office. "On second thought, why don't we go see Juan, talk to him now if you have time?"

"Sure, sounds good."

Al and Tony walked back to Juan's office. Juan looked up and saw them standing at the door and invited them in.

"Come in, make yourselves comfortable. What's up?"

Sitting down, Tony asked Juan, "Remember, we discussed removing Al from collections and placing him with the muscle group?"

"Yes, I think that's what we decided to do," Juan replied.

"I told him we would come and discuss it with you if you have time. Have you had time to talk to Dennis Martinez, crew leader of the muscle group, yet?

"No, I was waiting to talk to you again before finalizing this move."

"Who did we decide on for Dennis's replacement?" Tony asked.

"If memory serves me correctly, it was Bobby Baker. He works for Carlos Munoz, the Chief Financial Officer of the loan company in the collections department," Juan said.

"Yes, I think you're right. What do you think of him as your replacement, Al? Do you think he is capable of handling your sector?"

"I know Bobby, but not that well. But what I've heard of him in the past is he would be a capable replacement. I think he'd be a good choice for the job."

"Okay, that settles that. I'll contact Bobby this evening, have him drop by tomorrow morning, work with you for a week or so, then reassign you to the muscle group, if that's agreeable with you?"

"Sounds like a plan to me," Al said.

"Okay, I'll get in touch with him before he leaves and have him meet with us in my office tomorrow morning at eight sharp."

Al and Tony left Juan's office. They walked back to where Tony was when Al came by and sat down. Before Al left, he and Tony discussed his new position inside the muscle group. It pleased Al making a change after the years he put in pounding and working the streets.

Juan, in the meantime, picked up his phone and called Bobby.

"I need you to drop by the new location at eight o'clock in the morning. You're being reassigned to collections."

This came as a complete surprise to Bobby hearing he had been considered for collections. It was a step-up in the ranks. Bobby was delighted at the very mention of the promotion. This made Juan's work easier having someone like Bobby interested, highly motivated, plus not reluctant to change on such short notice.

The next morning after Al arrived, in walked Bobby. Getting up from the table, Tony ushered both Al and Bobby into Juan's office to discuss Bobby's new role as a collector. Tony informed Juan that Al was ready to take Bobby out and get him started collecting. Bobby thanked Juan and Tony for giving him this chance to prove himself.

Al and Bobby walked out of Juan's office, ready to begin the daily routine of collecting. It was a good day for both Al and Bobby. Al was anxious in showing Bobby how to run a collection. It was not long before they reached their first stop. Before entering, Al explained to Bobby what to expect as he handed his small ledger to Bobby. It was Al's reference log used in collecting, a road map of the different businesses he collected from. It would be a tough week for Bobby, but the time had arrived. Both Al and Bobby were ready for change.

Meanwhile, back at the office, Ivan arrived with a million things on his mind to accomplish that day. First, he called Juan to his office to discuss more of his duties and responsibilities as a partner. Ivan told him he must be cognizant of the different groups and what each entity within that group entailed. It was not simple as Juan had envisioned. Most jobs in the association were not your everyday run-of-the-mill occupation. Plus, most of the workforce inside the organization was ever evolving, changing from day to day, week to week, month to month, never staying the same, as Juan soon came to learn.

Ivan looked over at Juan and told him, "Get your notepad out, write down what I tell you. It will be helpful to you in the coming days and weeks. After I explain in detail what you can expect, study your notes, learn as much about each group as possible. It's a huge commitment on your part. You will need to call a meeting soon of each group leader, explaining what you expect as individuals and as group leaders.

"Clarify to them what your expectations are and consequences if your principles are not followed. Once they understand what you expect, meet one-on-one with each group leader, listen to what they have to say. By the time you finish with each leader, you should feel in total control. Also, you should have a good perception of how each group leader feels, how their job fits within the realm of things within the association. It behooves you to let them in no uncertain terms are accountable to you and you alone. Tell them you will not put up with bickering between the rank and file. Be firm. Let them know if there's a problem inside their ranks to let you know immediately and not let it fester. It's not only bad for the group but the organization overall."

"I'll get started right away. If I have any questions later, I'm sure I can depend on your assistance," Juan replied.

"Anytime you have a question, feel free to come into my office to discuss it," Ivan told Juan.

Leaving Ivan's office, Juan was ready to accept his new challenge but could see the handwriting on the wall. This new position was more demanding and daunting than he earlier surmised.

Juan was having second thoughts as to what he had gotten himself involved with—so many challenges, new problems to cope with. It would be a miracle if he succeeded.

He thought to himself, *Am I really ready for the responsibilities Ivan just added to my list which was already full?*

Back in his office, he sat behind his desk, looking over the notes he had written down. As he sat mulling over, separating groups, job descriptions, he formed a mental concept of each group's function as they fit within the confines of the organization. He spent the remainder of the day studying and learning about each group prior to meeting with them. At day's end, he was absolutely exhausted with the workload on his shoulders, which Ivan placed there.

He summoned the Irishman, who was sitting in the lobby at the table with Tony.

"Bring the car around. I'm ready to leave."

A little later, the Irishman returned and picked up Juan, then drove him to one of his favorite restaurants called the Sportsman's. Juan had been there on several occasions with Ivan, where he enjoyed both the atmosphere and food. The Irishman dropped Juan off while he parked the car. Juan entered and was seated at Ivan's favorite table while he waited for the Irishman to join him. The Irishman, as he came in, spotted Juan and walked over to where he was seated and sat down. A waitress soon made her way over to their table where she took their drink order.

After giving her their drink order, she gave them time to look over the menu before she returned. After dinner, the Irishman drove Juan to his hotel, dropping him off for the evening. Once inside his room, Juan took a long relaxing bath. Afterward, he crawled out of the tub, dried off, then headed to bed, where he slept undisturbed the remainder of the night. He awoke the following morning feeling refreshed and eager to begin a new day. He called the front desk once he was dressed, asking the desk clerk on duty, "Is my driver in the lobby?"

The desk clerk answered in the affirmative, "Yes, he's been here about ten minutes."

"Thanks, tell him I'll be right down."

He walked down the steps to the lobby, where he met the Irishman.

Before leaving the Irishman asked him, "Where to this morning, boss?"

"Let's try the diner near downtown on Indiana Avenue, next to the Holiday Inn. Are you familiar where it is?"

"Yes, boss, I know the place."

Juan was pleased with his new driver. He knew he had made the right decision choosing him. He felt comfortable around the Irishman, knowing he had his back and was accessible in any predicament he found himself involved. The Irishman was laid back, but had this air about him that he would not put up with nonsense if push came to shove. He was big and strong and gave anyone around him the impression he was quite capable of handling himself, thank you. Juan felt his selection of the Irishman as his personal driver was one of his better choices. Both Juan and the Irishman were well matched as a team. Neither appeared to have that bad-boy attitude; they were a perfect team.

Reaching the diner, Juan and the Irishman exited the car, which had been parked alongside the diner, and they had to walk around to the entrance. Once inside, they found a table near the back of the diner where they sat down. From this vantage point, they had an unobstructed view of everyone coming in and going out. After breakfast, the Irishman drove Juan to the office where he began another long and hectic day.

Once inside, Juan walked back to Ivan's office to confer with him about the day's agenda. Juan wanted to find out from Ivan if he had any loose ends that needed his immediate attention.

"Yes, I want you and the Irishman to check on one of the collectors who's having a minor problem with one of his clients. The client has become rather belligerent lately, causing a problem among several of the local businesses in the area. The owner has assured the collector, in no uncertain terms, he's paid his last dues for protection and told not to return. I want you and the Irishman to take a ride over there. See if you can persuade the shop owner to pay up. I want you to talk to him, convince him to stop his nonsense. I need you to quell this problem before it gets out of control."

"Okay, we'll ride out there this morning and see what we can do in correcting the problem. Is there anything else we need to check on while we're out?"

"Nothing I know of at the moment, just get this problem resolved as quickly and quietly as possible."

Juan left Ivan's office, looked over at where the Irishman sat talking to Tony, and told him, "Get the car. We have an errand to run this morning."

They drove out to meet the collector named Junior, who filled Juan in on the problem collecting from the owner of a local tavern. After hearing Junior's plight, the three walked across the street and entered the tavern.

Approaching the bartender, Juan asked, "Is the owner in this morning? If so, I need to speak with him."

"Yes, he's in his office. Hold on while I go tell him someone wants to see him."

"Tell him Juan Grajales is here to pick up the dues he owes."

The bartender stepped from behind the bar, walked back to the office, where he stuck his head in, and told the owner, "There is a Juan Grajales with two associates in the bar waiting to see you. He told me to tell you he came to collect the dues you owed."

"Okay, send the scumbag in."

Juan entered the office alone, and when the owner looked up and saw Juan, he immediately started cursing giving him a load of BS about paying dues. Then told Juan to tell his boss, "I refuse to give him any more of my money. You can take that to the bank, you bunch of jerkoffs."

Juan, in his mild manner ways, looked the owner straight in the eye and said, "I am the boss. I've come to collect the money you owe the organization for protection. I also understand you've been causing Junior problems with other clients of ours in the neighborhood. I'm here to stop this foolishness today and collect the two weeks' dues you owe."

"F——k you! I'm not scared of you. I don't intend paying another dime to you and your rip-off organization. Now get the f——k out of my office, off my property, and take those two goons you brought with you. I'm not paying another dime, understand?"

Juan walked to the office door, where he told the Irishman, "Start removing the bottles from the top shelves, break every f——g bottle until I tell you to stop."

The Irishman immediately stepped behind the bar and told the bartender, "Get out from behind the bar."

He then started picking up liquor bottles off the shelves one by one and throwing them onto the floor where they broke spilling their contents. After clearing the bottles from the back bar, he proceeded doing the same to all the bottles in the well. He threw one bottle at a time from the rack against the opposite wall, where it shattered into a thousand pieces before falling onto the floor. After breaking all the bottles in the well, he picked up a thick shaker glass throwing it against a large mirror on the back bar, destroying it. He then grabbed the dispenser used for fountain service, ripped it from the bar, and threw it to the floor.

Juan, once again, told the owner, "I'm here to collect your dues. I'm not leaving until I get the money."

"Screw you, asshole, and that other SOB at the bar busting my chops."

"Okay, if that's how you want to play this game, then it's time I upped the ante."

Juan walked behind the desk, picked the man up from his chair, punched him one time in the face, and knocked him to the floor.

Juan then looked around the office and spotted a large trophy sitting on a nearby shelf. He walked over, picked it off the shelf, and walked back to where the owner lay on the floor. He raised the trophy over his head with one hand, swung it down, hitting the owner across his right shinbone almost breaking his leg. The owner screamed out in pain yet remained defiant. He then threw the trophy across the room, breaking a large picture that hung on the opposite wall of the small office. Juan turned back, looking at the owner lying on the floor in excruciating pain. Leaning over, Juan picked the owner off the floor, smacked him again, then threw him in his chair.

Juan again asked, "Are you ready now to fork over the dues you owe?"

"Hell, no! You can kill me before I pay you another dime." Juan yelled to the Irishman who was still taking care of business at the bar and told him, "Start working on the bartender, maybe that will knock some sense in this idiot."

The Irishman grabbed hold of the bartender by the neck and punched him a few times in the face and midsection. The owner slumping over in his chair with his head resting on the desk heard what the Irishman was doing to his nephew. He meekly whispered for Juan to stop doing any further damage to his nephew or tavern.

"My nephew had nothing to do with this. It's my decision, mine alone in not paying up. Just stop this madness, you've done enough damage. I'll pay what I owe. I'll also stop spreading discontent around the neighborhood. I'll address the situation to the other tavern owners and business in the area about paying their dues."

With that, Juan released his grip on the owner, who got up out of his chair and hobbled over to his safe. After trying a couple of times to open the safe, he finally succeeded, reached inside, retrieved the envelope addressed to Boss Man, and handed it to Juan.

Juan told the owner before leaving, "If I have to return, I will not be so understanding next time, capisce?"

Juan, with the payment for dues in hand, turned, motioning to the other two it was time to leave. The three walked out of the tavern, stopping outside briefly.

Juan handed the envelope to Junior and told him, "If you have any more trouble from this bar owner or other business owner's in the area, call me. I'll return and do what it takes to straighten things out, okay?"

"Yeah, thanks. It was getting a bit messy out here, and I need some backup."

Juan and the Irishman returned to the car and headed back to the office while Junior returned to collecting.

Back at the office, Juan walked into Ivan's office and told him, "We addressed the problem Junior was having and should not have any more trouble with the tavern owner. I think the owner saw our point, paid the two payments he owed, which I handed over to Junior. Convinced the tavern owner not to withhold protection money next time Junior came calling."

Ivan was pleased with the way Juan handled the somewhat-volatile situation.

Ivan said to Juan, "I've decided to let you do the hiring and firing for the entire organization. I think you're ready taking on the everyday activities of the association. That includes running interference for the loan company collections using the muscle group. Meet with Dennis. As of today, you're in total control of that group too. You need to set up ground rules concerning that group. They must understand when we loan money out, it must be paid back within a reasonable time frame. If not, you and the muscle group are to do whatever it takes to collect payments. This is one of the organization's most lucrative business, also the most dangerous. So make sure they understand the ground rules first and foremost. Are you ready to take on the additional burden of running the muscle group and handling the rest of the workload I'm piling on you?"

"Well, it'll take time to adjust to my schedule, but as long as I have the Irishman at my back and with your help and guidance, I'm sure I'll manage. After seeing the Irishman operate, I was impressed. But I need to talk to Al, get him firmly established inside the muscle group. Will be good having someone in that group I can rely on and trust."

"Good, I think you and the Irishman will do well together. With Al, I have reservations, but if you think he's the right man for the muscle group, that's your call. I know Al. He's been one of my most loyal people. Sure he will be loyal to you, no matter where he's assigned. You might give him consideration once he learns the ropes at being your number one go-to in that group. He is fair but uncompromising when he has a job to do. I've learned from the past that once he's committed, nothing stands in his way. That's why I've kept him in collections as long as I have. He's a good man to have around.

"After you get settled into your routine and the muscle group, I'll give you the ledger I keep on different companies I've loaned money. Look it over, learn which companies were good investments and ones not living up to their contract. We need to start applying pressure on the businesses with delinquent debts by ramping up the muscle group in their collecting obligation, letting them earn their keep.

"You can begin by meeting with the muscle group. Have them start with the oldest outstanding debts, working their way forward. We need to whip those companies back into line, and I know with your help and the cooperation of the muscle group, it will get done. It's been difficult for me these last few years getting good help in following my orders and doing as they were told.

"Here's a list of several companies you and the muscle group can begin with immediately. The muscle group needs to start applying pressure on delinquent debts owed today. Once we've collected the outstanding dues, we should start showing a profit once again. I'm counting on you to take care of the business since I feel my time is running out. We can use the extra money right now since we've had such a large outlay of money lately.

"I know you will not let me down. That's why I chose you above all the others in selecting a partner. I saw the fire in your belly and determination in your eyes. I knew you were special."

"Thanks for believing in me. I appreciate you taking me into your confidence. I have a purpose now for getting up every day. Having people like you believing in me makes my life worthwhile. If it had not been for you and Al, I would still be living out of garbage cans and sleeping in boxes in some cold, wet alleyway. I owe it all to you and Al."

"Get a move on it. You have a lot to do. We can't waste time pussyfooting around here. We haven't got all day. Now get to it."

Juan walked out of Ivan's office and back to his. He sat down at his desk and started writing a list of the projects Ivan just dropped on his lap. It would have been too much, too fast for most people having such an enormous burden placed on them at once, but he was ready to take the ball and run with it.

Juan took the next several days to meet with different groups within the organization. He explained to them what his expectations and concerns were since becoming chief cook and bottle washer. When meeting with the muscle group, he made sure they were all on the same page and brought them up to speed with his requirements and concerns. He wanted them to understand collecting from some of the larger companies; they, too, had their own muscle to call upon called a union. It was a tremendous challenge for Juan as a newbie CEO running a company this size, but if Ivan could do it, so could he.

CHAPTER 21

Juan sent word to Al to drop by his office later that afternoon; he had an important matter to discuss with him. Al, after dropping off his collections to Ivan, walked next door to see what was so important Juan wanted to see him. When Al stepped inside his office, Juan signaled for him to have a seat, indicating he would be with him after he finished his phone conversation.

Al sat down and waited patiently while Juan finished talking on the phone and hung up.

Juan leaned back in his chair and said to Al, "I appreciate you coming by this afternoon. I have a few things I need to confer with you concerning your replacement and new position within the organization. Firstly, let's talk about your replacement. How well do you know Bobby Baker, and secondly, in your opinion, is he capable of handling collections?"

"I would say so, yes. He seems motivated and has adapted well in his new job. I think he'll do well with his new assignment. I heard recently after going to work at the loan company, took to it like fish to water. He's a natural, like you when you started working with me," Al expounded.

"Good. After you finish training Bobby by Friday, I'm moving you to the muscle group on Monday. By the end of this week, Bobby should be up and running. I know you're ready for the change.

"On Monday morning, I want you in my office no later than eight o'clock. I'll have the Irishman take you and me out to meet the muscle group. We'll meet them at the abandoned old warehouse by the train tracks down by the river. I think you know the place. I want you there when I explain what to expect now that I'm running the organization. After I finish my spiel, I'll introduce you, letting them know you've been reassigned and part of their group starting immediately. I'm sure you'll fit right in. You know the collecting business as well if not better than most.

You and I know the only difference between collection on the streets and working with a group is having backup while on assignment.

"I've not met Dennis, the group's leader. I would like yours and the Irishman's assessment of Dennis after the meeting. I need to know what you two think of his leadership ability. I need a strong leader in that group. If I find Dennis is not capable, I'll replace him."

"I'll watch him like a hawk. If I don't think he is your man, I'll be up front and give you my honest assessment" Al replied.

"I appreciate your honesty and wait for your input, looking forward to your evaluation of him. I have nothing else at this time, so I'll see you bright and early Monday morning."

Al stood up, shook Juan's hand, and left his office. Al stopped by to chat with Tony and the Irishman before leaving. Al finished with the chitchat and left for the weekend. After Al's departure, Juan called the Irishman into his office, telling him, "I'm ready to close up shop and go have dinner. Why don't you get the car and meet me out front in five?"

After dinner, Juan was driven back to the hotel where he was staying. Once in his room, he cleaned up, sat in his big chair relaxing, and began thinking about moving from the hotel and finding another place to relocate. Living so close to Al was not good for him or Al. He felt he needed more personal space—a place he could relax, not bothered by Al when not working.

The next morning, the Irishman was waiting for Juan in the lobby as Juan came down the stairs.

He said to the Irishman, "Today, I've decided to look for a new dig for myself. This place is becoming too confining with Al in such close proximity. I do not want to create animosity between us if I can avoid it. It is best I move out and find myself another place to live."

After breakfast, the Irishman drove back to the office where Juan was to meet Al at eight o'clock. Entering the building, Juan walked over to where Tony and Al sat.

He told Al, "Sit tight, Al. I'll be right back."

Juan proceeded back to Ivan's office.

"Good morning, Ivan. I wanted to let you know I've set up a special meeting with the muscle group this morning, I'm meeting with Dennis and afterward introduce Al to his new associates."

"Good. I'm glad you're handling this matter early. I have not had the manpower or the right people around me lately to spend much time on that end of the business. Don't think you'll have any problems, but if you do, let me know. I'll help any way I can."

"Okay, I left Al sitting with Tony, think he's ready to get started on his new job. I have a long day ahead, need to get my thinking cap on before rallying the troops, ha ha."

Yes, and let me know how things turn out when you return to the office."

"You bet, I'll drop by your office later this afternoon and fill you in."

"Great, I'll be anxious to hear how it went with Dennis and Al and how you fared overall with the group."

Juan walked out of the office and went over to where Tony and Al sat. Juan put his hand on Al's shoulder and asked, "Are you ready for a little ride this morning?"

"Yeah, boss, I'm ready. Let's do it."

Al got up, following Juan outside where the Irishman waited. Juan sat in the back; Al climbed in the front passenger seat. They drove to the outskirts of town to an abandoned old warehouse near the river's edge. When they arrived on scene a little after nine, the Irishman stopped near the abandoned old structure where Juan exited.

He motioned for Al to get out, then told Al, "Follow me." Entering the abandoned warehouse, Juan found it dark, damp, and musty-smelling. It would have to do. There were few places left in town that a group like this could meet without drawing undue attention.

The muscle group had arrived earlier and was waiting inside for Juan's arrival. The small but elite group of misfits Juan encountered that morning looked like a bunch of treacherous-looking loners, to say the least.

Once inside, Juan met Dennis; his first impression was disappointment. Juan was not impressed, actually, quite the opposite.

Dennis's conduct and behavior from the get-go was made known to Juan the minute they shook hands. The handshake exposed a lot about Dennis, especially what Juan could expect from him going forward. After conferring with Dennis before the meeting, Juan discovered Dennis was self-centered, confrontational loner, not a team player by any means of the imagination. How he ran the elite group as well as he had was a total mystery to Juan.

After their short meeting, Juan called the rest of the group together, introducing himself along with Al and the Irishman. Once the introductions were over, the group seemed to drop their ambiguity toward Juan, accepting him without question, catching Juan totally off guard. He thought he would have a tougher time connecting with this group but felt the camaraderie immediately. He felt at ease with the group at large, but then there was Dennis, standing on his right side as Juan addressed the group.

Juan told the group what he expected; they seemed relatively comfortable with his expectations concerning the group as a whole. Near the end of the meeting, Juan told them if they needed anything to call him anytime, day or night, he was available. He then looked over at Dennis and said, "I'd like to have a word with you in private before I leave."

Dennis and Juan walked back to a vacant corner of the warehouse where Juan stopped, looked once again at Dennis, and said to him, "I expect you as a team leader to keep me abreast of any problems within the muscle group. I do not want you overstepping your bounds, understood?"

Dennis acted a bit perturbed at Juan's innuendo and said nothing. Juan felt the tension between Dennis and himself after their one-on-one meeting. The impression Juan had of Dennis when told what he expected had not been favorable.

Juan explained to Dennis, "There are changes to be made if the group is to continue."

Dennis stood silent, not uttering a word or acknowledging anything Juan said.

"I want us to keep in contact weekly. That way, you can update me on your progress."

Again, nothing but silence. Dennis only nodded his head.

Juan felt from the outset Dennis was not the right man for the job but wanted Al's and the Irishman's feedback before making any hasty judgment about the team leader.

After the meeting, Al had a chance to meet with several of the group, including Dennis. Dennis accepted Al into the group without showing any malice, but Al too felt tension between himself and Dennis. It was something Al could not accept and would inform Juan once they returned to the office. Overall, it was a good experience for Juan meeting the muscle group.

Back in the car, Juan asked Al for his thoughts of the group and his assessment of the group as a whole.

"I see no problem. I knew a couple of the guys. The rest accepted me without reservations. Don't think I'll encounter any problem going forward. If I do, I should be able to handle anything that arises."

"Good. When we get back to the office, I want you and the Irishman in my office. I need your feedback on Dennis. Having met him, I have my own opinion, but your opinions and assessments of Dennis will weigh heavy in my decision."

Back at the office, they passed Tony, sitting alone at his table playing cards as usual. Juan assumed since Ivan's new driver Johnny was not sitting at the table that Ivan must be out of the office.

"Hello," Tony said, as the three passed by his table.

The Irishman acknowledged Tony as they continued to Juan's office. Closing the door to the office, Juan told them to be seated.

"Now that you've met Dennis, what are your thoughts of him, and what's your first impression or opinion of how he handled himself around us and the rest of the group?"

Al was the first to respond to Juan's question.

"He's definitely a loner. Could see right off the bat he does not accept authority easily. He appeared defiant in unreceptive ways, arrogant attitude, which signals to me, it's his way or the highway in an impetuous sort of way. You need to watch this one close. He is trouble looking for a place to happen."

"And you, Irishman? What was your first impression meeting Dennis for the first time?"

"Meeting Dennis, basically the same as Al described him. I had the feeling the majority of the group did not like or trust him as far as they could throw him. I have to agree with Al. I personally think he should be replaced by someone not so impulsive. I'm sure he does only what is needed in keeping the group in line and together. But in my honest opinion, someone else should be in charge of that group. Dennis is downright scary and could cause you and the association a lot of headaches if he continues as the leader of that group."

"I thank you for your input. I need to talk to Ivan. Get his response to our opinions and concerns about Dennis. I will let you know later what he says."

The meeting ended on that note. Al and the Irishman left Juan's office, walked back to where Tony sat, and joined him.

Juan walked over to Ivan's office, noticing he had not returned. Returning to his office, he began writing down a few names for Dennis's replacement, names which he felt could take over the muscle group and run it right. But only if Ivan agreed with his assessment of Dennis.

Later that afternoon, Ivan arrived back from taking care of a few things he had slacked off doing lately. Since Juan had taken up a lot of the slack, Ivan had time to tie a lot of loose ends together with other investments he had neglected lately. He seemed in a better frame of mind upon his return, showing not only in his demeanor but his uplifted spirit.

Juan walked once more over to Ivan's office, shutting the door. He sat down and told Ivan about the meeting at the warehouse and his impression on meeting Dennis and his overall assessments of the muscle group.

"In my honest opinion, Ivan, Dennis is not the man for that job. I'm leery of him heading such a vital part of the organization."

"I told you when you accepted the partnership, you do what you deem is right. If in your opinion you feel Dennis needs to be replaced, that's fine with me, just do it. I want a group that operates as one, with the interest of the entire organization, not personal satisfaction or individual gain."

This was going to be a game changer replacing Dennis as group leader, not an easy decision especially for Juan being the newbie. The reaction from Dennis during their initial meeting, Juan knew it was a necessary move to replace Dennis as soon as possible. It was in the best interest of the association getting the group back on track, operating like professionals as they were meant to be.

Returning to his office, Juan sat down, drafted a letter to Dennis explaining the new changes he was making within the group.

It's essential at this time to inform you that you're being replaced as team leader of the muscle group. I'm informing you are officially relieved as team leader of group. If you would like to talk to me about my decision, drop by my office anytime, and we'll talk. But only if you are interested in staying with the organization in a different capacity Juan added,

If you're interested working in the organization let me know. I'll personally look around and find a position suitable for you.

Signed, Juan Grajales.

Juan had the Irishman hand-deliver the message to Dennis at his home later that afternoon. When Dennis read the letter, he was not a happy camper. His position within the group had been terminated. The Irishman waited for a response and could see Dennis was visibly upset and highly agitated.

Suddenly, Dennis told the Irishman in no uncertain terms, "You can tell Juan Grajales I have no intentions of working at a lesser job, definitely not interested in talking to him."

The Irishman returned to Juan's office, relaying Dennis's reply after reading the letter. Juan, hearing what Dennis told the Irishman, without question or hesitation, accepted Dennis's verbal reply, refusing any future offers or meetings with Juan. Dennis was officially off the payroll, permanently terminated from working for the organization.

Juan had to find a replacement for Dennis from within the muscle group if possible. Looking over the list he compiled earlier, a couple of names jumped out. One was Al, whom he trusted and respected. The other was a member of the group named Mario DeMarco. Mario was Dennis's second in command.

Before deciding whom he would choose for the opened position, he first wanted to talk with Ivan, see if he had a preference filling the empty slot. Juan got up from his desk, walked over to Ivan's office, poked his head in, and asked, "Ivan, do you have a moment to discuss my choices for Dennis's replacement?"

"Yes, come on in. I'm not busy at the moment."

Sitting down next to Ivan's desk, Juan removed a piece of paper from his pocket where he'd written down two names for Dennis's replacement.

He placed the piece of paper on Ivan's desk with the two names under consideration for the job opening in the muscle group. Ivan reached over, picked up the piece of paper, and read the two names.

Juan said to Ivan, "I need your opinion on the names listed as a replacement for Dennis. I'm especially interested in Mario, whom I met briefly after the meeting at the warehouse. I want to know a little more from you about his character and demeanor. And if you agree, Mario would be an acceptable candidate and capable of handling the job? I want to know about his past work ethics since coming aboard. You know Mario as well as anyone, who better to ask than you about Mario?"

"Yes, I know Mario. He's trustworthy, dependable, and good at his job. He's one I could count on in any given situation without hesitation. I've never had a complaint about him since coming to work for me a couple of years ago. I think he is a fine choice."

Ivan looked once again at the piece of paper at the only two names listed.

"Of course, I've known Al from the get-go. He came to work for me when I first started the organization. He's as honest and trustworthy as the day is long. His work ethics is top-notch. It's a toss-up who would be better-suited to fill the slot. But since you've asked my personal opinion, Mario would be my first pick. He's worked with the group and has extensive experience. I'm still leaving this matter in your hands. It's your decision. You will have to live with the decision you make. I'll trust your judgment in this matter. I know you'll make the right choice."

After Juan's brief time in Ivan's office, he accepted Ivan's nominee to replace Dennis, but it was his choice, his choice alone whom was selected as the new leader of the group. This was the second-biggest decision he had to make since becoming a partner. Making the right decision was imperative. It was strictly a judgment call on Juan's part, choosing between two qualified people. Both Mario and Al were motivated, respected, and aware of what the job entailed, a tough call no matter which one he chose.

Juan thanked Ivan for his time and input. As he left, he told Ivan, "I'm going to give this matter a bit more consideration before making my final decision, but as of now, I'm leaning toward Mario. It's a tough decision no matter which I chose to lead that group. I want the one, when I make my final decision, to be a team player. That's an essential part of my selection. It's not an easy decision as you know. I'll consider their weaknesses and strengths and weigh the pluses and minuses of each. Most of all, not let my personal feeling interfere with my final pronouncement. My choice boils down to whom I feel is most qualified."

Juan left Ivan's office and returned to his. After an hour of intense soul-searching, he finally reached his decision. He would call a special meeting for tomorrow morning to announce the name of the new leader heading the muscle group.

Juan called Tony back to his office.

"Yes, boss."

"I want you to get in touch with the muscle group, tell them a special meeting is scheduled at the old warehouse tomorrow morning at ten o'clock sharp. Tell them I have important information concerning a new team leader."

The next morning, Juan arrived at the warehouse at ten o'clock sharp and was immediately aware of some kind of disorder or confusion among the rank and file as they pulled up along the warehouse. Some of the men were standing around outside the warehouse talking. They appeared to be looking for some sort of leadership within their ranks. As Juan alighted from the car and approached the small group, Al stepped away from where the group had assembled and walked over to speak to Juan. As Al drew closer to Juan, he asked, "Did you hear the news concerning Dennis last night?"

"No," Juan answered.

Al proceeded to tell Juan about a chain of events, which led Dennis getting into an argument with a pool player where eventually a fight ensued. Apparently, Dennis, in one of his drunken stupor, killed one of the local union members. The union member and Dennis had been rivals after a bitter confrontation at the union member's workplace a while back. Dennis had in the past threatened this particular union member numerous times with violence if he had any more trouble with him when he came to collect.

Apparently, the last time they met bad blood surfaced; last night, it came to a head. It all began when Dennis and the union member began arguing over a silly pool game. This time the argument escalated into a heated battle royal. Dennis was the one who instigated the fracas as far as they know. He apparently picked up a long-neck bottle of beer and smashed it over the union member's head, busting the bottle. With the broken bottle neck in hand, Dennis shoved the broken piece of glass into the union member's face, stabbing him several times, before thrusting the broken bottle into the right side of his neck severing the jugular vein. Before the ambulance and police arrived, the union member had bled to death lying on the bar room floor. The police found Dennis outside in his car passed out and immediately arrested him. The police took Dennis to jail where he was booked on a second-degree murder charge.

Dennis, sleeping off his drunken stupor, woke up in jail and learned of what he did and the charges filed against him. All the police could do was allow him his one phone call. He called a former group member to notify Juan or Ivan to get him lawyered up, or he was going to spill the beans on the organization.

Hearing the turn of events of last night sent chills up Juan's spine.

Juan said, "Why would Dennis even think of involving the organization? It had nothing to do with his situation. It was a personal beef between him and a rival."

The only thing Juan could think of after hearing the news was, if they refused his request in finding him a lawyer, he would cut a deal with the prosecution for a lesser charge by turning his murder charge into a corruption investigation by turning state evidence on his former employer.

Juan and Ivan had a real problem on their hands. Juan had to advise Ivan about the dilemma they now faced. They had to move swiftly before this became a scandal and destroyed the organization.

What had he gotten himself into?

CHAPTER 22

Mario saw Juan when he arrived at the warehouse and immediately walked inside the warehouse along with a few of his group. After everyone was assembled inside, Juan called the meeting to order informing all those present that Mario was replacing Dennis as group leader along with Al as his second in command. Upon hearing the appointment of Mario as new group leader, they showed their approval with a loud and long applause, showing not only their unity but agreement with Juan's choices.

Juan, after telling the muscle group of his choices, looked at Mario and asked, "Would you like to step forward and say a few words?"

Mario answered in the affirmative. He stepped up, looking out over the group by saying, "I want to thank Juan for this opportunity to serve you as leader of this small but elite group. I will do whatever it takes in maintaining the highest standards and excellence Juan expects from us. We are a force to be reckoned with when it comes to doing our job. Don't ever forget that. I am proud to be associated with a group of individuals as this who go about their work with purpose and fortitude."

Mario continued, "I'm not like Dennis. I will treat you as individuals, not as a toy to discard when I'm done using it. I have only the utmost respect for each and every one of you. And when it comes to delegating authority, I will be fair, have your backs no matter the circumstances." With these said, he again received an even bigger round of applause.

After the meeting concluded, each member came up to congratulate Mario, telling him how much better they felt now he was in charge. After all the handshaking and individual attaboys given to Mario, Mario walked over to Juan and asked to speak with him alone.

While walking away from the group, Mario asked Juan, "Have you heard the latest about Dennis and the trouble he has gotten himself in?"

"Yes, Al mentioned it to me when I arrived. But you can fill me in a little more if you would."

"Dennis was arrested at one of the local bars for killing a man last night."

"I hear he's locked up in the county jail facing an involuntary manslaughter charge this morning."

"That's not what I want to hear, especially now. Thought we were finished with him and ready to move on without him. Can't believe he's done such a thing, are you sure?"

"Yes, I heard it from a reliable source first thing this morning."

Mario, after accepting his promotion, was told by Juan, "Now that Dennis is in jail, I'm sure the association will come under extreme scrutiny, not only by the press but also lawyers. You and your group need to remain under the radar as we wait on the outcome of Dennis's fate. Any changes you have for the group will have to be put on hold until this debacle is over. Your hands, like mine, are tied until the ugly mess is settled. The last thing you or the organization wants is bring added attention to the association."

"Yes, I understand."

This was not the way Juan and Mario expected their day to begin but accepted the unwanted news and ready to move forward. All they could do at this time was march in place, just one more hurdle to overcome. It would be a difficult time for Mario and Juan, but a necessary evil they had to accept. This was an enormous and awesome burden for both, but they had no choice until Dennis's faith was decided.

Inexperienced in such matters, Juan had a lot riding on his ability maintaining decorum within the organization. It would take spunk and a lot of luck keeping this ship upright and on an even keel if he was to weather this latest storm. It was no easy chore fora newbie like Juan. It would have been a difficult task even for the most-seasoned veteran.

This whole affair could have been avoided if not for Dennis's foolish actions. Everything seemed to unravel after Juan and Dennis's first meeting. Dennis, from the get-go, resisted Juan's authority. Butting heads at their first introduction, quickly disintegrating into the toilet afterward. The evaluation of Dennis by Juan, the Irishman, and Al had come full circle. Dennis was a loose cannon; he had to be replaced with someone less volatile, more suited for the job. Dennis had become a ticking time bomb, flying off the handle at the least provocation. Juan was thankful Dennis was no longer employed by the organization when this horrendous act occurred.

Juan and Ivan were caught in the middle of this seemingly no-win situation all because of Dennis. If Dennis, which was highly unlikely, admitted guilt prior to going to trial, maybe, just maybe, a good defense lawyer could negotiate with the prosecution for a lesser sentence. That was the only way Dennis could possibly be spared a life sentence. A lot was riding on this trial not only for Dennis, but the organization itself. They had to humor Dennis hoping he would not bring the association into the fracas he personally brought on himself.

Would furnishing Dennis a lawyer be enough to appease him not to involve the organization?

Juan returned to the office after the meeting and walked into Ivan's office. He told Ivan about appointing Mario to head the muscle group and Al as his second in command. Ivan was satisfied with Juan's first big decision since becoming a partner, replacing Dennis with Mario. With Mario's appointment to head the muscle group, he would run it as a business not a self-serving entity like Dennis ran it previously.

Juan ask Ivan, "Have you heard what happened last night involving Dennis?"

"No, what's the story on Dennis this time?"

"I hate to be the bearer of bad news, but Dennis apparently had a beef with a pool player prior to leaving a bar last night. There had been bad blood between the two apparently, and last night, it came to a head. Dennis, having drank too much, lost his cool after he challenged [a local union member] on a shot, which led to an argument, and escalated to a fight. Next thing, the union member lay dead on the floor. Dennis was arrested, taken downtown, booked, and charged with involuntary manslaughter.

"Dennis woke up this morning in jail, learning of the charge against him, and allowed to make his one phone call. Instead of calling the association, he called one of his buddies from the muscle group informing him he needed a lawyer. Dennis told his buddy in no uncertain terms,

'If the organization does not provide me a lawyer, I'm going to spill the beans on the entire organization.'"

Juan looked at Ivan and asked, "What do you want to do about his threat? Do we take it seriously, find him a lawyer, or just forget him? What do we do?"

"Guess we need to hook him up with a lawyer and hope he does not involve us. We sure as hell don't need that kind of publicity now that we are in the process of turning the organization around. I can't believe that SOB would turn on the association, but you never know people until push comes to shove. I'll call the association's lawyer and ask him what recourse we have."

"Is there anything I can do to help resolve the problem?"

"Nothing I know of. Damn Dennis anyway. I never liked the SOB, and now I hate m——f——r even more."

"Yes, I know the feeling. If there is anything I can do to help, let me know? I distrusted him the first time we met, can't believe he would turn against us like this. He's just a lowlife, a no-good asshole, a real loose cannon, and a loser."

"Sounds like he will do anything to protect himself no matter who gets hurt. He apparently has no conscience, only animosity against any form of authority. I'm sure he will do whatever it takes to get the best deal, no matter whom he steps on. We'll have to watch our step while he is incarcerated awaiting trial. No telling what he will do or say," Ivan told Juan.

"I think you are right," Juan replied.

Suddenly the phone rang; it was Big Sid from the Silver Dollar Saloon.

"Good morning, Ivan. I've just heard what happened last night with your boy Dennis. I called to find out if there's anything I can do?"

Ivan related the story of Dennis's rampage last night and what he was demanding the association do for him.

"If you need my help, I'll do whatever it takes to silence Dennis if he gets out of hand. I have eyes and ears around town, and it would be my pleasure to eliminate your problem. You just say the word, and your problem is history."

"I appreciate the offer, Big Sid, but I think we can handle this without more bloodshed and violence, but if not, I'll call. Thanks."

Ivan hung up the phone, telling Juan what Bid Sid suggested if things started going south.

"I told him, 'we'll handle it,' but if I find out he's going to become a stool pigeon and begins crying to the prosecution or police about the organization, we may take Big Sid up on his offer. But until then, we have to keep our noses clean. Our only hope is for no outside interference from Dennis."

"If there is nothing else, I think I will head back to my office, catch up on some of my work that's been piling up lately. If you need me for anything later, let me know."

Juan left Ivan's office, returning to his in order to finish the mounds of paperwork piling up and needing his attention. By the time Juan finished with all his paperwork that morning, it was time for lunch. Walking out of his office, over to where the Irishman sat talking to Tony, told him, "Get the car. I have a couple of errands to run before stopping for lunch."

The Irishman soon returned with the car and picked up Juan. He then drove Juan over to check on the new hire Bobby Baker. Juan wanted to see how Bobby's day was going and if he had any problems or needed anything. Juan spotted Bobby as he walked down the sidewalk, heading to the shoe repair shop to collect. While approaching Bobby, the Irishman rolled down his window and shouted across the street at Bobby. Bobby acknowledged the Irishman and crossed the street where the car was, opened the passenger door, and crawled in the front next to the Irishman. He turned around, looked at Juan, and asked, "What's going on, boss?"

"I wanted to talk to you. Find out if you are having any problems collecting."

"No, everything is going smooth. Nothing unusual to report," Bobby said.

"Also wanted to know if you've heard anything about what happened to Dennis last night."

"No, what happened?"

"He got drunk last night at one of the local bars, apparently had an argument with someone whom he had a running beef with and killed him."

"You don't say?"

"Yes, I wanted you to be aware of the situation and the unfavorable spot this has put the association in. I need you to keep your eyes and ears open for any problems on the streets. We need to be aware of rumors or threats you may hear. We need to lay below the radar for a while, keeping a low profile. Don't want to rock the boat until this blows over, understood?"

"You got it, boss. If I hear of anything, I will let you know."

"Thanks. We may get some heat from the police since we've been cited in the past running collections. Watch yourself. Keep a lookout for any signs of union unrest. The situation Dennis is in is of great concern to us. We must be prepared to face whatever turn of events happens during this temporary setback, okay?"

"Yes, I understand. You can count on me, boss."

"Okay, Bobby, I'm counting on you. By the way, if you have time, would you like to go with me and the Irishman for lunch at the deli around the corner?"

"Sure, I was getting hungry and planned on taking a break after my next stop anyway."

"Irishman, drive over to the deli. We'll have lunch now."

The Irishman took a couple of turns, and suddenly, they were in front of the deli. Inside, they found a table away from the front door and sat down. They looked over the menu, but it was difficult to decide what to order with so many interesting sandwiches and soups to choose from. The waitress came over and took their drink order along with their food order. It was not long until their sandwiches and drinks were brought to the table.

During lunch, Juan asked Bobby, "So, Bobby, tell me how do you like collecting so far? Have you had any problems?"

"Not yet. A few seem reluctant at times to pay up, but nothing I've not been able to handle."

"Good, that's what I wanted to hear."

After lunch, walking outside, Bobby told the Irishman and Juan goodbye as they returned to the car. They left him to continue on his route.

The next stop on Juan's list was a visit to a local hotel not far from the office, just a few blocks south of the circle downtown. Reaching the hotel, the Irishman stopped the car.

As Juan exited, he told the Irishman, "Wait in the car. I'll be back shortly."

Juan walked inside and approached the sign-in desk and asked the clerk, "Do you have any available units for rent, and if so, what's the cost of a two-bedroom unit for, let's say, six months?"

After looking over the price list for long-term guests, the clerk looked back up at Juan and told him, "Five hundred a month, plus the first and last month's rent, paid in advance."

"That sounds good. Is it possible for me to see the unit before making up my mind?"

"Sure thing."

The clerk removed the key to unit 1010 from the keyboard hanging on the back wall and handed the key to Juan. Juan walked over to the elevator where he pushed the call button. Once inside the elevator, pushed number 10 on the chrome panel. The elevator began its slow ascent to the tenth floor. Reaching the tenth floor, the elevator door slowly opened, he stepped off and proceeded down the hallway to unit 1010. Taking the key in his hand, he inserted it into the lock and entered. It was much nicer, bigger, and brighter than the unit he now occupied. He looked around; it had all the amenities he required, so decided to take it. He liked the idea it was an end unit with a view of a small park across the street. After checking out the unit, Juan returned to the lobby. He walked back to where the desk clerk stood waiting his return and told him, "I'll take it."

The clerk had him fill out a long-term rental agreement, then asked how he wanted to pay. Juan pulled his wallet out of his jacket pocket, opened it, removed fifteen-one hundred dollar bills. He handed them to the desk clerk, who appeared surprised at the wad of money now in his hands. The clerk finally located a receipt book, where he wrote a receipt for fifteen hundred dollars. The clerk handed Juan a carbon copy and kept the original. Juan thanked the clerk and left the hotel.

Back outside and in the car, Juan told the Irishman, "Drive me back to the hotel I've been staying. I have a few things to pick up."

Arriving back at the hotel, Juan stepped out of the car and walked into the hotel lobby. Stopping at the desk, he picked up his key from the desk clerk, then proceeded to his room. Once inside the small room, gathered up what clothes and toiletry articles he had. Placing the items in a small suitcase recently purchased, along with the a few clothes accumulated while working for Ivan. Once he had all his belongings, he headed back downstairs.

He stopped at the desk and told the clerk, "I need to settle my account. I'm checking out."

The clerk checked his records, told Juan he still owed one week's rent plus tax. The total came to sixty-five dollars and thirty-nine cents. Juan reached inside his jacket, pulled out his wallet, removed seventy dollars, and handed it to the clerk.

He told the clerk, "Keep the change."

Picking up his meager belongings, left the hotel, returned to the car placing the small suitcase on the back seat along with the loose clothes.

Juan told the Irishman, "Drive me back to the office."

When they arrived back at the office, Tony was sitting at the table playing cards. He heard the front door open. Looking up, saw Juan.

Tony stopped Juan as he passed and said, "Ivan left a message for you." He gave Juan the note. Juan opened and read it. It stated,

I'm not feeling well and have gone home for the day. Will not be returning this afternoon. I may take off tomorrow too if I'm not better. I'm leaving you to hold down the fort and take care of business until my return.

Juan thanked Tony and proceeded to his office.

Soon, after entering his office, the phone rang. Juan answered; the voice on the other end asked to speak with Ivan. Juan told the caller Ivan was not around, he'd gone home for the day and asked not to be disturbed. Juan asked who it was that was calling.

"Yes, my name is Steven Wasserman, the lawyer for the association. I had spoken to Ivan earlier about locating someone to assist Dennis with his involuntary manslaughter charge."

"Yes, he told me he called you. I'm Ivan's partner. Maybe I can be of help?"

"Okay, Ivan hired me several years ago. I'm on a retainer to assist and represent the association in any legal matters concerning the association. I've just gotten off the phone with a local attorney willing to take on the case against Dennis, but he told me he would need five thousand dollars up front before continuing."

Juan thought about what the attorney told him and said, "Do you think this attorney is capable of representing Dennis in such a high-profile case as this?"

"I do."

"Has he been involved in any murder cases prior to taking Dennis's case? Is he skilled enough to spend the time arguing Dennis's case before a judge who is not shy about calling a spade a spade? The judge as I understand is not known as a lenient judge by any means of the imagination. Dennis has dug himself a very deep hole that will be hard to get out of," said Juan.

"Yes, so let me give you a little background on Justin Muller. He's been around town for a while, has a good track record in several murder cases, and a fair rapport with most judges he has appeared before. And he's the only attorney I've talked to who showed any interest at all in this case. Since this case involves one of your former employees, the trial could become a huge problem for your organization. I've learned Dennis is a foul ball as I'm sure you know. A difficult case, at best, for any attorney willing to represent him. It is going to be hard for any attorney to convince a jury of his peers as to his credibility. If and when the case goes to trial, and your association becomes involved, it's going to get nasty. It will not be just another involuntary manslaughter but a three-ring circus. By that time, it will be more complex and extremely complicated. I'm sure you can understand Atty. Justin Muller's position?"

"Yes, I understand. Will you call Mr. Muller? Have him call me or let him come by my office tomorrow so we can talk. I need to find out what he thinks he can do to help Dennis."

"Certainly, I'll call him as soon as we hang up. I'll have him get in touch with you, and you two can set up a time and place to meet."

"Thank you, Stephen, I appreciate the time you've spent hooking Dennis up with an attorney."

Juan realized after conferring with Stephen just how few attorneys appreciated stepping into an arena with such a volatile and unpredictable individuals like Dennis.

Juan after his conversation with Stephen told him, "I'll let Ivan know you found Dennis an attorney willing to accept his case. I'm sure he'll appreciate your endeavor and choice of attorney."

After hanging the phone up, Juan began gathering papers pertaining to Dennis, his work ethics, personality, and anything else he could find for Justin when he arrives to pick up his retainer fee. Not a lot of papers of interest, anything that shed light on Dennis's conduct would help Justin understand Dennis's irrational behavior.

After his talk with Stephen the phone rang again; this time it was Justin. They talked briefly and made arrangements to meet in Juan's office at nine o'clock sharp the following morning.

As Juan hung up the phone once again, it rang almost immediately. It was Becky, Ivan's wife, calling to tell Juan that Ivan had been taken to the hospital and was not doing well.

She explained to Juan, "Ivan had had a mild heart attack last night and transported to a local hospital for observation. I'll call you back when I learn more about his condition."

"I appreciate you calling and letting me know he's in the hospital. Keep me informed. If there is anything I can do for you or the family in the meantime, call me. I'm here for you and your family."

Learning of Ivan's sudden medical emergency, Juan was mentally ill-prepared as he faced the future alone. Thank goodness Ivan had added his name to accounts at the bank requiring a signature in the day-to-day operation of the organization. At least he can sign checks, pay bills, and keep the organization afloat until Ivan's return.

Late that afternoon, as street collectors began arriving, he was the go-to person accepting their daily pickup of dues. After the last envelope was handed to him, he took the entire batch received to Ivan's office, where he removed the daily ledger from the safe. He proceeded to sit down at Ivan's desk and signed off on each envelope and collector, accounting for the money received. After he finished signing off each item, he placed today's booty inside the safe. The ledger was used by Ivan to record his ill-gotten monies, a slush fund of sorts, double bookkeeping at its best. The money collected for protection was only for emergencies, or crisis, such as the one involving Dennis.

As soon as Juan finished signing off the ledger and putting the money in the safe, he walked back to his office where he cleared his desk.

Leaving for the evening, he and the Irishman had dinner at a small restaurant on Indiana Avenue where he occasionally ate when living on the mean streets. It was difficult to forget where he came from even though it was painful recalling those dreadful times in his past. It was important to him to remember how he survived prior to working for the association.

After dinner, Juan told the Irishman, "Drive me to the hotel a few blocks south of the circle downtown. I'm tired and ready to relax after another hectic day. The Irishman dropped him off at his new place."

And before leaving, Juan told him, "Meet me in the lobby in the morning around six. We'll stop and have breakfast before heading to work."

CHAPTER 23

In his new dig at the hotel, he cleaned up before returning to the living room and crashing in a chair and propping his feet on the ottoman. Somewhat relaxed sitting in the chair, he could not stop thinking of the numerous things to complete at work. Before long, he got up, walked over to the small TV, and turned it on. Juan thought watching TV would take his mind off work, but it was not to be. Getting off his chair, he walked over and turned the TV off. He was not able to dismiss the feelings of the unexpected series of events that suddenly surrounded him. He decided it was time to get up and head to bed. Once in bed, it did not take long before the thoughts were gone and he fell asleep.

The next morning after a restless night's sleep, he crawled out of bed, shaved, brushed his teeth, took a hot bath, and was ready to face another chaotic day at the office.

Later he met the Irishman in the lobby, had him drive over to the Clock restaurant for breakfast, then to the office. Juan anticipated a busy day and needed an early start in order to accomplish the many things on his agenda.

Tony arrived earlier and was talking to the new secretary Sheila Williams at the front desk when Juan arrived. Juan had not met Sheila, so as he walked in, he proceeded to where she and Tony stood talking and said, "Good morning, Tony."

Juan turned to the new secretary, addressing her, "Good morning. We've not met. My name is Juan Grajales, and you are?"

"My name is Sheila Williams. I'm the new secretary."

After the introductions, Sheila told Juan, "I've received several calls this morning, Mr. Grajales." She handed him a list of names along with phone numbers."

"Thank you, Sheila," he replied, taking the list with him. Juan quickly walked to his office.

Being in charge of a such a large conglomerate, Juan felt things were becoming grueling and, at times, taxing exercise in futility. This was going to be another frenzied and chaotic day, not knowing sometimes which way to turn or whom to turn to.

Looking over the phone list from Sheila, he wondered how Ivan was able to adapt to such an active regime yet lasting as long as he had alone. Inside his office, he took a seat at his desk and immediately began dialing the first number on the list. The phone rang several times before it was answered.

It was Mario who answered. Juan told him, "Good morning, Mario, what is it you need to speak with me about this morning?"

"I've encountered several minor issues with the group and need your opinion on certain matters brought to my attention, just need a second opinion."

"I told you, when I appointed you as team leader, you are in total charge. Whatever you need to do to correct situations that arise, use your own judgment, go with your gut. I have total confidence in your decision. If there is anything you cannot handle after exhausting all avenues, I'm available. If this is one of those times, I'm here, ready to help, but if it is a decision you can make, make it."

"I am also involved with a misunderstanding between Al and me. We seem to be at an impasse on most issues within the group, and not sure we'll be able to work it out and reach some sort of an amicable solution. Sorry to bother you with such trivial problems, but will handle it. Thanks for listening."

"That's okay, glad I was here to use as a sounding board. You be strong. Don't take any guff from your subordinates, even Al. Stand your ground. You're in charge, don't forget. If you think you are right, make the decision, don't waver. You'll find it gets lonely at the top."

"Right, boss. Sorry, I bothered you."

After their short conversation, Juan hung up.

Next on the list was none other than Al. Juan dialed the number, and after a few rings, Al answered.

"Hello, Al, this is Juan. What's the nature of your call this morning?"

"Oh, hello, Juan. I called to say Mario and I had a difference of opinion about a problem within our ranks. It's becoming messy. I told him I would not work with someone who was so narrow-minded, at which he became confrontational, plus he rejected my opinion. He told me to get out of his face, not to come back until I was ready to accept his authority. He was not happy at all with my brashness about an incident I had with one of the members. The member was spreading rumors about me. That's when I told him to go f——k himself. This apparently struck a nerve with Mario, and he got pissed at me."

"Go talk to Mario, get this petty situation straightened out. I have enough to worry about than picky shit like this. I want you two to stop this bickering, or I'll make some changes neither of you'll like, understood?"

"Yes, boss."

Juan hung up, then dialed Justin's number.

After a short briefing on the status of Dennis's upcoming trial, Justin asked Juan, "When I come by later this morning, would it be possible to pick up my retainer fee?"

"That'll be fine. I'll have your money ready before you leave," Juan told Justin.

Juan hung up, walked over to Ivan's office where he opened the safe. He stuffed five thousand dollars into an oversized envelope, sealed and addressed it: Justin Muller (Retainer Fee…Dennis).

Juan took time out to call the hospital, to get an update on Ivan's condition. A nurse at the hospital picked up the phone. Juan asked the condition of Ivan and was told that "he's resting comfortably at the moment, but had had a restless night and not out of the woods yet. We'll let you know if his condition worsens."

He thanked the nurse and told her, "If there's anything I can do, let me know."

At nine o'clock sharp, Atty. Justin Muller walked into the lobby and approached the desk where Sheila sat busily typing away. As Atty. Muller has approached her desk, she looked up and asked him, "Can I help you, sir?"

"Yes, my name is Justin Muller. I've spoken with Mr. Grajales earlier. I believe he is expecting me."

"Yes, give me a minute to tell him you are here."

"Thank you."

Sheila hit the call button on the intercom and announced, "A Mr. Justin Muller is here to see you."

Suddenly, the intercom came back on telling Sheila, "Send Mr. Muller in."

She pointed to Juan's office and told him, "Mr. Grajales will see you now."

Justin entered the office. Seeing Justin enter, Juan got up and walked around his desk to meet him. He reached out his hand, and they shook hands. When all the pleasantries were passed around, both took a seat and got down to business. Justin Muller was all business as he discussed Dennis's case to Juan, pointing out the ramifications and difficulties the case presented him as a defense attorney.

Juan was surprised at the amount of details that had to be worked out prior to Dennis's going to trial. After their meeting, Juan picked up the envelope and handed it to Justin Muller.

As Juan handed Attorney Muller the retainer, he told Justin, "I'm expecting big things from you. Dennis needs all the help he can get in getting out of this mess. And as you've heard by now, Dennis brought all this on himself because of his bad judgment, behavior, and temperament."

Attorney Muller agreed with Juan's analyses, telling him, "I'll do everything in my power to help Dennis with the involuntary manslaughter charges he's facing. But as you know, in cases like this, there are no guarantees. Since this is a highly publicized case, several witnesses have already stepped forward who were present at the bar the evening of the incident. They are all willing to testify against Dennis. The prosecution is going to have a field day with this case, so don't expect miracles."

Before the meeting ended, Attorney Muller stood up, shook hands once again with Juan, assuring him he would do whatever he could to help Dennis.

Juan told Attorney Muller before leaving the office, "I want to be keep informed as to the progress in this case."

After Juan's last comment, Attorney Muller turned toward the door and left Juan's office.

CHAPTER 24

The phone rang as Attorney Muller was leaving Juan's office. It was the hospital calling to report to Juan on Ivan's condition. "

This is Ms. Victor. The nurse at the hospital calling you back to inform you Mr. Cohen has been rushed to the OR for emergency surgery. The doctors are not sure what caused him to relapse but doing what they can to determine the cause. That's all I have at this time. I'll call you back when I have more information."

After hearing what the nurse said, Juan thanked her and told her he appreciated what they were doing to keep Ivan alive.

What would happen if Ivan could not return to work, or God forbid, he passed away?

Juan's day had not started out good and seemed to continue downhill as the morning progressed. He felt time was running out for Ivan since hearing his condition was waning.

Juan must make arrangements soon for an assistance to help him through the next few weeks since Ivan was not going to be around to help. Maybe someone within the organization he trusted and capable of taking up the slack, giving him more time for running the business.

After some soul-searching, he decided to ask Tony if he would be interested in assisting him in the interim. Tony had been close to Ivan, aware of his comings and goings around the organization. Juan decided to call Tony to his office and present him with the dilemma he faced.

He told Tony, "Since Ivan's in the hospital, we don't know for how long, I'm going to need someone with knowledge and expertise of the interworking of the association to assist me while Ivan's away. Would you be interested while I look for a full-time assistant?"

"No, not really. I'm happy where I am. I'm not interested in learning a new job at this stage of my life. I'm sure you understand? Since you know Al, why not ask him? I've heard he's not thrilled with his new position."

"Thanks, I'll ask Al and see if he's interested." Tony left the office and returned to his job.

Juan, after several calls, found Al back at the hotel and told him, "Meet me in my office this afternoon. I have a proposition for you."

"Sure, I'm not busy this afternoon," Al replied.

"Okay, I'll send over the Irishman to pick you up. We need to talk."

Later that afternoon, Al and the Irishman returned to the office. As Al passed by where Tony sat playing cards, he waved, said hi, and continued walking toward Juan's office. Al knocked on the office door and was told to come in. Al entered the office, closing the door behind him, and told to have a seat.

Juan looked up, "I'm glad you could make it this afternoon. I need to talk to you about helping me around the office while Ivan is in the hospital. It looks like he will not be back for a while. I need someone to help me in the short-term. Do you think you would be interested?

"Sure, boss, it's better than putting up with that asshole Mario and his BS."

"Yes, I hear you. I'm surprised you two didn't hit it off."

"Guess we are too much alike. A conflict of personality thing, you know?"

"I'm glad you are willing to help me out here in the office. It will take a lot of stress off me and make my job less taxing. If things work out, maybe I'll elevate you to office manager. How does that sound?"

"Sounds like something I'd be interested in."

"Okay then. First, let's begin this afternoon by me showing you a few small run-of-the-mill tasks I need completed. Once those have been mastered, I'll start assigning you more challenging responsibilities. All I want you to do for starters are these.

"Number 1—this afternoon, you need to check on the daily collections after everyone has been accounted for, bringing me the envelopes along with the ledger to my office.

"Number 2—answer my calls when I'm out or busy with a client.

"Number 3—make daily work schedules out for those employees whose job changes day to day.

"Number 4—help Sheila with payroll.

"You know most of the collectors, that's a plus. They like and trust you. Do you think you can handle what I've told you?

"Sure, boss."

"Okay, let's get started. I am limited on time, so first, you need to familiarize yourself with the office setup. I need you up to speed as soon as possible. Let's not waste any more time. Get started, familiarize yourself with the office before the collectors start arriving.

"This will be your office. I'm moving into Ivan's once I finish here. Get yourself ready for collections. By the time they arrive, you should be up and ready to receive the day's take. This is something you are familiar with, so it should not be a problem for you, right?"

"Right, no problem, boss. I can handle that part with my eyes closed. I've seen it done thousands of times with Ivan."

"Good, here's the ledger. You'll need to document each and every collection. Once the collections are received and documented, bring the ledger along with the envelopes to me. I'll double-check your numbers before I put the monies and ledger away. Familiarize yourself with the ledger while you get comfortable with your new surroundings. Are you ready to get started?"

Juan left the office as Al looked around at his new surroundings and pleased with his new job. He finally had a real position inside the association. At last, he had achieved a position he could be proud of. No longer just a collector or working for the muscle group; he had a real title. If he were capable and knowledgeable enough to excel in this position, it would be the crowning highlight of his career. He was anxious to finish the day, go home and celebrate with his wife on his advancement, not facing the dangers working day to day as a collector or muscle group on call twenty-four seven.

Once in Ivan's office, Juan began rummaging through the unfinished business lying on Ivan's desk. He had a lot to learn himself about Ivan's business dealings. It was much more complicated and intricate than he imagined. Juan began working his magic through the maze of paperwork, with the help of others in the office. Working his way through the labyrinth of paperwork; approaching it as just another task undertaken since starting to work for the organization. The mission ahead appeared insurmountable, but with time and persistence, he would overcome this adversity.

If Al did not work out, he'd find a qualified office manager. But he would give Al the benefit of the doubt before starting to look for a replacement. Time was the most cherished element required at this point.

The afternoon was the most frustrating, taxing day Juan had faced since being hired. As he blindly marched forward into the belly of the beast at warped speed, not only did he learn to run a business in the blink of an eye but also oversee two dozen employees, delegate authority, and accomplish monumental tasks. He wondered if time was his best asset.

Sheila and Tony were given additional responsibilities. They were to become his eyes and ears, all working in unison if the association was to succeed. It would be difficult for each group in the association to take on added responsibility, especially those in and around the office.

Juan had no choice but pass on more work to those reporting to the office. The office staff would be doing the grunt work and work yet to be discovered. Juan took the reins as leader; there was no turning back at this point. He was the one who had to be strong, yet fair with every employee starting from the bottom up. They must understand from the beginning what he said was final. His authority was not to be questioned. If challenged, the one doing the challenging would become history. It was not going to be easy, but nothing in his life had been without consequences.

The first problem encountered as he organized the pile of paperwork left by Ivan was the bills for stud fees, which had not been paid and several months overdue. He called each owner of fillies sent to the farm and impregnated in Lexington.

After contacting each owner and explaining who he was and the reason for the call, Juan asked the owners why they had not paid the stud fees, which had been outstanding for months.

Discussing the unpaid fees, each of the owners said, "It is an unintentional failure on our part, and fee will be paid by week's end or sooner."

Juan told them that if he did not receive payments by Saturday, they could expect to be slapped with a lawsuit. They had a legal and binding contract, which they broke, and needed to pay up or face the consequences, and hung up.

Juan noticed a letter from the association's accountant concerning a tax deduction listed on the latest monthly charges, which needed to be amended or corrected.

He contacted Sheila over the intercom, asking her, "Are you familiar with the latest charges we sent the accountant?

"Yes," she replied.

"Do you have the register with the totals in your files, the one showing our paid accounts for last month? If so, bring the file into my office. I need to look at it before I contact the accountant."

After their conversation, Sheila walked over to one of the file cabinets along the back wall, retrieved the register in question, then took it to Juan's office.

Handing the file to Juan, she asked, "Is there anything else you need while I'm here?"

"No, thank you, that will be all for now."

As Juan looked over the file; it did not take long until he found the error in question. Calling the accountant, he explained the situation. Juan gave him the correct total listed in the register. The accountant, after hearing about the error, looked at his copy of the tax report and told Juan it was a typical clerical error. He would resubmit the report and that should take care of the problem.

The accountant told Juan, "I will send you a corrected copy once I finish and send the amended copy to the tax people next week."

Juan hung up and ended his call with the accountant. He called Sheila again into the office.

"Here's your register back. I'm finished with it."

With the mountain of paperwork to read, review, and process, it was a daunting and overwhelming, but someone had to do it, and guess what? He was selected.

When the mail arrived later that afternoon, Sheila separated and cataloged them into different stacks. Letters she thought pertinent, needing Juan's immediate attention, she took to his office. Laying the mails on the right side of Juan's desk to sort through at his convenience.

He thanked her as he continued with the letter he was reading before she interrupted.

The notice was from a collecting agent demanding the organization pay their outstanding debt for two rental vans—the two vans used for their trip to Grand Isle and back to New Orleans after their fishing trip. He searched through his files looking for the original paperwork for the rental agreement, but was not able to locate it.

Once again, Juan called Sheila on the intercom, "Sheila, do you know where the rental agreement is for the two vans we rented while we were in New Orleans on our trip?"

"I remember the trip. I'll look up the contract. It should be in my files. When I find it, I'll get back with you."

Not long after his inquiry on the rental contract, Sheila appeared in the office and handed the rental agreement to him. He looked at the rental agreement and immediately called the collection agency. He explained the circumstances surrounding the office and why it had been an oversight on their part not paying in a timely manner.

He told them, "You can expect the check in the mail by day's end," and hung up.

He called Sheila again on the intercom, "Sheila, come to my office and pick up the rental agreement. I've talked to the rental company, explained to them the mistake was ours. Told them we would have a check in the mail by day's end."

When she returned to Juan's office, she picked up the rental agreement and told Juan, "I will cut them a check, send it by express mail. They should receive it by Friday at the latest." Then left the office.

Later that afternoon, collectors began arriving with their daily receipts. As they entered Juan's office, they were pleasantly surprised to see Al behind the desk. It was good seeing him as they renewed old friendships. Seeing Al, once one of them, made them feel good. They saw Al as a beacon of hope, giving them incentive to accomplish more out of life than just collecting. If Al could do it, why not them?

At day's end, the collectors came and went. Al finished with the collectors, took their contributions along with the ledger to Juan's office to be rechecked. After rechecking Al's work, Juan found that it looked like everyone had paid so far, which in any business would be considered good. Juan had finished with his calls, appointments, and immediate issues were addressed. He was ready to check once again Al's figures before putting the ledger and monies away.

It had been a productive day overall, and it was time to close for the night. Getting up from the desk, Juan walked into the lobby and told everyone, "I want you to know you have done an outstanding job so far, and I'm proud of you. I could not have done it without your help, thanks."

Everyone appreciated his sincerity, his ethics, and work habits. His was nothing like Ivan. The organization was changing; it was fun once again for employees and no one seemed anxious in leaving even though it had been a long trying day for all. Having Juan at the helm was so different. It was more hectic but seemed less demanding in a way that was hard to describe. Pleased with Juan and his overall attitude running the business made their job easier. They worked harder, but the work seemed less grueling, plus they were eager to please Juan no matter what the circumstances.

Juan looked over at the Irishman and told him, "I'm ready to leave. Bring the car around."

When they closed the office, everyone said good night, each heading in separate directions.

Juan told the Irishman, "I want to go to the hotel to relax a bit before dinner."

Meanwhile, Al, upon arriving home that evening, was excited to tell his wife of his promotion.

Tony, on the other hand, was glad he refused the office job but happy to continue working the lobby.

Sheila, meanwhile, was thinking more and more of her new boss. She felt things between Juan and her were changing, certain feelings and innuendos were beginning to surface.

Juan found himself reacting differently, enjoying the interest and attention she showed him when around her.

You could tell there was interest growing between the two. It was more obvious as time went on. There was a physical attraction in play, but only time would reveal the extent of the magnetism.

The next day was to be another chaotic day. Hopefully, with the troops in place, Juan would have a better handle on the daily routine. It should not be as taxing as the previous days on him or the office staff. The mountain of work that had piled up since Ivan's heart attack had slowly diminished. Juan was anxious to see the business running like the business he and Ivan envisioned when he became a partner.

The next morning Juan arrived at work, Tony spoke up as he passed by and said, "Sorry to be the bearer of bad news, there has been complications with Ivan earlier. He's suffered another heart attack and is in a coma, not expected to survive the day."

This was not the news Juan wanted to hear. It came as a shock, totally unexpected. How was he to continue this hectic pace without Ivan's help and knowledge? So many questions and no answers.

As a partner, it was up to him to take full responsibility, continue operating business as usual because options were nonexistent. Luckily, he had a great office team surrounding him.

He went into the office, sat down at his desk, wrote down the most important items needing immediate attention. Other matters would be dealt with as time allowed. In order to maintain the high standards, he had to set forth rules for the organization early on. The main responsibility at this juncture was to put the business back on an even keel. There seemed to be no light at the end of the tunnel with things going from bad to worse at every turn.

As Sheila arrived at work, Tony came to her and said, "The situation concerning Ivan's health had once again taken turn for the worse. Juan expected the office staff to do their part in keeping the office running as smoothly as possible. They are to be issued new directives concerning certain business matters not normally handled by office staff. Things were changing at the office on a minute-to-minute basis. Everyone was expected to pull their own weight during this unsettling time."

When Al arrived, was told about Ivan's earlier heart attack.

Tony explained to Al, "We need a lot of coordination and cooperation among the office staff. Satellite staffers need to work together in order to hold the company together as well."

Al, desperately trying to do his part, was having his own difficulty keeping up with his duties. He was the cog in the wheel slowing down the office, something had to give and soon.

Juan informed the Irishman of Ivan's condition earlier. Beginning immediately, he would be required to run errands for the office staff, deliver and pick up essential items as required. They were minor compared to other directives handed out to office staff that morning.

The Irishman took the new directive with a grain of salt. He did not mind the extra workload; in fact, he liked the new job description. It gave him something to do rather than sitting around all day, playing cards and twiddling his thumbs waiting for Juan.

Later that morning, Juan called a meeting of the office staffers to inform them of a new direction for the association's survival. After the meeting, still reeling from the turn of events of late, the office staff returned to work. Not long after the meeting, the office staff was again firing on all cylinders. Amazing how adaptable and flexible this office staff had become in the face of adversity. How? Without fanfare, each staffer took his or her new responsibilities and ran with it, with the exception of Al.

Later that morning, Juan called Ivan's wife at home, but she did not answer. The maid answered. She informed him Becky had returned to the hospital to check on Ivan. After his brief conversation with the maid, hung up. Then he placed a call to the hospital and informed Becky was in the waiting room awaiting word on Ivan's latest condition. When called to the nurse's station over the Public Address System she had a call, Becky rushed to the nurse's station where she was handed a phone.

Juan asked her, "How is Ivan doing?"

Becky told him, "Ivan's not doing well. The doctors have little hope he'll last the day."

Juan reminded her again, "If there's anything I can do, let me know."

Thanking him for calling, she told him, "If I hear anything new about Ivan's condition, I will contact you immediately," and hung up.

It was midmorning when Sheila received a call from Dennis's attorney, Justin Muller, calling to speak with Juan, so she transferred the call. When Juan picked up the phone, Attorney Muller had more bad news.

"Dennis decided to turn against the association in hopes of a lesser sentence. Dennis's case is becoming a fiasco, not only for the judicial system, but for you, me, and the association. You must move quickly in order to clean up the association and turn it around. If your organization is admitted into the proceedings, it must be presented in a way that shows it as a legitimate entity. Not a business associated with loan sharking or racketeering, etc."

"How can I present the association as legitimate business if introduced?"

"You'll have to clean it up if you plan on continuing to operate after the trial," was Justin's recommendation.

After his conversation with Justin, Juan called Al, Tony, and Sheila to his office for a roundtable discussion about legitimizing the business.

"I need input, recommendations on cleaning up the association on the surface so it appears to be a legitimate entity. Do any of you have any suggestions?"

After an hour or so, the decision was to restructure the businesses. This time it involved all field employees. It would take time, and the time frame was critical. They had to act fast. This was the only way the business would survive if Dennis testified against the association. It was a long shot. If Dennis's testimony was admitted in court against the association, he could potentially throw the association under the bus.

After the meeting, Sheila walked to her desk and started going through her files of the different entities owned by the organization, jotting down names, dates, places. When she finished, she presented her list to Juan. Juan looked over the list, plus his own folders, trying to figure out a workable solution to the pressing problem. Somehow they had to incorporate certain employees into legitimate businesses run by the organization. Among the group of employees, only "the muscle group" could not be reassigned. They had a reputation and was impossible to hide if Dennis brought them into play.

Juan decided to continue paying the muscle group under the table while they lay low until the mess with Dennis was over. He was glad it was a small group, only five individuals on standby, paid only when called upon for duty. He believed the association could avoid being dragged through the mud if he placed collectors in other businesses owned by the association until things settled down.

With that in mind, he called the association lawyer to ask his opinion of the situation he faced. Juan wanted to know if it was plausible to turn the association around, if he integrated several employees into the legitimate businesses owned and operated by the association.

The attorney told Juan, "It depends on how much Dennis knows about the association's loan business and overall operation if allowed to take the stand."

Attorney Steven Wasserman then asked Juan, "Send me a list of businesses the organization runs. That way, I'll have a better idea what avenue you must follow. I'll get back to you with my recommendations as soon as possible."

Since Dennis decided to turn on the association, Juan called Attorney Justin Muller to ask his opinion about the association's obligation in furnishing Dennis with an attorney going forward.

Justin Muller recommended, "Why not let Dennis get his own court-appointed attorney? Why should you give the SOB a free ride since it sounds as if he is going to try hanging the organization up by its gonads in order to save his own ass? The SOB deserved whatever the court hands down. I don't think it should be the association's problem any longer."

"If that is what I should do, that settles it. Let's drop him and see what happens," Juan replied.

Attorney Justin Muller also told Juan, "I'm going to submit my withdrawal from the case to the court this afternoon. I'll be available in case my services are required going forward. If you need me, call. I'm still on a retainer until this thing is settled anyway."

Juan thanked Attorney Muller, then hung up the phone. Since Justin Muller was no longer representing Dennis, Juan had other obligations to address that were more important than who represented Dennis.

Later that afternoon, Juan's phone rang. It was Steven Wasserman. He had been informed of this latest debacle concerning Dennis and Attorney Justin Muller. He told Juan he was glad to see he and Attorney Muller decided not to pursue representing Dennis at this time.

"Why should you represent the bastard who's looking to destroy you and the association? The association had nothing to do with his incarceration in the first place. He is an ungrateful SOB. You've tried to help, but as usual, his greed surfaced once again. He is one of those people who would turn on his own mother if it benefited him. Let him wallow in his own excrement and suffer the consequences. He is a user, nothing else. I'm glad you decided to go this route. Maybe he will learn his lesson, again maybe not. Time will tell."

CHAPTER 25

Dennis no longer had ties with the association after releasing Justin Muller. Juan began relocating certain field employees to other groups inside the organization. Juan sent word out to all collectors working the streets to meet in his office the following day for reassignment.

The next morning, the collectors gathered in the office. Juan asked them here so he could explain his relocation strategy to them. This was a complete surprise to those working the streets. After explaining to them how the repositioning was to be carried out, told those in attendance to revisit each store they collected from and tell the owners they were getting a reprieve but not become complacent because they would be returning.

Excusing the group, Juan contemplated on which organization within the association could absorb help without being overly taxed. The first option was a Oasis, the restaurant the association owned. He decided to send two collectors there: one to work in the kitchen; the other, behind the bar or as a server. The restaurant had a large turnover of employees; it was always in need of new trainees or fulltime help.

Juan transferred one of the collectors to the loan company to use him as a COO, to execute the company's business plans and become an inside informer. The new hire there would be Juan's eyes and ears inside the loan company. He needed information as to the validity and trustworthiness of the employees working there. This had to be someone from the group of collectors, who was business savvy, yet stay in the background as an informant.

During this meeting with the collectors, Juan discovered who that person was for that job. His name was Alex, a college graduate who minored in business and finance at Indiana University. Alex had fallen on hard times lately before running across the job as a collector. Alex had exceptional knowledge of business as he talked to Juan after the meeting.

Juan was impressed with Alex from the get-go and chose him to fill the position at the loan company. Alex was more qualified than the manager now running the establishment. It was a no-brainer for Juan. Alex was given a promotion plus a substantial salary increase. Alex was elated at his new position and promotion. The advancement of Alex was a choice Juan would not regret.

With three collectors still needing to be relocated, he decided to send them to the farm outside Lexington, Kentucky, the most profitable and prized possession among the association's enterprises.

Juan knew the horse farm required a lot of help, man-hours, and money to operate properly. Miles and miles of fencing had to be constantly maintained. There was also the constant upkeep of the grounds and maintenance of the barns, stalls, and lastly, the feeding and grooming of the animals. Each job on the farm was an essential part of the business. Work on the farm never stopped; it was continuous and around the clock. And of course, the farm must be ready in having the registered animals available at a moment's notice for breeding service. Upkeep on the farm was an ongoing, tedious, and laborious daily routine.

Juan's relocation of the last three street employees to the farm gave the association credence of legitimacy if summoned to appear at the trial of Dennis. With this last relocation, his list was complete. Juan could sit back, run the business, and not worry about the legitimacy of the association until after the trial.

Completing the relocation, Juan walked out into the lobby and informed everyone, "The Irishman and I will be out of town for the next couple of days. I'm leaving it to you to hold down the fort while we're away. If you need me, contact the foreman at the farm or the hotel where we'll be staying in Lexington."

He handed Sheila his itinerary with pertinent information needed while he was away. He told the Irishman, "Get the car ready by tomorrow. We'll be driving to Lexington in the morning."

The Irishman spent the biggest part of the afternoon having the car serviced, ready for the drive to Lexington.

The following morning, the Irishman parked the car in front of Juan's hotel and went inside, asking the desk clerk to "call Mr. Grajales, inform him his driver is waiting downstairs in the lobby."

It was not long after the call when Juan emerged from the elevator. Juan was eager to get on the road, but first they would have breakfast. After breakfast, they hit the road on their way to Kentucky. Driving into Lexington later that afternoon, the Irishman located the hotel where Sheila had made reservations. Not far from downtown in case the need arose in locating an accountant, lawyer, or other professionals while in town. Not having visited the farm since taking over, he was not sure what to expect once he arrived.

After dinner that first evening, he and the Irishman went back upstairs to for the evening.

Juan told the Irishman, "Meet me in the dining room no later than six thirty tomorrow morning."

The next day, Juan was up early. He showered, dressed, and headed downstairs for breakfast. Here he would meet the Irishman for before continuing to the farm. After breakfast, they headed down the highway toward the farm. About a half hour later, Juan saw a sign—The Stables—indicating the farm was just ahead on the right. The Irishman slowed the car down as they reached the turnoff, turning off the highway onto a dirt road, which lead to the farm.

Juan's first impression was how beautiful the farm was. Approaching a pristine large white-painted barn, Juan spotted someone whom he thought might be the foreman, busy feeding horses.

Juan told the Irishman to stop the car. Juan exited the car and approached the man.

Luke, who in the meantime, had stopped what he was doing and asked, "Can I help you?"

"I'm Juan Grajales. I came down to meet you and inform you Ivan Cohen is in the hospital after having a serious heart attack. He's still in guarded condition at a local hospital back in Indy. I'm in charge of the association until he returns. I wanted to come down to visit the farm and meet with you. I'd appreciate if you would show me around, explain the different aspects of running a farm this size."

Luke was surprised at hearing Ivan was gravely ill and at the unannounced visit from Juan.

"I was worried about Ivan since I've not had contact with him in a week or so. I had it on my list to call him next week if I did not hear from him soon."

After introductions and small talk, Luke asked Juan, "Ready for a tour around the farm?"

"Yes, and afterward, I would like to look at your books to see what the financial condition of the farm looks like."

Luke escorted Juan around the farm, explaining what a breeding horse farm entailed.

After seeing all that he wanted to see, Juan told Luke, "Okay, let's go to your office, you can show me your books."

Once inside Luke's office, he removed several books from a file cabinet and began showing Juan the financial statements from last year. Looking over the financial statements, Juan thought everything seemed to be in order. The farm, in general, seemed financially sound. The business overall was profitable, which was good news.

After being shown around the farm and going over the books, Juan told Luke, "I'm sending three new employees down next week. The association is in the process of relocating several employees and thought the farm could use the extra help. You can expect them next week. Use them in any capacity you deemed necessary. It's up to you to keep them occupied. Looks like you could use a couple of extra hands. I'll need you to furnish me a job description and work location on the farm of each of your employees. A daily log of their duties and the number of hours worked weekly. I'm going to require a weekly report sent to my office detailing the work performed by each worker. My office will assume the duty of making out the weekly checks starting next week. My office will send you the checks for distribution to the workers. Are you okay with that?"

"Sure, whatever you want me to do, I'm comfortable with it."

"Fine, I think I've seen enough and believe it's time the Irishman and I head back to our hotel. I've seen what I came down to see, so.

I'll be leaving now and let you get back to work. I'm impressed with the way the farm is running, if you needed anything, anything at all while I'm in town, let me know."

Juan and the Irishman left the farm and returned to the hotel. The trip to the farm had been enlightening. Juan had been impressed with the farm and hoped eventually the other entities owned by the association ran as well. It was a tall order but plausible.

On his return to Indy, Juan learned of Ivan's passing the night prior to his arrival back in town. It was a sad day for all concerned, especially him. He called Becky expressing his sincere condolences for her loss. And if there was anything that she needed him to do, all she had to do was ask. Becky thanked him for calling and would be in touch.

What was he to do now?

Juan had more on his plate than ever in running the association. Being solely in charge, the first thing he wanted to do was try and reorganize the entire organization. Begin by placing reliable people in key positions within the association.

With the transition from being a partner to CEO, he was going to need assistance.

He informed Sheila, "Type a memo, send a copy to each satellite business and person in charge to attend an informal meeting in my office tomorrow morning, eight o'clock sharp. The meeting would begin then. If they're not on time, they need to start looking for other employment. I'll not tolerate excuses. I want to meet with all key personnel of each sector to discuss how association business will be accomplished in the future."

The memo was typed and sent to all concerned before the end of the workday. Everyone the following morning appeared on time. The door was closed to Juan's office, and the meeting began. It lasted for over two hours as Juan explained in detail what he expected from each and would not tolerate hypocrisy among the rank and file.

Juan spoke while Sheila took notes as each head of a sector gave their assessments of their operation. He got a feel for the person as to whether they were the right person needed in that sector.

After going back through the list, Sheila compiled. He got a clearer picture of the individual and if they were the right individual for the job. Eventually shuffling people around in the different sectors making changes he thought would be beneficial to that division. At least he felt the right people were in the right positions and who he could depend. During this transformation, because of uncertainty there would be confusion the first few days until everyone grasped what he was doing and things settled down.

A couple of managers were left hanging as the meeting ended. They were unsure what was going to happen to them as Juan continued reorganizing the association.

After the meeting, Juan called Ivan's wife, Becky. He could tell she had been crying and sounded depressed.

He offered his condolences once again, by telling her, "You know, Becky, if I can be of assistance, I'm always available. I know it is a sad time for you, but is there anything I can do to help you and your family at this time?"

"I appreciate your concern and would like to take you up on your offer. Can I ask you to take care of the funeral arrangements? It had been Ivan's last wish for you to do so. He knew it would be too difficult for me to do on my own. Can you help me?" Becky asked.

"Yes, I'll be more than happy to handle the arrangements. Is there anything else you can think of?"

"No, I just want to get this behind me so I can move on. Without Ivan in my life, I feel so alone. Did you know we have been married for over forty years?"

"No, Ivan never told me that. I understand how you must miss him. If you think of anything else that I can be of service, call me."

"Thank you, Juan, you don't know how much I appreciate what you're doing in my time of grief and for carrying on with Ivan's legacy. We'll meet after the funeral and settle the more important things concerning Ivan's will, et cetera. Let's keep in contact."

"I will. You take care of yourself. I'll get started right away with the funeral arrangements. Is there any particular funeral home you wish to have his body taken?"

"No, I'm leaving that up to your discretion."

"Okay, I'll get back to you as soon as I find a funeral home and learn the particulars. I'm sure the funeral home will want to contact you for more pertinent information about what you would like done for Ivan."

"Okay."

"Becky, don't worry about a thing. I'll take care of it."

After hanging up the phone from talking to Becky, Juan paged Sheila on the intercom.

When she answered, Juan asked her, "Sheila, have you had any connections with funeral homes in the area lately?"

"No, I'm not familiar with the ones around here. I can call around."

"Would you? Thanks."

Several calls later, Sheila found a funeral home that met Juan's criteria. She informed Juan while placing the funeral administrator on hold. She told him to pick up the phone and talk to the funeral director directly. Picking up his phone, Juan asked the funeral director several questions. The director answered each of Juan's questions. The director assured Juan they could handle any and all requests and would be privileged to handle Ivan's funeral. The director promised to do whatever was necessary to measure up to the standards called upon them to perform.

Juan told the director, "Go ahead and get started on the arrangements. I'll be in to finalize the paperwork this afternoon."

He called Becky back after talking to the funeral director to let her know the arrangements for Ivan's funeral were being implemented at this time and he was personally overseeing the prearrangements.

He also mentioned to Becky, "The funeral home I'm dealing with is on the outskirts of town not far from where you live."

Becky seemed pleased with his choice and how quickly he expedited Ivan's request of taking care of the funeral arrangements. Again, she thanked Juan for all he was doing for her and her family in their time of sorrow.

After the funeral, things began to quieten down around the office. Juan received a call from the attorney taking care of Ivan's affairs. Atty. Wasserman asked that Becky and he come to his office soon to take care of the living trust Ivan set up prior to his death. They made a tentative time to meet the following week at 10:30 a.m. on Tuesday.

When Tuesday came, Juan and Becky met with the attorney in his office. As Becky and Juan sat listening to the attorney read the trust and hearing the stipulations included in the trust, she was in agreement with Ivan's wishes. Juan learned Becky was to retain Ivan's original 51 percent of the partnership, while he retained 49 percent.

Becky told Juan before leaving Atty. Wasserman's office, "I want nothing to do with running the business. It is yours to run as you see fit."

Becky wanted only to be a silent partner, and for Juan to send a monthly statement to her accountant, so the accountant could see how the business was being handled. The accountant, in turn, would inform her of the results. She would be in contact if the accountant detected anything in the statements needing her attention. Juan agreed to Becky's terms and reiterated he would be up front and straight forward with her on every aspect of the business henceforth.

Returning to the office, he had a lot of catching up to do. The only way he knew how to accomplish this monumental task was to jump in head first.

He called Dennis's attorney to find out how the situation with the preliminary hearing was and if there had been any new developments in the case.

The attorney told him, "I talked to the prosecuting attorney and after talking with Dennis, he had no substantial information concerning the association's criminal deception, only hearsay of its involvement in unscrupulous business practice. Barring any new evidence, the association seemed to be under the radar and in the clear.

"Dennis does not stand a china man's chance in hell of getting out of this involuntary manslaughter charge. He put all his eggs in one basket and botched his chances of acquittal or a lesser sentence. That's the way the cookie crumbles when one lets his mouth overrule his derriere. Dennis has made his bed and now had to lay in it."

Juan was happy with the news coming from the attorney concerning the association's involvement. It had taken a huge weight off his shoulders to learn this declaration; he could now move on to running the business without worrying about Dennis.

CHAPTER 26

Juan arrived at work to discover someone had broken into the building, entered his office, riffled through his files, and tried peeling the door of the large safe. Though not successful, it still left a huge mess behind to clean up.

Juan called the police. After police arrived, they took fingerprints, pictures and questioned employees who worked in the office. Consequently, little evidence was found at the scene in which to follow up on. They told Juan that if new evidence was found, they would inform him. After the police finished their investigation, vacated his office and building, Juan called Al, Tony, and Sheila to his office.

He told them, "I need you to keep your eyes and ears open. If you hear any kind of rumor about the break-in, I want to know."

After the break-in, things began happening inside and outside the office that defied logic. Strange things continued with more frequency, such as when the Irishman went to the garage to retrieve the car and found its battery missing. In another incident, a member of the muscle group was accosted and beaten up for no reason. The door to Sheila's apartment had been jimmied and ultimately entered; nothing was missing as far as she could tell. Another strange thing happened when Tony discovered the deck of cards he played solitaire daily were missing. It was a small incident, but noteworthy. Why were these things suddenly happening?

The farm also was not without its problems. For unknown reasons, in the last three months, it had begun incurring more and more debt. Things inside the organization were beginning to go awry. The farm appeared to be slowly drowning in debt unexpectedly. Why?

Learning of the debit problem, Juan called to confront the foreman, Luke.

The foreman told Juan, "I have no clue as to why suddenly the farm is incurring more debt lately. I'll ask the accountant here if he can find the problem. As soon as he does, I'll get back with you."

When Juan confronted Luke about the sudden decrease in revenue over the last three months or so, he evasive rather coy.

Luke told Juan, "I have no clue as to why the cost of running the farm has dramatically increased over the past few months. The horses are healthy, vet bills are minimal, and feed cost has not increased. The wages have increased slightly but only because of the three new hires you sent. Don't know of any other reasons."

Juan explained to Luke, "The decrease in revenue indicates a major problem, plus a substantial cash flow problem now exists. Further investigation by me and my accountant here have discovered several accounting errors in your accountant's monthly statements dating back to the demise of Ivan. This shortage is leading us to believe the cause of the shortage is due to accounting mistakes.

"The association's accountant found evidence the accountant working for the farm may be altering or cooking the books. It appears to have begun prior to Ivan's demise. So I've decided to get to the bottom of this infraction by coming down, along with my accountant, and confronting your accountant. It's blatant in the way he has falsified certain entries the past few months. There's no way he is clever enough to cover up the flagrant paper trail he's submitted the last few months. It's too obvious.

"Expect my accountant and I at the farm in a day or two. I need to talk to you and your accountant about the infractions in the monthly statements we received. I suggest you get your ducks in a row before we arrive. I need to get to the crux of things and straighten out this problem immediately. Do I make myself clear?" "Yes, I'll do what I can on my end in helping solve the problem."

Arriving in downtown Lexington two days later, their first stop was to the accountant's office. Juan and his accountant, without announcing their presences, walked right in, past the secretary who was taken aback as they blatantly walked straight into her boss's office, surprising the accountant, Jay

Juan introduced himself and his accountant and told Jay Beery in no uncertain terms, "After reviewing your last-three monthly reports, which were sent to my accountant. We've become aware of several accounting errors that adds up to several thousand dollars missing from the farm's account. We need to see your latest files along with the receipts Luke's sent you. We need to compare your receipts with the ones we received from Luke.

Jay had his secretary retrieved the files Juan asked to see. After rummaging for the files and accompanying receipts, she brought them into Jay's office. The secretary placed the files along with the receipts on the table where Juan and his accountant sat with Jay. Juan and his accountant began the long and arduous task of scanning the files and checking each against their copies. As they gleaned meticulously through the files and receipts, they began noticing the same pattern emerging as the files sent to Indy.

At that point, Juan confronted Jay with what they were finding. Jay had no rational explanation as to why the statements were flawed and no idea what happened to the missing money. Juan knew Jay was lying the minute he opened his mouth, spouting out unbelievable excuses. He pretended to have no knowledge how the money disappeared. Juan decided to up the ante by putting pressure on Jay, threatening him with bodily harm if he did not come clean.

Jay had been caught red-handed. Knowing Juan meant business, Jay decided to tell Juan what he and Luke conjured up prior Ivan's death. It was not long until Jay spilled the beans. Juan learned the story behind why the farm was short on cash the last few months.

Juan told Jay in no uncertain terms, "I want all the monies you and Luke skimmed from the association put back in the farm account by the end of today. If not today, you no longer will be able to do accounting or any other work for a long time. Have I made myself clear?"

"Yes, but it's going to take me more than a day to come up with the money. I promise I'll have the money back in the farm's account by the end of the week, if that's acceptable?"

"I'll give you the benefit of the doubt. I'll give you two days, two days only. If the money has not been replaced in the farm's account, I'm returning and you will not like what follows, understood?"

"Perfectly clear, Mr. Grajales."

"Two days," Juan reiterated.

Juan and his accountant stayed in town the next couple of days keeping close tabs on Jay, making sure he did not leave town before returning the money.

At the end of the second day, Jay was not able to come up with the monies skimmed from the farm's account. He was still short several thousand dollars. Time had run out for Jay; it was time to pay the piper or suffer the consequences.

The Irishman met up with Jay as he was leaving work on the second day, escorting him to the waiting car where Juan waited. The Irishman opened the door to the back, pushing Jay inside and shut the door. Jay was at a loss for words. He knew his sham was over. It was all downhill from here.

Jay got the gist of what he was looking forward to. Looking at the Irishman then at Juan, he realized he was in for a wild ride with these two. They drove out to the farm to meet Luke, who was in the barn raking fresh hay around the stalls when they arrived.

Luke was surprised when he looked up and saw Jay get out of the car along with Juan. Luke talked to Jay only yesterday and knew Jay had been confronted by Juan about the missing money but thought Jay was smart enough he could take care of the problem. But suddenly, they appeared back at the farm. Luke was now frightened, wondering what he had gotten himself into with Jay.

Luke wondering to himself, *Why are they here? What's going on? Why had Juan brought Jay, especially this late in the day?*

As they approached, Luke stopped raking hay and asked, "What do I owe this unexpected pleasure? What brings you out this way so late in the evening? Is something wrong?" he asked.

"I think you know why. I want to talk to you and Jay in your office now!"

The Irishman followed as they walked from the barn back to Luke's office to discuss the missing money and the bottom of this charade between Luke and Jay. Once inside Luke's office, Juan decided to lay the cards on the table and to the crux of the matter quickly, giving them no time to think up some unbelievable cockamamie story.

Juan was suspicious once the accountant found the obvious mistakes Jay made on his accounting reports. It was apparent the two were in cahoots, running a scam. Without admission of guilt from Luke, he had Jay's story. Juan was not sure which one was the biggest problem but determined to find out. It would be a matter of time until Juan learned if his theory about both were true.

Inside Luke's office, Juan asked both Luke and Jay to sit down. Nervously, they sat down and watched the Irishman pull from his waistband a large metal pipe and held it in his right hand, tapping it against his left hand in a menacing gesture.

Juan asked Luke, "I'm going to ask you one time and only one time. Luke, have you and Jay been working together, skimming money from the farm's account?"

At first, Luke denied the accusation, telling Juan, "No, boss, I know nothing about what you are referring to."

Juan could tell Luke was lying by his actions. Juan looked over at the Irishman and signaled with a nod. Suddenly out of the blue, the Irishman drew back the pipe in his right hand, striking Luke on the right shinbone with such force causing Luke to yell out in excruciating pain. Luke, feeling the agony of the pain caused by the pipe, could not help but scream.

Juan said to Luke, "I told you I was only going to ask you one time about skimming money from the association's account set aside solely to run the farm."

Luke looked over at Jay with terror in his eyes, then said to Juan, "Yes, but it was Jay's idea. He thought it would take you time to get up to speed and we would not get caught in the interim."

After hearing Luke tell both he and Jay were responsible for taking the money, Jay felt relieved that he was not the only one involved in the rip-off.

Juan then turned to Jay, "Is what Luke said true?"

Jay looked up at the Irishman, who by now was towering over him with the dreaded metal bar still clutched in his hand ready to do him bodily harm if he did not tell Juan what he wanted to hear. Jay wanted to find a hole to crawl into, but there was no place to run or hide. He felt remorseful, but it was too late. It was the time he paid the piper for his misdeed.

Suddenly, without warning, he too was struck with the terrifying force of the iron pipe on the right shinbone, this time breaking the tibia. The pain endured by Jay was beyond description. As he reached down, he was grimacing with pain, holding onto his broken leg. As the pain increased, he started screaming at the top of his lungs. A short time later, after the pain subsided a bit, both men settled down.

Juan asked Luke, "Do you have enough personal money set aside to pay the balance of what Jay needs to satisfy your ill-gotten funds."

"How much is still needed to placate our debt?"

"The total amount owed the association by you two is eight thousand dollars."

After the pain subsided some more, Luke looked up at Juan, "Yes, there's enough money in the office safe to pay the remainder of the debt owed. I stashed the money I received from Jay in the office safe. I was going to use it for a rainy-day fund. Guess I learned the hard way today, my rainy-day fund just ran out."

Slowly getting out of the chair, Luke slowly limped back to the safe to retrieve the money. Then back over to Juan, he handed the money to him.

Juan looked at both men and told them, "You are both finished with the association and farm. Now get up and get your sorry asses off the f——king farm. I don't want to see your ugly faces around here again, understood?"

"Yes," both answered in unison.

Jay slowly got up, holding on to Luke as they stumbled powerlessly out the door to Luke's car. Both crawled in, never making eye contact with Juan or the Irishman. Luke began the long drive down the picturesque lane leading from the farm, never looking back.

Juan was now in a quandary; he needed a replacement to run the farm before heading back to Indy. At the farm that evening, Juan called a meeting of the employees who lived and worked on the farm. He briefed them on what happened to Luke and Jay.

After informing them he had fired Luke, Juan told them, "I'm looking for a foreman to replace Luke to run the farm. Is there anyone among you here acquainted with or know someone locally qualified in running a farm of this size?"

Bobby Baker (one of the collectors recently sent from Indy to work on the farm) spoke up, "I've had a lot of experience having been raised on a farm in southern Indiana. I can help out until a replacement can be found."

Juan took Bobby aside and talked to him briefly about the possibility of him taking control and running the farm. During his brief meeting with Bobby, Juan discovered Bobby had a wealth of knowledge at running a large farm. Bobby was familiar with all aspects of horse farming, and Juan liked what he heard. So Juan appointed Bobby on the spot as the new foreman replacing Luke.

Returning to the meeting, Juan informed the group, "I've appointed Bobby Baker as your new foreman starting immediately."

Everyone seemed to take the appointment of Bobby in stride. Bobby with his knowledge in horse farming was the idea choice.

Bobby, excited about his promotion, readily accepted the position. Who would have thought in the midst of all the confusion, Juan would find a replacement this quick? Bobby was given the chance of a lifetime, running a first-class stud farm in the bluegrass state of Kentucky.

Bobby thanked Juan for the opportunity, promising, "You'll not regret your choice."

Juan told Bobby again about what happened to Luke and Jay, telling him, "I do not want a repeat in the future. I'm sure you understand the ramifications. Understand if you violate that trust, what can and will happen?"

"You can count on me, boss, not to be involved in such things. I would never do anything to jeopardize the association or your trust in me."

"Okay, as long as we understand each other, and I can count on you to be up front and honest with me, the job is yours. I will find someone local to help you learn not only what's involved running a farm this size but keeping records of everyday expenditures and incomes. You'll also be responsible for the hours a farmhand works so the management company has the information needed when it comes time to file income taxes.

"The accountant sends me a copy of the monthly report. Another copy is given to the management company. Plus, I'll need a copy of the stud fees collected so I can send a copy to the management company. In turn, the management company will notify the owner by sending the necessary paperwork on the lineage and genealogy of the procedure for their future reference.

"As you know running a farm of this size is not just taking care of farm animals, farmhands, but what's in the best interest of the association, etc.

"Is there anything else I can help you with before I leave? If not, get yourself acquainted with your new job as quickly as possible. You have a big responsibility ahead of you, and not a lot of time in getting up to speed. I expect you to send me a report each week while you are learning the procedures, letting me know how well you are getting along."

"Okay, boss, I will. It'll take me a month or two to get into the swing of things. Just have patience, I'll not disappoint you."

Before leaving, Juan gathered the farmhands once again to finish his pep talk.

He told them, "If you have a problem, talk to Bobby. He's your go-to boss and sounding board. If there are no more questions, I'll be leaving. Good luck to all of you."

After getting things settled on the farm, Juan, his accountant, and the Irishman left, heading back to Lexington. Tomorrow was to be another busy day. Juan had to find a new accounting firm to take over for Beery who had been fired along with Luke for misappropriation of farm money. He did not have a lot of time to spend looking for a new accountant; he had to locate one quickly. It would not be easy since he had no time to do research or background check for a qualified accountant; he must do it on the fly.

After dinner that evening and a good night's rest, Juan was up early the next morning making calls. He contacted several accounting firms in the area. He finally settled on an accounting firm owned by a Mr. Jim Logan. After meeting with Mr. Logan, he decided to hire his accounting firm. After signing the necessary paperwork, it was time to head back to Indianapolis, busying himself with more association business, which required his undivided attention. It had been a long, exhausting trip to Lexington, but it turned out better than he could ever imagined after all was said and done.

CHAPTER 27

Back in Indianapolis, Juan was ready to buckle down, meet head-on the problems brewing locally. The Irishman dropped him off at the office. Juan had a lot of tweaking to do within the organization but was slowly getting a handle on the overall operation. With the problems in Lexington out of the way, he could concentrate his undivided attention to the remaining issues facing the association.

First thing he needed to do that morning was contact Big Sid and find out what was happening around town while he was away.

When reached Big Sid, he was told, "There's a new group in town out of Chicago. They arrived the day you left for Kentucky. They're making waves offering some of the smaller businesses more protection for less money. As far as I know, no businesses have signed up yet. Now that you are temporarily out of the collection business, you've made it convenient for the Chicago group to muscle their way in. You need to decide soon which direction you are heading with your organization. Whether you are staying in the collection business or not. I know it is a difficult time having the association dumped in your lap and Dennis's trial hanging over your head, but we as a group have a real problem and need your help."

After the phone conversation with Big Sid, Juan invited his office staff to his office to learn what they thought about going legit.

When the office staff assembled in his office, he asked each one individually, "What do you think of eliminating the collection group entirely? If we do, we can become a legitimate entity, except for the muscle group who is needed to collect overdue debts from some of the larger companies we make loans. It would behoove us to make the move now rather than later, but only if you think it's the right move.

It would enhance the image of the organization, provide a better work environment, and a company we could be proud to be associated with."

During this lengthy discussion with the office staff, he told them, "The revenue generated by other entities within the organization is substantial. By removing the collection business, the other businesses in the group stepping up their game plan, eventually offsetting the lost revenue generated by collectors. Eliminating that small group would not affect our bottom line that much. I'm thinking we need to terminate the group completely. That would be one less headache to contend with on a daily basis, but with one exception, the muscle group. They are a necessary evil. We need them to collect the larger debts incurred by the loan company.

"Since Dennis has been incarcerated, he has become a huge burden hanging over the association. He is capable of causing the association a lot of trouble. But I understand from talking to the attorney that was hired to represent him, anything he says in court concerning the association is hearsay, and not permissible. Knowing what we do now about the case, luckily we are not scheduled to participate in the hearing. So at this time, I think it wise for us to begin turning the association around. It would be in our best interest going forward. And the more I think of it, changing the image of the association, the more appealing it is to me."

After his meeting with staff, they all agreed it was a good idea taking the association in a new direction. It would be easier since the collection group was inactive, and Dennis was out of the picture. Without the collection group running around the city stirring up trouble, the association would be at liberty to take on a new persona and remain a viable entity.

Juan called Becky Cohen after everyone had left the office. He wanted to run this idea by her, knowing she would have no objections to his proposal. She wanted only to be informed in case anything happened, she was still in the loop. As long as things were running smoothly and business was profitable, she did not mind what Juan did in maintaining the association's image.

It was a big step for any association revamping its objective, but if handled properly, the goal he had in mind was attainable. If they run a legitimate operation, other business groups in the area would be willing to support him and his endeavor. This would solidify its survival.

Juan was getting close to informing his parents of his achievement. Learning of his success, they would be proud. He wanted to earn their acceptance since his banishment from home. He looked forward to the day he was able to contact them to tell them his story. He yearned for their forgiveness for his past actions; it had been a heavy burden on his shoulders over the years. He wished that after making contact, they would invite him home for a visit. Having no correspondence with them since leaving home, he missed them terribly. This was his new goal—having a close relationship with his parents once again. Maybe after the situation involving Dennis was over, he would surprise them by a phone call.

Now came the hard part—the complete overhaul of the association.

Calling Al to the office, he asked, "Al, do you know anything about optimizing the organizational structure or improving the potential of the association?"

He told Juan, "Sorry, boss, I'm not familiar with organizational procedures, only the collection aspect of the old organization. I have no idea about such things as partnerships, hybrid organizations, et cetera."

Juan thanked Al for his time and honesty, then told him, "I'll talk to you later."

Juan needed to restructure the organization but decided to continue the business as is until he had time to streamline it properly.

Meanwhile, after his third meeting with the staff, Sheila reflected on what had to be accomplished within the organization going into the future. She seemed impressed with the turnaround proposed by Juan. She was ready to help in any capacity to turn it around.

Juan called the Irishman to his office and said, "After our meeting this morning, I'm going to shift a lot of employees around but as far as your job, I've decided you'll remain as my driver and righthand man if that is acceptable to you."

"That's fine, boss."

"As far as Tony's position within the organization, I'm still uncertain. I have vacillated over what I should do in keeping Tony on board since his job will no longer be required. I need to talk with him about his future within the association. I'm sure he would be satisfied with any decision I make. He mentioned not long ago he had contemplated on retiring and enjoying what few years he has left. I need to find out soon so I can move forward.

"Johnny Leopold [Ivan's driver] will stay on as Al's driver, but I have doubts that Al's the person needed to handle the job he was assigned. He's not capable in helping me with even the mundane daily operations. The menial responsibilities I've given him are more than he can comprehend or handle. The more tasks I give him, the less he is able to do. I've got to get myself a good office manager. Al is on his way out."

As the wheels slowly turned, the association began turning the corner. The organization was heading in a new direction. Everyone enjoyed the new direction in which it was headed. Juan no longer wanted the worry about groups such as the Chicago group trying to muscle its way in on his territory. He was finished with that lawless and reckless bunch of cowboys.

It was not long until Dennis's trial was to begin in earnest. The most serious of all the counts against him was the involuntary manslaughter charge. It was a time of anxiety for Juan and would continue until the trial was over and a just verdict rendered. Juan could see no reason the court would permit Dennis to involve the association; it had nothing to do with his case. One could never predict what would happen until the fat lady sings. Juan was hoping against hope it would not be Dennis who would be singing.

Becky called Juan and told him, "Luke called me today, asking me if I heard what happened at the farm? I told him no. So he told me he and the accountant [used by the farm] had been confronted about mismanaging funds, beaten up, fired, and ran off the farm. He wanted to know if there was anything I could since I was still involved."

Juan told Becky, "Luke and Jay Beery [accountant for the farm] were caught red-handed skimming monies from the farm's account prior to Ivan's death. They were hoping not to be caught, but they were wrong. The accountant who takes care of the association's books here and I took a ride down to the farm last week and met with Luke and Jay Beery. I explained to them what the accountant discovered while auditing the files sent to him. The association's accountant discovered spread over a few months' time thousands of dollars missing from the farm's account.

"When confronted with the allegations, they eventually admitted taking the money for their own personal use from the farm's account. We used a bit of persuasion, but in the end, we learned the truth why the money was missing. At that point, I fired both and told them they were finished working on the farm and to never step back on the property.

"I was able to replace Luke with a new foreman on site by the name of Bobby Baker. I had previously sent him down to the farm to work, along with two others after closing down the collection group. He is a person we can count on and trust. Also, before leaving Lexington, I hired a new accountant, Jim Logan, I think you will approve. If you would like to meet or talk with either Bobby Baker or Jim Logan, I can arrange them to come up to meet you."

"I appreciate the effort you've put into keeping the association afloat since Ivan's passing. No, I don't need to meet them at this time, maybe later. It would be a good idea having them come to Indianapolis sometime in the future to sit down and talk if that is agreeable?"

"Sounds good to me. I want to keep you up to speed on everything going on within the association. It would behoove you and I to meet once every quarter or so and talk, would you agree?"

"Yes, that's a splendid idea. You have always been up front, and I appreciate what you've accomplished since Ivan's demise. Now that I know the truth about what occurred at the farm, I will inform Luke I've talked to you, and aware why he and the accountant were dismissed. At which time, I'll tell him not to expect any assistance from me and not to call again. Thanks again, keep in touch."

CHAPTER 28

Al was overwhelmed with the workload and was quickly falling further and further behind. He was at his wit's end when he walked into Juan's office before starting work.

He said to Juan, "Good morning, boss, I need to talk to you if you have time?"

"Sure, Al, come in. What's on your mind?"

"I think you realize I'm not capable of handling the rigorous duties of an office manager. I think you should look around for an office manager to fill that position. I'm swamped and totally lost with the amount of work in front of me day after day."

"I appreciate your frankness, Al. Can I ask you to stay on until I can find a replacement?"

"Sure, but you need to find one soon."

"Okay, I'll have Sheila look for a replacement today. Maybe we can find one by next week if you can hold out till then?"

"By the way, would you know if there's any other position within the organization I might qualify for?"

"No, Al, every slot in the association has been filled since closing down the collector's sector. There's nothing I'm aware of at this time, but I'll look around."

A few days later, Juan called Al back into the office and told him, "Once I find a replacement for the office manager's position, I'm sorry to tell you your services will be no longer be needed. I'm terminating you."

This hit Al like a ton of bricks, completely shattering his world; he had nowhere to turn. His life as he knew it was over. This did not set well with Al, already irritated with himself not being able to handle the stress of his office job. Al now found himself in a catch-22 and did not know which way to turn. He was having marital problems at home and now this. Disenchanted with himself, plummeting out of control, being terminated from the only real job he's ever had, decided to end it all.

At the end of the work day, Al left the office dejected, ignoring everyone as he walked out the office for the last time. He walked through the entry door, out onto the sidewalk, reeling at the turn of events in his life lately. Realizing now he had nothing to look forward to or live for, he decided earlier in the day to put an end to this feeling of hopelessness and despair.

The next morning, Juan received a call from Al's wife, asking him, "Do you know where Al is? I'm worried about him since he did not call or come home last evening."

"No, I've not seen or heard from him since he left the office last evening."

"This is not like him not to call me if he's staying in town or going to be late."

"I'm sorry, but when he left last night, he did so without saying a word to me or the office staff. If I hear anything, I'll call you," Juan replied and hung up.

Later that morning, Al's wife received a visit from the local police department informing her they found her husband earlier, floating face down in White River. He apparently had taken his own life since nothing at the scene indicated otherwise. The medical examiner who examined Al's body found his lungs filled with water indicating he either fell or jumped into the river and drowned. Her worst fears had been confirmed. After the police left, she called Juan and told him of Al's demise.

"If there is anything I can do to help, let me know. I'm deeply sorry for your loss. I know how much Al meant to you and your family. It's a tremendous loss not only for you and your family but to all of us who knew him. I offer you my sincere condolences for your loss," Juan expressed to her.

Hanging up the phone, Juan walked into the lobby and informed the office group of Al's passing. They were shocked as well, but everyone knew he was having a difficult time coping lately. It was apparently more than he could take at one time and decided to end his anguish.

Juan felt bad for Al's family, but it was not his fault. Al was not capable of handling the workload that came with the territory. It was a matter of basic economics. Al had to be replaced.

Learning of Al's demise, Juan asked Sheila, "Call the employment agency and find me an office manager."

Sheila immediately picked up her phone, called the local employment agency, and inquired about the availability of an office manager.

The clerk at the employment told her, "Can you hold a minute, let me check my list?"

"Certainly."

"Oh, yes, here we are. A gentleman recently dropped off his résumé along with his credentials, said he was looking to relocate to Indy from Muncie. According to his résumé, he's highly qualified and would be available soon for relocation. If you would like to contact him, I can give you his office number in Muncie."

"Yes, I'd appreciate you giving me his number. That way, I can contact him this morning and set up an appointment this afternoon. I'll get back with you as soon as I find out anything concrete."

"Yes, do that."

Sheila wrote down the number the employment agency gave her. She called the number as soon as she hung up from talking to the employment office.

A male voice answered.

"Is this Mr. Palmer Long?" Sheila asked.

"Yes, may I ask who's calling?"

"My name is Sheila Williams. I'm Mr. Juan Grajales's secretary at Cohen Enterprises located in Indianapolis. I've just talked to the employment agency here. They provided me with your number and told me you were interested in relocating to Indianapolis."

After a brief conversation, he agreed to drop by the office that afternoon around four thirty for an interview.

At promptly four thirty, Palmer Long entered the building that housed Cohen Enterprises. When he approached Sheila's desk, she looked up and was immediately impressed with whoever it was that just walked in.

"Good afternoon, my name is Palmer Long. I'm the gentleman you spoke with on the phone earlier this morning. I'm here for my four-thirty meeting with Mr. Juan Grajales concerning the office manager's job that's available."

"Yes, Mr. Long. He's expecting you."

Sheila hit the intercom announcing, "There's a Mr. Palmer Long here to see you about the office manager's position that's available."

"Yes, send him in."

"Go right in, Mr. Long. Mr. Grajales is expecting you."

"Thank you."

Palmer Long entered Juan's office. When he looked around, the first thing that caught his attention was a large safe along the back wall left of Juan's desk. He was more than a little curious as to why such a large safe? The place was not a huge department store or amusement park needing such a large safe to keep its money safe. He thought only places like that needed safes this big. It seemed strange a company such as Cohen Enterprises needed such a strong large fireproof cabinet and a complex locking system for storing valuables.

Juan stood up from his desk as Palmer entered, extended his hand across the desk, and shook Palmer's hand. He told Palmer to have a seat, pointing to the chair nearest his desk. After talking for over an hour with Palmer, Juan was satisfied with Palmer's extensive training, knowledge, and expertise in office management.

And after the interview, Juan asked, "When will you be available to start work?"

"I'll need to finish my obligation with the firm I'm presently employed. It will be at least a week before I can start." "Is there a chance of starting earlier than that?"

"Only if the firm I'm working will release me from my contract."

"Okay, if they will, let me know. We need you as soon as possible. My last so-called manager walked off the job and left us in a mess."

"I'll give your secretary a call later if the company agrees in letting me leave sooner."

"That's fine. Check with Sheila before leaving, give her the information she needs to get you into our system before your return."

"It's been a pleasure, Mr. Grajales. I look forward to working with you."

Later that afternoon, Juan received a call from Ted the veterinarian about the horse Ivan purchased and later died from presumptive pulmonary failure. He called to tell Juan his original diagnosis had been misdiagnosed; Ivan had been right. The horse had been given a relatively new experimental medication, which was not thoroughly tested or approved. It was used in testing results on older horses with (COPD) pulmonary failure only. Ted in his diagnosis did not realize his mistake until recently as he was conferring with an owner who mentioned using the same medication on one of his younger horses, which also died.

After some in-depth research, Ted found the drug dexamethasone should have been avoided at all costs if a horse was subjected to multiple risk factors. Apparently, those risk factors had not been duly noted on the horse's medical chart prior to Ivan purchase. It had been an oversight of the previous vet's treatment prior to the sale of the horse to Ivan.

He wanted to relate his findings and consequences of this medication to Juan. It was used only as a last resort on any horse. Juan thanked the vet, telling him he appreciated his honesty and veracity.

"I'll pass this information on to my foreman in Lexington, so he is aware of the consequences of using this particular medication."

The breeders' association had been up front with Ivan when he purchased the horse. It had been an honest mistake by a vet. Ivan's the one who paid the price for the vet's mistake. This was a case of live and learn, a valuable lesson when dealing with horses. Juan wanted Bobby, his foreman, to make sure his vet knows what he is administering, plus keeping a detailed record to show owners if questioned.

Al was laid to rest four days after being discovered in White River. Juan, along with the office staff, and several employees attended Al's funeral. After the funeral, Juan tried consoling Al's wife, but she had nothing to say or do with him. She believed Juan was responsible for Al's death after learning of his termination. Juan tried making her understand the situation, but she was too distraught and had no interest understanding his plight.

He did tell her, "If there's anything the organization or I can do, let me know."

She turned away without saying a word and walked over to her family to give them comfort. After the eulogy was given at the grave site and the casket lid close for the last time, Juan and the Irishman returned to the car and drove off, leaving behind Al's family to grieve in private at their loss.

The following day, Jimmy Kapos the foreman at the breeders' farm dropped by to see Juan. He wanted him to know he overheard several members of the breeders' association talking about the farm in Lexington which was a major concern to Juan.

Jimmy told Juan, "I overheard the Bull and several of his cronies saying something about taking over the farm in Lexington and dumping your organization. I don't know the full inside scoop why but wanted to warn you something big was in the works."

Juan thanked Jimmy for dropping by and giving him a heads-up and told him, "I appreciate your information. Keep your ears open. If you hear anything else, let me know."

Jimmy got up, shook Juan's hand, then left the office. Juan contacted Bobby the foreman at the farm to see if there had been visitors to the farm from the breeders' association lately.

"Yes, as a matter of fact, last week a couple from the breeders' association arrived unannounced, checked the roster of horse's we stable at the farm. They didn't indicate to me what they were here for, but I noticed them taking notes as they checked the roster."

"Okay, if they come back, I want to be notified immediately. Don't give them any information other than what is on the roster, understood?"

"Yes, boss."

Juan hung up the phone, called to the Irishman to come to the office. After the Irishman arrived, Juan told him, "Get the car. We're taking a ride out to the breeders' farm. I have some business I need to address with Tony the Bull."

The Irishman returned shortly with the car. He picked up Juan and headed to the breeders' farm. Arriving at the office, Juan got out, walked into the office, and approached the secretary.

He told her in no uncertain terms, "I'm here to see Anthony Stefano."

"Have a seat Mr.—"

"My name is Juan. Juan Grajales."

"I'll inform Mr. Stefano you are here and check if he's available to see you."

A few minutes later, Tony the Bull informed his secretary to send in Mr. Grajales. It did not take long after meeting with Anthony Stefano for Juan to recognize the Bull was a no-nonsense person. He had a job to do and stopped at nothing until it was completed.

Anthony Stefano's first question out of his mouth was "Who the hell you think you are coming in here like this, demanding to meet with me on such short notice? Do you think you are better than anybody else? What is it you want? Tell me what it is, then get the hell out of my office."

Juan began by saying, "I want to know if you and the breeders' association are contemplating taking over the farm in Lexington, which belongs to the organization I run? If it's true, why and how do you plan on accomplishing such a feat?"

"It's been brought to the attention of the association several horses on your farm are not properly documented by the breeders' association as stud horses. That is a breach of contract Ivan signed when he purchased the farm several years ago. I do not intend to let this breach of contract continue. Our association is presently drawing up the necessary paperwork to remove you and your organization from our roster, at which time assume total responsibility for the farm."

"You don't have the right to do that. How can you legally take over a business that you have nothing invested in other than some contract signed with Ivan, who is now deceased? Seems like with a new administrator running the organization, an addendum or a new contract updating the contract should have been in order?"

"Oh, but we have every right, an ironclad contract signed by Ivan. You need to read the contract. It states: If the farm is used for any purpose other than those stated in the contract, it breaches the contract and forfeits the farm to the breeders' association. Including, all real estate, horses, monies collected in the future from breeding, etcetera, etcetera."

"That's bullshit and you know it. You can't do that. You have no legal authority. I'll fight you tooth and nail. This is a major part of the organization's income. I'll not give it up without a fight."

"Don't threaten me with your crap. No matter what you say, we'll remove you and your group from the farm. The only thing I can suggest to you is, start looking for another line of work. Your days are numbered, asshole."

"You best be ready for the fight of your life if you decide to go forward with this matter. I don't need your BS or your association telling me what kind of horses I can or can't have on the farm. It's none of your f——king business. Also, don't send any more of your cronies to the farm. They're not welcome any longer. Stay away from the farm and out of my business. Do I make myself clear?"

"Guess you'll learn the hard way, sonny boy. Have it your way."

First thing Juan did after returning to the office was called the organization's lawyer, Steven Wasserman. He told Atty. Wasserman what the breeders' association was trying to pull on the organization and needed his input as to what avenue to take in stopping such a hostile takeover.

Atty. Wasserman told Juan, "I'll look over the contract Ivan signed and see if I can find a loophole giving the organization an out according to the contract. I will need a little time to study the contract. I will get back to you when I have something positive to report."

CHAPTER 29

After talking to Atty. Wasserman, Juan busied himself with other matters piling up on his desk for lack of an office manager. He was having trouble in keeping up with the different aspects of the businesses, finding himself playing catch-up most days now. It was becoming much more difficult without a full-time office manager coping with the daily business by himself and Sheila.

Juan learned that running a legitimate business was tougher than running a corrupt one. In a legitimate business, every *Is* had to be dotted, every *Ts* crossed. Whereas in the previous unlawful business, you could run it more or less willy-nilly. And record-keeping was much less stressful the old way. But, now committed, Juan was determined to forge ahead with this new concept.

It was a matter of time until Palmer finished his commitment in Muncie and head to Indy where he would begin cleaning up some of the mess Al left behind. Palmer would play a huge role once he started working on the backlog of paperwork now accumulating. Palmer could began to free things up so Juan had time to concentrate more on overseeing the operation than worrying about paperwork. The paperwork was completely out of hand, along with other problems like the farm, the breeders' association, and Al's death. The business was suffering immeasurably. Once Palmer came onboard, it would allow Juan to focus on more important aspects of the business.

A week passed since Al died. Things in the office were no better, maybe worse. When Juan showed up to work Monday morning, his new office manager Palmer Long awaited his arrival. Juan could not wait to get Palmer started on the backlog of correspondence, which continued accumulating daily. Juan took Palmer into his office, showing him the chaos, which awaited his attention. Juan outlined the most significant to the less mundane aspects of paperwork on the desk needing consideration. Once Palmer was briefed by Juan, understanding the enormity of the backlog of paperwork confronting him, Palmer slowly begun the daunting task of separating, sorting, and getting things in some semblance of order.

Given the enormous amount of work, it would be a long arduous process wading through the mountain of delinquent bills, some requiring immediate attention, past-due correspondence needing response to like yesterday. This was Palmer's challenge, but being an organizer, he jumped in with both feet and went to work. It took him most of the first day sorting through the mounds of correspondence, but at the end of a long and exhausting day, Palmer had separated the paperwork, which now laid in neat stacks, covering not only his desk, but any flat surface in his office.

It had been a monumental task, but Palmer being the first-rate accountant "as advertised" in his résumé was that and more. By the end of the next day, he should have a good start clearing up the chaos that inundated his office. Pleased with himself and his accomplishment, he now had a concept of just how big and complex the many businesses existing within the organization were. But from the looks of the paperwork lying around his office, it was way bigger than his first impression implied.

First on Palmer's agenda arriving to work the next morning was giving Sheila the outstanding bills to pay, while he posted and filled the remaining paperwork. He kept Sheila busy cutting checks and paying delinquent bills the entire morning.

He set aside those bills running the association. The bills not crucial and certain correspondence with later dates would be answered, paid, or filed away on a need-to basis. After the second day, Palmer finished sorting, rearranging the paperwork, and was ready to call it a day. He unquestionably put in a full day's work, earning his pay, that's a given.

Juan, highly impressed with Palmer and his work ethics, was excited at having him aboard. Palmer, a godsend making Juan's life tolerable and bearable once again. The rest of the week went without a hitch, the paperwork was whittled down to where it had become rather mundane for Palmer, or at least manageable.

The following Monday afternoon, Attorney Steven Wasserman called Juan, "Good afternoon, Juan, I found that loophole I was looking for. The one we can use in getting the breeders' association off your back. If and when the breeders' file their lawsuit, we will be ready to burst their bubble."

"I appreciate your due diligence in finding the loophole and learning the contract Ivan signed with the breeders' association was not ironclad as they thought. At least now, we have wiggle room and able in breaking the contract."

"If you hear anything else or something comes up later, call me," Atty. Wasserman told Juan.

As the next few weeks passed, things in the office settled down. The association was beginning to run smoothly and things were falling into place. The overall state of the organization was shaping up. Everyone from the office staff to the satellite businesses had taken on a different demeanor. Those working for the association no matter what capacity were handling themselves with more professionalism, a first for the association.

The restaurant, the loan company, and even the horse farm was running smoother with few exceptions, but nothing the association could not handle. The organization itself had come full circle. Juan now had time to visit different venues and keep closer tabs on the day-to-day operation.

Becky, Ivan's widow, was kept up to date monthly by statements from the accountant or Juan's weekly calls. She was pleased with how Juan handled the business and often expressed it to him on occasions.

One day, as she talked to Juan, she told him, "Before anything happens to me, I want a new contract drawn up designating you as the sole owner of the business in case of my demise or some unforeseen or unanticipated cataclysm happens. Also, I want to set up a living trust for the two boys."

"Not a problem, Becky. I'll contact our lawyer and have him draw up the living trust for the two boys. And a new contract between us in case there is some sort of crisis occurring in the future. I'll have him send you a copy for your approval. If it meets your expectations, we'll meet at his office so we can sign off on it."

"Thank you."

After talking to Becky, Juan called to inform the association's attorney to draw up a living trust and a new contract between him and Becky.

Atty. Wasserman told Juan after hearing what he wanted, "I'll start on it right away, but first I have to talk to Becky about certain aspects of the living will that need included in setting up a living trust for her sons."

After his conversation with Atty. Wasserman, Juan told the Irishman, "Get the car."

The Irishman returned as Juan was walking out the front entrance of the office.

Once inside the car, Juan told the Irishman, "Today let's have lunch at the local restaurant the association owns. After looking over last month's budget, I noticed the manager had not posted several daily receipts. I need to know why they were not included. If the manager does not have a good reason, he's out of there. I'm not going to put up with any excuses, only facts. If he can't work by the rules, then he can find other employment."

Juan arrived at the Oasis Watering Hole. As he and the Irishman entered, Juan found the restaurant exceptionally busy but was able to find a table and sat down. Soon they were greeted by a very friendly waitress.

Juan looked up at her and asked, "Is the manager available?"

"No, the manager is out of town for the day. He went to Cincinnati to River Down's horse track and won't be back until later this evening.

That's, if he returns to the restaurant." That did not set well with Juan who then asked, "Who's in charge of the restaurant while the manager is out of town like this?"

"No one. We do what we have to do until he returns."

"How often does the manager go to the horse track in Cincinnati?"

"At least once, sometimes twice a week."

"You tell him the next time you see him to come see me. I need to talk to him."

"Sure, but who should I tell him wants to see him?"

"My name is Juan Grajales. He'll recognize the name."

Juan and the Irishman ordered lunch, and as they ate, they noticed two men entering the restaurant who looked out of place. They were either out-of-towners or locals looking for trouble. They found a table not far from where Juan and the Irishman sat.

Suddenly, one of them yelled across the restaurant at the waitress, "Hey, sweetie, yeah, you, bring me and my friend a cold beer. We're thirsty."

The waitress looked around and told him, "Just hold your horses, partner. As soon as I have a moment, I'll be there to take your drink order."

He yelled at the waitress again. Reaching over to the table next to him, he picked up an empty long-neck bottle off the table, broke it on the table, yelling once again for a cold beer, and told the waitress, "I don't have time to f——k around waiting."

Everyone in the place was startled. At this time, the bartender (Joe Lucas) walked out from behind the bar and walked over to where the two sat.

Joe told them, "You'll have to settle down or leave."

That was not such a good idea; the bartender learned quickly. The man with the broken bottle in his hand stood up, laid the broken bottle top on the table, grabbed the bartender by his shirt, punching him so hard in the face knocking him off his feet and onto the floor. At that moment, the waitress screamed and told them she was calling the cops. Suddenly, the Irishman stood up and walked over to where the bartender lay on the floor. He stepped between the bartender and irate man, reached down and helped Joe off the floor.

The Irishman asked Joe once he was standing up and holding his bleeding nose, "Are you all right?"

"Yes, I think so. My nose feels like it's broken, but otherwise I'm okay, thanks." The Irishman turned and faced the man standing nearby, reached over, grabbed him by his coat, drew back his fist, and slugged him with a haymaker. It caught the attention not only of the perpetrator but his buddy. The Irishman punched him again in the rib cage, knocking the wind out of him. He felt the full fury of the Irishman's encounter. He stepped back with his hands held over his head and palms forward, indicating he had had enough. Juan, by this time, had had enough of the two also. He walked over to find out who they were and why they were here.

Juan asked, "Who are you, and what's your problem?"

"We are with the Chicago group. We were sent out to stir up a bit of trouble with locals."

Juan told them in no uncertain terms, "You are not welcome here. You go back and tell the Chicago group for me that this type of intimidation would not be tolerated here or anywhere else in town. Tell your boss he needs to leave Nap-town and return to Chi-town, capisce?"

The Irishman pointed to the door, telling the two to get out and not to come back. The two bolted toward the door, never looking back. This was their first encounter with the group from Chicago, but Juan knew it would not be the last.

After the two men left, Juan told the waitress if there was any more trouble to call him. He wrote his number down on the back of her receipt pad and handed it back to her. He turned and walked back to the table and sat down along with the Irishman. After lunch, Juan paid the check, leaving the waitress and bartender a bigger-than-normal tip. He exited the restaurant and headed back to the office.

The next morning, the manager of the Oasis Watering Hole came into the office and spoke briefly with Sheila at the front desk.

He told her, "My name is Hector Otego. I'm here to see Mr. Grajales. He left a message with one of my waitresses at the Oasis Watering Hole yesterday, said he wanted to see me."

Sheila hit the intercom button, announcing that the Oasis Manager, Hector Otego, was there to see him.

"Yes, send him in."

When Hector walked into Juan's office, Juan told him, "Have a seat, Hector. We have a few things to discuss, like what have you been up to lately? And I want to know how you manage the Oasis when you are off playing the horses?

"Looking over last month's report, I found several receipts missing. Upon further investigation of previous months, there's a pattern emerging. Once, sometimes twice, a week certain entries are missing and a handwritten entry is inserted along with a notation telling the receipts are missing. I've not gone back farther than four months, but may not have go back farther if you explain to me what's going on?"

"Don't know what you are talking about, Mr. Grajales. I've given an account of all the daily receipts to the accountant as instructed. He must have misplaced them and written them in," Hector told Juan.

"No, Hector, don't think so. I think you are addicted to the horses and skimming money from the restaurant by cooking the books. I'd like for you to tell me why you pad one or two receipts each week, then drive to Cincinnati's Riverside race track where you blow it on the horses."

"No, you're wrong. When I go to the horse track in Cincinnati, I used my own money."

"How many trips did you make to the track last month when you were supposed to be working?"

"Maybe four times if memory serves me correctly?"

"That's BS, and you know it. I've learned you go at least once and sometimes twice a week. When you leave, there is no one in charge of the Oasis. Does the association not pay you enough not to steal money from the restaurant to feed your habit? I'm going to look back when I have time and see how long this skimming of yours has been going on. When I figure out how much you've stolen, I expect you to pay back every penny you've taken from the organization. Is that clear?"

"You'll not find anything in previous reports showing me skimming off the top."

"Until further notice, you no longer work for the association until this situation is cleared up. I do not want you to return to the Oasis, understand? I don't want you anywhere near the place. If I hear of you going back, I'll come looking for you, and it will not be a pretty sight when I find you. Now get the f——k out of my sight, you lowlife SOB."

Hector, with no further excuses, got up and walked out of the office. His job, his livelihood had come to a screeching halt. As he left the office, he wondered what his life would be like going forward. He had skimmed thousands of dollars in the past from the Oasis, and it was payback time. Paybacks are hell, he thought, but he had not been able to resist the availability of the money at his disposal; it was just too tempting. Not only had he been barred from the Oasis, but now a huge debt loomed over his head to repay. He could not forget the bookies in town he owed money. With no sign of income, how was he going repay his debts? His life changed forever that morning. What had he gotten himself into? How was he going to repay his debts? He found himself in a deep honey hole with no way out; the easy life he once knew was over.

After Hector left, Juan called the Oasis Watering Hole, and asked to speak with Joe Lucas.

When Joe answered the phone, Juan told him, "My name is Juan Grajales. I'm CEO for the company you work for. I was there yesterday when the two men came in and caused you and the waitress trouble. I saw how you tried handling the situation and was impressed as you tried to quell the situation by yourself even though you were outnumbered and no one there to assist or back you up. I also had a talk with Hector this morning, and I am wondering, Would you be interested in becoming manager of the Oasis? It means a lot more responsibility, but after seeing you in action, I think you are a perfect fit. I was impressed. If you think you might be interested, the job is yours, and you start today. We'll need to find a new bartender, but I'm sure you know someone who could take over for you behind the bar on short notice?"

"Yes, on both questions. I have a friend who works down the street at a local establishment. I will call this afternoon and have her come in tomorrow if that is okay with you?"

"Great, Joe, do what you have to do, but keep me informed if you run into any problems between now and then. I'll drop by from time to time to check in on you. Good luck."

"Oh, by the way, Joe, I fired Hector. He is not to enter the establishment. If he does, let me know."

"Thanks, Mr. Grajales. Don't know what else to say. This happened so fast, but don't worry, Mr. Grajales, I'll do you proud. I promise."

"I know you will, Joe. I believed in you from the minute I saw you in action."

CHAPTER 30

Things were reaching a low point as Juan and Palmer delved further and further into the accounting practices of the Oasis's manager. After finding more entries missing, they began checking other business practices inside the organization. As their searched continued, more and more graft among the different organizations were discovered. The organization at first glance was riddled with fraud and appeared throughout the entire system. Juan had to find a way to stem the flow of corruption before the organization became insolvent.

At first glance, he had his doubts if it was possible getting it under control. Would he be able to reverse the association's direction in time? The fraud and graft were worse than he imagined. He and Palmer were only looking at the tip of the iceberg, knowing it went much deeper and more serious than first realized.

Since Juan had taken control of the organization, everywhere he turned, he saw exploitation. It started at the top and trickled down. The fraud and graft were evident in every facet of businesses within the organization. Each entity checked appeared corrupted in one way or other. Each business presented its own unique set of problems, each requiring immediate attention.

As Juan and Palmer delved deeper and deeper, all they could do was look at each other in disbelief and shake their heads. Juan never in his wildest dreams imagined how corrupt the different groups within the association were prior and after Ivan's death.

How could the individual groups be so corrupt when Ivan ran it with such an iron hand? Ivan must have been so overwhelmed before his demise that he was not able to see the forest for the trees.

It was something that could not be turned around quickly. Before reaching that pinnacle of no return, Juan had to weed out these practices before continuing in turning around the organization. With Palmer's help, they painstakingly went through each organization's file, finding all kinds of palm-greasing, wheeling and dealing, and mismanagement of funds. Checking further into the loan company, they found kickbacks, dirty dealings, and corruption. They loaned money to companies and friends with little or no collateral to substantiate the loan. There was no way some of the borrowers could ever repay the high interest on the loan they received, let alone pay the debt itself back. They were bad debts from the offset, and these unlawful practices had to be addressed ASAP.

After several hours of looking over the loan company's books and finding so many disturbing entries, Juan told Palmer, "Continue your search. I'm going to visit the loan company and meet with the accountant who handles the books."

Arriving at the loan company, Juan found the accountant working diligently in his office. Juan entered the accountant's office highly agitated, demanding to see the latest files he and the office manager checked off on. When he looked over those files, Juan discovered more telltale signs of deception, misuse of funds throughout the loan department. He asked the accountant why certain loans had been approved. He also told the accountant he wanted to see the latest applications, contracts, etc. on file.

The accountant retrieved the last two months of applications and contracts from his files and handed them to Juan. As Juan looked them over, he found more discrepancies. Juan had the manager Jordan and assistant paged to the accountant's office. When the manager entered with his assistant, Juan looked up at the manager.

And Juan said, "I would like you to look at these files and explain what these inconsistencies are on the highlighted entries I found on your recent applications."

The manager could not substantiate the discrepancies. Jordan gave Juan a few lame excuses but could not explain why they were there. Juan immediately fired Jordan on the spot, turned around, and appointed Carlos Munoz, Jordan's assistant, as interim manager with the understanding, if he turned the business around, he would be promoted full-time manager.

Carlos was told "Stop loaning money to undesirables. If I find out you are loaning money underhandedly, you too will be history, understood?"

"I understand. I'll clean up the loan company and stop the corruption and dishonesty now prevalent. I'll make you that promise."

"I'll be checking on you from time to time, and if I find any back-scratching or shadiness in any of the loans going forward, you're out of here, capisce?" At that, Juan left the loan company and headed back to the office.

Carlos appeared to be a team player. Juan seemed satisfied with his choice as interim manager. He would now wait on hiring a new loan manager if Carlos stepped up to the plate and turned the loan company around. If that happened, the manager's job was his.

Juan next contacted the horse farm to talk to Bobby the foreman, asking him, "Have you run across any problems since taking over as foreman with corrupt or dishonest sales people lately?"

"Yes, I ran across one drug company salesman selling vitamins and nutritional supplements, who was doctoring orders with generic ones, not the ones ordered, but was still charging for the more expensive ones. When I questioned him, like always, he had an excuse when confronted. His excuse was the drug company substituted a lesser expensive or generic version and still charged the higher price, same lame excuse as always. The salesman resubmitted the order, as always got mixed-up in the shuffle, and nothing was ever resolved. I stopped buying from him after finding a new distributor. Also, I learned one of the original farmhands had been making deals with other horse breeders in the area, selling sperm from some of the best stud horses on the farm. It was hearsay, but I wanted to find out for myself before I did anything. After a few inquiries, I learned it was true. I fired his sorry ass and found a replacement immediately. This kind of conduct will not be permitted on my watch."

"If you run into any other problems on the farm you find too difficult to handle, let me know."

"I will. Things are slowly turning around down here. Think I'll be okay."

Why, after all the things I had incorporated into the association, how was it possible that this can of worms had weaved its ugly head into every sector? Juan saw the handwriting on the wall; the organization was headed for ruin if he could not stop this travesty. It was up to him to turn the businesses around, heading it in a new direction. Not an easy task to ask anyone to perform, but hopefully by appointing new managers at the restaurant, the loan office, and farm in Lexington, he could began turning it around. With new appointees in place, the association should start seeing a turnaround; that is, if he made the right appointments.

He called Sheila into his office and told her, "Call the employment agency. Ask them to send over a few qualified people so I can interview them for jobs at the loan company and restaurant. I need a check-and-balance group in each of those sectors, giving me a second set of eyes. I need new blood in the system if we are to stay viable and operational."

"I'll get on it right away."

The next day, several persons of interest showed up for job interviews, and by day's end, three new people thought to be qualified, trustworthy filled the existing vacancies left by previous scumbags who were fired. He would turn the organization around one way or the other; he had to get it back on track. Satisfied with his three new choices, it was the time to set a new course, not the sleazy, immoral, corrupt group of late, but an entirely new legit organization.

Setting a new course, heading in the right direction had a definitive impact on the employees, old and new alike. Even Sheila showed more pride, especially in her appearance around the office. She showed more self-importance in her work, a new attitude with those she came in contact with. This immediately caught Juan's eye. It was not long afterward he asked her out for dinner after work one evening.

Juan had the Irishman drive them to a nice restaurant on the outskirts of town where they enjoyed small talk, drinks, and dinner. When finished with dinner, the Irishman dropped her back to her apartment, and Juan to his hotel.

Juan was feeling things inside his body he never felt before after his dinner engagement with Sheila. When he returned to his room at the hotel, the first thing he did was take a cold shower and then to bed. It had been a wonderful evening. Juan had been enamored with Sheila's company. It was something new for him, and he looking forward to doing it again soon.

The next morning, the Irishman arrived at the hotel at his normal time to pick up Juan. He drove Juan to another of his favorite café for breakfast before heading to the office. After breakfast, and on his way to the office, Juan reminisced about the evening he spent with Sheila. Somehow or other, he had to get his mind set on business rather than Sheila, but he was finding it difficult.

Sheila had turned his world inside out and upside down. Once inside the office building, Juan noticed Sheila working behind her desk as he entered.

He stopped and said, "Good morning, Sheila. Did you enjoy your dinner last evening?"

"Yes, thanks to you. It was a real treat. I enjoyed it muchly."

"We will have to do it again soon?"

"Fine with me. I have no objections."

"Good."

Once inside his office, it did not take long before he was kneedeep in paperwork needing his immediate attention. After seeing Sheila, knowing she was just outside in the lobby, his concentration was not in his work but her. He had to get hold of himself, settle down, and do some work, reminding himself, work comes first. He reached over, picked up the phone, and called Carlos over at the loan company.

Carlos answered on the second ring, "Carlos Munoz speaking. May I help you?"

"Good morning, Carlos, Juan Grajales here. I wanted to touch base with you this morning to see how things are going. Also, if the new hire I sent you arrived?"

"Good morning, Mr. Grajales. Yes, he arrived earlier and is at work doing catch-up work for me. I interviewed him briefly after he arrived. So far, I'm pleased with your choice. He fits well within the guidelines you set up for the loan department."

At that Juan smiled. He next called the Oasis to check on the new hires he sent Joe as well.

Joe answered, "Oasis."

"Joe, good morning. Juan Grajales here calling to see how things are going at the restaurant this morning?"

"Great, Mr. Grajales."

"Have the two new employees I sent over arrived yet? And if so, are they acceptable?"

"Yes, I've placed one in the kitchen to help prepare the noon meals, and the female I put behind the bar. She will be cleaning and stocking the bar before opening, then help Sonny the remainder of her shift bartend. I think both trainees you sent over will work out well. Both seem to be motivated, which is a plus."

"Okay, Joe, if you need anything, anything at all, call later."

Juan hung up the phone; everyone seemed pleased with the new personnel sent from the employment office. The restaurant and loan company once again had ample help and heading in the right direction. Hoping nothing new on the horizon showed up to derail this train as it continued full speed down the track, Juan was on a roll finally. Things should start looking up soon.

After talking to Joe at the Oasis, Juan asked the Irishman to come to his office and told him, "I want you and Tony to drive out to the breeders' farm and find Jimmy Kapos. I need to know if he's learned anymore about who the breeder is purchasing sperm from one of our farmhands on the farm in Lexington. If anybody knows, it would be Jimmy."

Palmer was soon knocking on Juan's door. Juan looked up to see him standing in the doorway with a small pile of paper in his hands.

"Come in, Palmer."

"I've compared invoices from the farm against what we have, and I've run into a small problem."

"What kind of problem?"

"It looks like Luke added a dummy company to the purveyor's list, a waste management company, supposedly hired to haul away refuse that's nonexistent. The farm already had a contract with a similar company to remove farm refuse. The bill is entered each month in the amount of three hundred dollars, listed only as a rubbish pick-up. Luke, writes a check each month, then sends it to a PO box in Bay St. Louis. I've looked for the company in Bay St. Louis, and no such company exists. What do you want me to do?"

"There's not much we can do now. Luke is no longer working for the association. Have Bobby stop writing the check and hope it's the last we hear from Luke, and you find no more bogus accounts."

"Okay, the rest of the accounts and receipts seem to be in order. I'll still keep a close eye for other anomalies or discrepancies but think this was the only one. But you never know when or where one will turn up. I can't believe Luke was so blatant with this one, takes all kinds."

Palmer returned to his office in order to finish checking the other accounts and receipts from the farm. It had been a daunting day for Palmer, but he slowly and meticulously was beginning to get things in order for the association finally.

Juan continued keeping Becky abreast of the changing situations within the organization. Becky was aghast at learning how dishonest Dennis, Jordan, and Luke had been not only with Ivan but with Juan. She was under the impression Ivan ran a tight ship but learned since Juan came aboard, was taking a crash course in corruption. He never knew just how corrupt and deceitful those he appointed to run the different entities really were. She was glad to see Juan cleaning up the mess left by Ivan but surprised how wide and deep inside the organization the deceitfulness and dishonesty ran.

Juan was captivated at running the organization, seeing how its interworking functioned and how much work it took in managing it. It had been his calling; he enjoyed the chase and removal of the bad seeds found along the way. He was on the last leg of his journey of turning the association in a new direction. The organization was running on all cylinders. The business concept envisioned was finally coming to fruition. No longer the sleazy entity involved in violence and crime he found to be repulsive and evil. Learning early on running a business involves violence, thugs, dishonesty, and liars made his job problematic and difficult. That type of business went by the wayside with probation, gangsters, and mob mind-sets, which he wanted no part.

It was noon when Juan told the Irishman to bring the car around; he was ready to leave the office and head over to the Sportsman's for lunch. Before finishing their lunch, who walked in but Big Sid from the Silver Dollar Saloon. Big Sid spotted Juan and walked over to where he sat with the Irishman. Juan stood up as Big Sid approached them, and they shook hands. Juan asked him to join them. Big Sid pulled out a chair and sat down while his driver sat next to the Irishman. Sitting there, the four of them made an intimidating-looking group, one you did not want to be on their bad side.

Big Sid, not only a restauranteur, but ran small-time racketeering, but nothing like the organization Ivan and now Juan ran. As they sat talking in generalities, Big Sid brought up the Chicago group who were still wondering around town causing trouble.

Big Sid told Juan, "The group from Chicago entered my restaurant recently causing a bit of commotion. It was quelled when my bartender removed a gun from under the bar, shooting into the ceiling, which got their attention, then told them it was time to leave. They gave him a spiel as to why they were there and eventually left but not before telling my bartender they would be back. I also heard through the grapevine later they infiltrated several small businesses around town, getting a foothold established. They were attaining quite a reputation as a force not to be f——d with. I've met with several local businesses lately trying to put a stop their invasion before it turns ugly. So far, little violence but we needed to get a handle on the situation before it gets out of hand. Can I have your support in heading this bunch of yahoos off at the pass?"

Juan was at first hesitant at Big Sid's request, but eventually, he agreed to do what he could to help stem the onslaught. They were at his side when push came to shove; it was only right he be there and help in their time of need.

"We are having a meeting Friday night at the Silver Dollar. I'd like you to attend. Can you make it?"

"Sure, I'll be there."

"Fine, looking forward to your input with the debacle we are facing. I'm sure with everyone's help attending the meeting, we will be able to quash this hostile takeover before the Chicago group gets too embedded."

CHAPTER 31

Juan left the Sportsman's and headed back to the office. He still had a lot of work to finish before leaving for the evening. Tony met Juan in the lobby as he entered, and he told him, "A group from the Chicago group came by earlier wanting to talk to you about hooking up with them. One of the fellows in the group left a phone number on the back of his card. Said that if you were interested, call."

Juan took the card from Tony. Immediately turning his attention to Sheila, he asked, "Would you like to have dinner with me tonight?"

"Yes, I have nothing planned. It would be my pleasure having dinner with you."

"Great, I'll be by to pick you up around seven thirty."

"Perfect, that will give me a chance to unwind and get ready."

"See you at seven thirty."

Heading to his office, first stopping to see Palmer who's busy as usual scrutinizing the monthly receipts from the farm.

"How does the paperwork from the farm look this month?"

"I'm almost finished checking receipts from the farm, and I've found no more bogus bills or entries raising a red flag. Think the rubbish account was the last. Think Bob has a good read on the activities on the farm."

"That's good news. Keep a close eye on that account a little longer. If you find anything suspicious on the balance sheet, let me know."

"I will."

Leaving Palmer's office, he walked to his office where heard his phone ringing. He hurried into his office and answered the phone immediately. He was taken aback by the voice on the other end; it was the Chicago mafioso leader asking to meet with him.

Juan told him in no uncertain terms, "I'm not interested in meeting or talking to you. You and your henchmen need to return to Chicago and forget Indianapolis."

The conversation was short and to the point, a total evasive move on the subject by Juan. He wanted nothing to do with the group and told them as much.

The rest of Juan's day was unremarkable. There was no further contact with the pushy Chicago bunch that day after the initial call. Juan left the office around five that afternoon and headed to his apartment to rest and freshen up prior to his dinner date with Sheila later. Inside the apartment, Juan relaxed in his favorite chair, reflecting back on the day's events, and what he could do to help the local businesses get rid of the group from Chicago.

As he sat relaxing, he remembered meeting someone in New Orleans by the name of Swamp Man, who mentioned to him, "If you ever needed assistance in Indy, give me a call."

That's when Swamp Man handed him his card with a contact number, which he placed in his wallet. Reaching in his back pocket, he removed the wallet and found the wrinkled card Swamp Man gave him with his number. Swamp Man lived just outside New Orleans and had a reputation for enforcing street law around New Orleans and Fat City.

While visiting Fat City, Juan heard through the grapevine Swamp Man was a no-nonsense, fearless individual with a group, a small contingency of undesirables, used to solve local disputes. Juan thought this maybe the answer to their local problem in Indy.

Juan reached over, picked up the phone, and dialed the number on the card. Swamp Man answered.

Juan told him who he was, that they had met while he was in New Orleans a couple of months back.

"You gave me your card, told me you were available, if we ever needed your assistance." Juan then told Swamp Man what was occurring lately in Indy and asked him, "Would you be interested in coming up and taking care of our problem?"

"I'd be glad to send a couple of associates to Indy and address your problem. Let me know when you're ready. We will take care of your problem and be back in Louisiana before the sun sets. If you and your group are interested, call me back when you make your final decision. It'll not take long."

"Thanks, I'll call as soon as I find out if our association is interested."

"I'll let you know as soon as possible."

Swamp Man ended the conversation with "looking forward to doing business with you all."

Juan had the Irishman drive up in front of Sheila's apartment at exactly seven thirty. Sheila was standing just inside the front entrance to her apartment building as they arrived. Picking up Sheila, they headed over to the Sportsman's, arriving at seven forty-five.

After a nice, quiet dinner and conversation, Juan turned to Sheila and asked, "Would you like to go back to my apartment for a nightcap?"

"Yes, that would be wonderful. I would like to see where you live."

"Great."

Leaving the restaurant, they drove back to Juan's apartment, where Juan told the Irishman, "Sheila and I are stepping off for a nightcap before she heads home. I'll call later for you to pick her up and take her back to her apartment."

"Okay, boss."

Arriving at Juan's apartment, Sheila and Juan exited the car, walked inside, and took the elevator up to Juan's apartment. Entering his apartment Sheila was genuinely impressed where he lived. His apartment was much larger than she anticipated, well-appointed with his own personal touches throughout.

He showed her around, and after the tour, asked, "What would you like to drink?"

"Drambuie over ice if you have it."

"Just happen to have a new bottle I bought earlier at the liquor store on my way home."

He opened the new bottle of Drambuie, filling a highball glass half full of ice, then pouring her a drink. He then made himself a scotch and soda. Juan handed Sheila her drink; they toasted to a wonderful evening and to more such evening in the future.

They spent the next hour or so talking about themselves, basically small talk, getting acquainted. Both enjoyed the evening, and after finishing her drink, she told him, "I must be going. It's getting late and need my beauty sleep if I'm to function tomorrow."

"I understand, but first, I want you to know how much I've enjoyed the evening and hope to repeat it again soon."

"Anytime."

"That settles it. We'll do it again real soon. I hope it doesn't bother you going out with the boss?"

"Why did you say that?"

"I've felt slightly apprehensive lately with so much going on at the office. Don't know whether I'm pitching or catching, if you get my drift?"

"Yes, I understand exactly what you're saying. You shouldn't feel that way. You are the kindest and most outgoing person I've met in years, I have a great deal of respect for you and what you do. I've just never considered you as being a self-doubter."

"I'm glad you feel that way. You've seen me for who I am not who or what I think I am. I will not bring the subject up again, ever."

"I find a distinctive quality in you I find attractive. It fascinates me. I'm drawn to you like a magnet. I've never felt like this before."

"Good. I'm pleased to hear you say that. I too am captivated by you."

"Well, I think it's time I leave. I hate to break up such a wonderful evening but duty calls. I must go and get some rest before work tomorrow."

Juan called the Irishman to come back and pick up Sheila. He arrived a short time later, picked up Sheila, and drove her back to her apartment.

He returned the car to the garage near the office and walked home. The Irishman had had it, he was ready for a hot shower before going to bed. After his shower, feeling refreshed, he crawled into bed and went fast to sleep.

On Friday evening after work, Juan wanted the Irishman to drive him to the local association's meeting, where they would decide what to do about the Chicago group. As soon as Juan entered the large meeting hall, he spotted Big Sid. Walking over to Big Sid to learn if anything had been settled about eliminating the Chicago group.

Big Sid told Juan, "The association has been getting a lot of flak lately from the Chicago bunch about joining forces. We've not decided on a plan how we are going to deal with them. I'm certainly not in favor of hooking up with them. Do you have a suggestion as to how we can get rid of them?"

"Maybe, I've called a fellow in Louisiana whom I met when we were there during the conference. He said he's willing to take care of our problem any time we give him the word."

Big Sid was highly interested in what Juan told him about the Swamp Man.

He told Juan, "If Swamp Man can deliver, it's worth the price. We as an association have no choice as far as I'm concerned."

It was not long that Big Sid called the meeting to order, where he eventually told the group about Juan's contact in New Orleans.

Then he asked, "Would you be interested in hiring a group from Louisiana who promises to solve our problem, eradicating the Chicago group in short order. We need to make a decision tonight. I'll make a motion we hire this Swamp Man to eliminate our most pressing problem, the Chicago group."

Someone in the audience seconded the motion.

After a short discussion, they took a vote, agreeing it was worth a try. They were unable to continue without assistance. After the meeting, Big Sid thanked Juan for his input and was hopeful the Louisiana group could quash the turbulent circumstances in Indy.

The next day, Juan called Swamp Man and told him they've decided to accept his offer to come to Indy and take care of business.

"We're ready for you to do whatever is necessary in taking care of our problem. Since I last talked to you about our problem, it has become much more dangerous. The longer they are around, it would only get worse."

"Don't worry about a thing. I'll get a small group together. They will be in Indy first part of next week if that's agreeable?"

"Thanks, if there is anything we can do in the meantime, let us know?"

"You don't have to do a thing. I have dealt with them in the past and know how to handle them."

"I will tell my associates the problem will soon be addressed. Let me know when you've eliminated our problem, and I'll have your money in the mail the same day."

After his talk with Swamp Man, Juan was relieved the problem with the Chicago group would soon be history. He called Big Sid and informed him what the Swamp Man said. Big Sid was elated with the speed at which the problem was being handled.

Big Sid asked me before hanging up, "Keep me informed when it's over."

I told him, "It'll be short-lived once we've committed to Swamp Man."

The following week, three men from Louisiana arrived early at the airport outside of Indy. They came prepared to close down the Chicago organization by running them out of town.

Once the New Orleans team was in place, they were notified by Juan that the Silver Dollar Saloon was contacted the day before for protection and would be returning the following day to collect their dues.

The following morning the Chicago group sent two of its collectors back to the Silver Dollar Saloon. Swamp Man's men were waiting in the wings to greet them as they arrived.

As they entered, they were approached by the three men sent by Swamp Man. The three men from New Orleans immediately confronted the two Chicago hoods, telling them they were not welcomed and leave.

Suddenly, without warning, it became a pushing-and-shoving match as a small brawl between the two groups broke out. After the confrontation, the collectors, bruised and busted up, limped toward the door and warned of the pending disaster if they continued business as usual in Indy.

The Chicago group returned to their control center telling their leader what occurred. This did not set well with him. The next day, he sent three men this time. As they entered the Silver Dollar Saloon, they were met again by the same three men from Louisiana, waiting near the entrance. Before they were able to enter, a hostile occurrence ensued outside. The three men from Louisiana beat the hell out of them causing one member of the group to need emergency treatment at a local hospital. They were told to go back and tell their boss it was time to leave. The next time, they would not be so merciful. Again, reiterating they were not welcomed in Indy and had to get the hell out of town while they were able.

When the Chicago men returned to their hotel, they told their boss what happened at the Silver Dollar Saloon. They explained to their leader they were told not to return; if they did, they would suffer the consequences. This was not what the Chicago leader expected, so he decided to visit the saloon again the following morning with a larger contingency of associates and settle the score with Swamp Man's men once and for all.

Arriving at the Silver Dollar Saloon early the next morning, the three from Louisiana were waiting outside in their car. It was not long until two cars pulled into the parking lot, loaded with extra muscle. The three from Louisiana waited until all the men exited their cars before getting out and confronting them. They were ready to do whatever to crush the situation and send this bunch of yahoos back to Chi-town with their tails between their legs. After the group from Chicago saw three men exit their car, they warned them to get back in their cars and leave town before things really got dirty and out of control.

The larger of the two groups now got out of their cars and readied themselves for the altercation that was looming. One of the men from Louisianan pulled a gun from his waistband, aimed it at the group leader, telling him in no uncertain terms to leave and not show his face around town after today. At that point, the group from Chicago began scattering, running for cover anywhere they could find a place to hunker down before the shooting began. Suddenly, bullets began flying; the war was on. It did not last long. Two of the Chicago group were wounded in the first volley of shots: one took bullet in the right shoulder, one took a bullet to the gut.

During the fracas outside, someone inside the restaurant called the police. Soon sirens could be heard in the distance. Just as fast as it started, the shooting ceased. The three from Louisiana jumped back in their car and sped off. The Chicago group did not have time to regroup before the police arrived on the scene. They were caught redhanded, with two of their group down and needing medical attention. One was treated at the scene while the other was transported to the local hospital for surgery.

There was no way the Chicago group was able to talk their way out of the mess they found themselves in. The police arrested the remaining group, taking them downtown for questioning.

After the incident, the police on scene began questioning the owner, employees, and customers who witnessed the confrontational and shoot-out. They all told the same story; no one really knew what happened. They were inside the restaurant and had not notice anything unusual or heard anything until shots were fired.

Someone called the police after hearing the first shot. It happened so fast, and by the time the police arrived on scene, it was over. The police spent most of the morning investigating the crime scene but came up with nothing on the group from Louisiana, no fingerprints, shell casings, footprints, cigarette butts, nothing to link them to the crime scene. They had come to Indy quietly to take care of business; when finished, they vanished just as quietly. It was like they were ghostly. They surprised the Chicago group, stunned at what happened, and left speechless as the police questioned them.

The three men from Louisiana finished their business in the parking lot, then drove straight to the airport, boarded their plane back in New Orleans. They were in Indy less than two and a half days. Their mission was accomplished, and they were out of there.

Arriving back in New Orleans, they were met at the airport by Swamp Man himself. Before parting company, going their separate ways, Swamp Man told them he was notified the Chicago group bonded out of jail and seen heading back north to Chicago. They were officially finished in Indy. That is, all but one, who was in the hospital where he remained for the next week recovering from a gunshot to the abdomen. The gunshot he took in the gut will keep him out of commission a while longer.

Swamp Man congratulated his group on a job well done.

The businesses involved with the collectors from Chicago were informed later that day about the Chicago group's involvement in the shoot-out at the Silver Dollar Saloon. The businesses forced by the Chicago group to pay protection money felt a sigh of relief hearing they had been ran out of town. They could once again carry on with business as usual, uninterrupted, no harassment, a non-issue since Juan stopped his protection. The Chicago group learned a valuable and expensive lesson, leave Naptown alone. Indy did not need their kind in this hard-working community trying to eke out a living, make ends meet, and pay for protection, for what?

With the problem of the Chicago group now quashed, Big Sid called a meeting with the different associations to ask for their contribution in paying their debt owed to the Swamp Man. Pleased with the job, but if ever faced with a similar situation, they knew who to contact. It was time to pay Swamp Man and his group for ridding them of the Chicago consortium as promised. They were more than happy to pay for his services. By that afternoon, the money was collected and delivered by Western Union to Swamp Man. There was no follow-up from Swamp Man or anyone from New Orleans. The task they were hired to do had been completed. Once the money was received, it ended all communication between Indy and New Orleans.

CHAPTER 32

Juan contacted Justin Muller later in the afternoon to see how Dennis's murder trial was going.

When Justin answered his phone, "Good afternoon, Justin. Juan Grajales here. I wanted to touch base with you to see how things are proceeding with Dennis's trial."

"Good afternoon, Juan, so far so good. Dennis, of course, is not happy with his newly appointed attorney, but there's little he can do now to undo the bad choices he's made lately. As I told you earlier, it was Dennis's idea if push came to shove. It was known if things started going south, he was willing to throw the organization under the bus for a lesser sentence. But that's become a fleeting memory since the prosecution has not given the defense an opening to bring in new evidence. Testimonies of the witnesses have not provided the prosecution just cause in which to introduce new evidence. The trial so far is not boding well for Dennis. He's learning a difficult lesson the hard way, finally realizing he was not as shrewd as he thought himself to be. Understanding now his blunder firing me turned out to be a bad move on his part and a disaster for his appointed defense team.

"His newly appointed defense attorney is young and inexperienced. He was not ready or able in laying out his client's defense accurately before the court. His new attorney's argument was: Dennis, inebriated at the time he committed the gruesome act, was unaware of his actions. If Dennis had not been drinking, this heinous crime would not have happened. In his condition at the time of the egregious act, he told the jury Dennis was not thinking rationally at the time of the manslaughter. If he had been fully sober, this dreadful crime would not have occurred, which was a lame excuse at best.

"The defense team's rendition of the incident did not hold water; even Dennis saw the writing on the wall. The prosecution was going to have a field day with his pretext. Everyone, including the judge, the gallery, including the jury, immediately saw where this case was headed. The evidence against Dennis was overwhelming, and Dennis had previously confessed to an involuntary manslaughter charge. There was no way out or light at the end of the tunnel for him. The only hope now was to cut a deal and involve the organization. But optimism at including the association was quickly fading, with little or no hope of a lesser charge being an option. Beating the system at this point in the trial had diminished to zero and impossible.

"Dennis was scared, and it showed in his behavior and demeanor as he sat silently listening to the overwhelming evidence given by the witnesses and prosecution attorneys. Witness after witness who took the stand all pointed fingers at him and only him. He had made a monumental mistake not letting me handle his case, but it's too late. It is time he accepted the inevitable."

"I thank you for the update and appreciate all you've tried to do for Dennis, but guess it was not meant to be."

"If I find out anything new, I'll call. Later."

Juan sat back in his chair, thinking to himself, Oh, *how slowly the wheels of justice turn but guessed it to be the way in which the legal system works.*

Time was not on Dennis's side and eventually he would have to face reality; the reality was, he's up a shit creek without a paddle, a dead man walking.

It did not take the jury long in reaching a guilty verdict after hearing the evidence and testimonies of witnesses. It was only a matter of formality once the jury was sequestered and debated the overwhelming evidence. They would have no recourse but find him guilty. Dennis, once found guilty of manslaughter, for all practical purposes, the life he once knew was over.

Juan thanked Justin again for his contribution and involvement being there when his help was needed.

Juan before hanging up, asked Justin, "Will you be available in the future if we are in need of your services?"

"Yes, anytime. Call me anytime I can be of assistance."

"Thank you."

Juan contacted Becky to inform her with what was happening at trial concerning Dennis. She was not shocked by the account Justin Muller gave Juan as to where the trial was headed. She felt Dennis would be found guilty but could not help feeling sorry for him even though he was not the smartest rock on the pile. The only thing she really knew about him was he treated Ivan with respect and she had always appreciated that.

Becky told Juan, "I knew Dennis was a smart-ass from the beginning. He could never keep his mouth shut. Always thought he knew best. He's always been that way. Ivan tried helping him, but he was such a know-it-all, such a stupid man Ivan once told her, but he's finally met his match."

"Yes, I think he's learned a tough lesson in life, not everything is black and white or me, me, me. You have to bend occasionally to survive. Guess he was absent the day that message was taught."

"I agree. He brought it all on himself. Life has not always been kind to Dennis. Guess he's always learned his lessons the hard way. But it was his way or the highway. I don't envy him. He's made his bed, and the rest is history."

"If I hear anything else of interest about the trial or Dennis, I will contact you."

"Thank you, Juan. You have been very forthright in our relationship and hope we can continue our working arrangement with the same transparency going forward."

"I'm sure we can, Becky. You have a wonderful day. If you need me, you know I'm always available."

"That means a lot to me and the children. Thank you again." After his conversation with Becky, he felt good that she had accepted him and the way he had managed the organization since Ivan's death.

With his efforts, the organization was slowly turning around and adapting into a respectable business—a first-rate organization anyone would be proud to work for. But before letting his guard down, there was work to be completed before his plan became a reality. Turning the corner had been a tediously slow process, but anything worthwhile takes time, and Juan was aware of the time factor involved, knowing one day things would jell and come to fruition.

"O, faith, ye of little faith," mumbling to himself, he chuckled as he quietly sat alone at his desk.

CHAPTER 33

Picking up the phone, Juan called Bobby to see how things were going down on the farm, and if he had had any more problems since the last time they spoke.

Bobby, answering his phone, said, "This is Bobby."

Juan responded by saying, "Hi, Bobby, how are things going down on the farm?"

"So far everything is great. I've not run into more shysters. The farm's running smoothly. The farmhands are content working together with little or no dissension among the ranks. They know their jobs. I have no problems in that department. I'm happy with the way things have turned out. It makes my job less stressful having good farmhands to work with. I'm sure it makes less work for every-one, including you, ha ha."

"Yes, including me. Okay, Bobby, since things are going well and you don't seem to need anything at this time, I'll talk to you later. I may try running down for a visit in a few days. Sounds like you are on top of everything. Keep up the good work and stay in touch."

It was early afternoon before Juan stopped and reflected back on the day's busy agenda. He had not taken time for lunch and decided to take a break. He asked the Irishman to bring the car around. It was time for lunch. The Irishman drove out to a restaurant that recently opened on the west side. As they entered the Town and Country restaurant, Juan was surprised by the sheer size of the place. It was large enough to accommodate two hundred people, at least. As far as he could tell, it had one large dining room and a party or meeting room off to one side. Once inside and seated, a waiter came over handing each a menu and took their drink order. Juan was over whelmed with the variety of entrées listed on the huge menu. It took several minutes to read over the entire menu. Finally, he decided on the fresh salmon served on a bed of rice, with broccoli and cheese sauce. The waiter returned with their drink order and took their food order.

Before the waiter left with the food order, Juan asked, "How long has the restaurant been open?"

"A month tomorrow."

"Glad you dropped by. I'm sure you will enjoy our food. Our chef is Tinos, an excellent chef from one of the most famous restaurants in Chicago. Think you will enjoy the salmon. He cuts it fresh daily himself."

"Thank you for the information. You've been very informative. I'm sure we will enjoy our lunch."

When the food arrived, it was as advertised. The salmon, perfect; the broccoli, fresh and al dente; the bed of rice included veggies scattered throughout. The cheese sauce spooned over the salmon was to die for; it was one of the better meals Juan had eaten bar none.

When he and the Irishman finished lunch, and it came time to leave, Juan motioned the waiter to the table and told him, "Give my compliments to Chef Tinos for such a wonderful and unforgettable lunch. I also would like to give you a little extra for being such a good waiter. Here's an extra five-spot. Thank you for making this such a remarkable dining experience."

"Thank you, sir, it's been my pleasure serving you. Do come again."

Juan and the Irishman left and headed back east. Once inside the lobby, Juan walked over and talked briefly to Sheila. He told her where they had lunch and asked her if she would be interested in having dinner there later that evening.

"Of course, it sounds wonderful."

"I'll pick you up at seven?"

"Seven it is. I'll be ready."

Juan then walked over to Palmer's office, stuck his head inside, and asked, "How are you doing? Find any more discrepancies from the farm or loan company?"

"No, everything seems correct and consistent according to the ledger entries."

"That's good news for a change. After you finish the grunt work, it will be easier, I'm sure, going forward."

"Yes, that's the day I'm shooting for, ha ha."

Juan returned to his office where he found a message on his desk. It was from Tony the Bull. Juan knew the Bull would not have called and left a message unless it was important. Juan picked up the phone and dialed Tony's number. After a couple of rings, Tony picked up.

"Hello."

"Tony, this is Juan. I have a note on my desk to call you."

"Yes, I have a proposition for you, if you have a moment to spare?"

"I have time. What is it?"

"I've been thinking lately about the farm your organization owns outside Lexington, wondering if you would be interested in leasing out part of the stables and pasture for about fifteen horses? We have several new members and need extra space to board their animals; the first place I thought of was the farm in Lexington. I know you have a lot of acreage there and ample room considering the number of horses you have stabled. Would you consider leasing some of your empty stalls?"

"I'll have to talk to my foreman Bobby and see what the situation is there. I need to find out If he has enough empty stalls, and farmhands to handle additional fifteen horses. I'll get back to you as soon as I find out."

"Great, I'll be waiting to hear from you, thanks." As soon as Juan hung up talking to Tony the Bull, put in a call to Bobby. Bobby answered and Juan explained what had just transpired with Tony from the breeders' farm in Indy.

Juan asked Bobby, "Do you think the farm can accommodate another fifteen horses?"

"That's a lot, fifteen additional horse to house and feed. But yes, think we can manage a few more horses down here."

"Thanks, Bobby, I'll call Tony and tell him you feel you have the extra space and pastures to accommodate fifteen more horses. If you need extra help, contact the employment agency in Lexington. I'm sure they can provide you with additional help. Call me back and let me know what you find out."

"Will do, boss. Looks like we have a lot of work to do before the horses arrive. Let me know when they are on their way so we are ready."

"Thanks, talk to you later."

Juan hung up the phone. It was getting late; time to stop for the day. Juan finished what few things remained on his desk, filed all the loose papers away, and was ready to close-up shop.

Using the intercom, he called Sheila.

"Do you have time to come to my office before leaving?"

"Sure, you caught me in the nick of time. I was about to finish up and walk out the door. Give me a minute."

Soon afterward, Sheila entered his office where he asked her, "Do you still feel like going to dinner later this evening?"

"Of course, I've thought of nothing else since you asked earlier. I'm so looking forward to it."

"Fine, I'll be by to pick you up at seven."

"I'll be ready."

Sheila returned to her desk and finished filling what few papers remained on her desk before calling it a day.

Juan called the Irishman to his office. "Get the car. I'm ready to go home and get ready for dinner. I'm meeting Sheila tonight at seven."

"Okay, I'll meet you out front in five minutes."

The Irishman before leaving told Tony, "I'll see you tomorrow."

Tony was ready to leave when Juan came by and asked, "How's things at home?"

"Fine, the wife and kids are doing great."

"I'm happy for you. If there is anything you need, all you have to do is ask. I am available to help in any way I can. But you know that by now?"

"I do and appreciate all you've done for me and the family. Just hope I can repay you some day for your kindness."

"See you tomorrow."

Juan walked over and told Sheila, "I'm looking forward to tonight. See you at seven."

He left the office and crawled into the waiting car. The Irishman drove him over to the hotel where he was dropped off. This was one night he was looking forward to. His only thought at the moment was being alone with Sheila; she was becoming a preoccupation, and he relished in the thought.

He could not wait to hold her in his arms and have her warm sexy body next to his. He had never felt this way about anyone in his life; it was puzzling yet exciting both at the same time. It was more exciting than collecting, when he felt that rush of adrenaline prior to engagement. His feeling for Sheila was euphoric, exhilarating, a new emotional state emerging from the depths of his soul frequently.

At seven sharp, he arrived in front of Sheila's apartment and quickly exited the car, taking the elevator up to the floor where she lived. Exiting the elevator, walking toward her door, he could feel his heart working overtime, could almost hear it as he walked down the hall. Reaching her door, he knocked twice and anxiously waited for her to answer. As she opened the door, he saw her; his whole demeanor changed.

Standing there in the hall, Juan was looking at this gorgeous person in front of him, and thought to himself, This is definitely the woman of my dreams. How could she be so beautiful, and I've never noticed her before?

Strange.

Standing in the doorway, she looked stunning in her new silky pantsuit, reminding him of some model on the front page of Vogue. He never dreamed she was so striking. As he entered, he took her softly in his arms. Consumed with desire, he hugged her gently, then gave her a passionate kiss before leaving. She smelled of heaven, her movements captivating, was open to every advancement he made. He held her in his arms, not wanting to let go. Oh, how wonderful this night was going to be. Bringing her closer once more, he gently kissed her soft lips. They were becoming more and more excited as the seconds passed, standing in the doorway holding on to her like a lifeline. He had to get a grip on himself and stop. If not, they would never get to the restaurant. They had plenty of time for extracurricular activity afterward. Once finished with this brief, passionate encounter of kissing and embracing, Juan released her. She then reached over where a chair sat near the door, picked up her wrap off the back of the chair, and handed it to him to place over her shoulders.

After putting on her wrap, he closed and locked her door and began walking arm in arm down the hallway toward the elevator. Reaching the lobby, they exited the elevator. Still arm in arm, they walked through the lobby to the waiting car. Juan was not letting go; she had become the most important thing in his world.

At the restaurant, he sat staring at her and admiring how beautiful she was. It was going to be a night to remember. After dinner, the Irishman dropped them off at Juan's apartment. As Juan exited the car, he then walked to the open window where the Irishman sat and told him, "Pick us up at the usual time in the morning."

The Irishman smiled back at Juan and said, "Six o'clock it is, boss. See you two then," he said, chuckling to himself as he drove away.

They walked into the hotel arm in arm, making a beeline to the elevator and upstairs. Once inside his unit, he helped remove her wrap and laid it across the back of a chair sitting in the living room.

He then kissed her tenderly and afterward told her, "Make yourself comfortable, and can I offer you an after-dinner drink? If so, what is your pleasure?"

"I'll have a Drambuie over ice, please. Last time it made me all tingly inside," she said, chuckling.

"Drambuie it is."

He poured her a Drambuie over ice, picked it up off the table, and handed it to her.

She made the comment, "I think before the night is over, I may need one more," as she seductively smiled at him.

He turned around, located the scotch bottle, and poured himself a double on the rocks. When he finished pouring his drink, he walked over to where she was seated on the couch. Setting his drink on the coffee table, he then sat down next to her. Reaching over to pick up his drink, he held it next to hers and toasted to a wonderful evening. Taking the glasses to their lips, they sipped from their glasses, a bit of nectar of the Gods before settling in for the evening of lovemaking.

The drinks felt warm and intoxicating as the warm liquid slowly passed through the esophagus to their stomachs. It did not take long for the drinks to begin sending them both into another dimension. Soon they were unable to hold back their desires, and each became very subservient as they kissed and gently caressed. Stopping momentarily, they reached over the coffee table to pick up their drinks and indulged in one more sip. Was this the sip that would finally push them over the edge? Setting their glasses back on the coffee table, they continued with their petting and lovemaking.

It did not take long until the petting progressed to the real touchy-feely portion of lovemaking. Juan had already become sexually aroused and was having a hard time keeping himself from going off prematurely. She too was aroused, letting her hands do the walking. As her hands slowly wandered over and around his muchly stimulated body. Slowly her hands moved farther down, finally reaching his trousers. She slowly loosened his belt, unbuttoned his trousers, and slowly unzipped his fly.

Meantime, Juan kept himself busy trying to remove her blouse and bra. Things were becoming alluring. They were reaching that point of no return. There was no turning back; it was too late.

As they continued with foreplay, each was now enthralled in another dimension called ecstasy. After removing her bra and caressing her breasts gently between his hands, he kissed her nipples, which were now standing erect and hard.

Sheila, in the meantime, was slowly working her way toward his stiff shaft, hidden beneath his shorts. Finally, she was able to wrap her hot hand around his stiff penis; he was almost to the point of yelling. The anticipation and intensification of their foreplay was over the top. Juan was now having a difficult time controlling his eagerness. Having never been in a situation quite like this, he was uncertain where she was headed with this.

Gently, with her right hand around his stiff shaft, she slowly began moving her hand up and down, gradually leaning down toward his opened trousers, eventually lowering her head between his legs. As she placed her hot, wet lips around his stiff shaft, rotating her head and tongue around slowly. She continued moving farther down his shaft until it was completely consumed by her soft, moist cavern. She continued until he no could longer hold off this feeling of euphoria, suddenly climaxing. As the euphoria began to wane and with shaky hands, he gently lifted her head from between his legs and from his now limp sex organ. He now caressed her warm body next to his and passionately kissed her.

Juan was surprised by the act; her erotic maneuvers were totally off the charts. After a time, she gently placed his still shaky hand between her separated legs, and he slowly rubbed his hand up and down on her wet and inviting vagina. Eventually, Sheila initiated him to insert his finger inside her, where he began moving it in and out, up and down on her clitoris, which stimulated her enough to give a soft, muffled, excited scream. She was becoming more and more aroused as his finger moved in and out, and all about, a real turn on for her. With head back, mouth open, breathing heavy, eyes closed, back arched, she was in her own world as Juan had been earlier.

Slowly opening her eyes, she looked up at him and said, "Let's move from the couch and into the bedroom and finish what we've started."

It sounded like a good idea to Juan. The couch was not advantageous to what they had in mind to do next. They got off the couch and headed to the bedroom where a king-size bed awaited their arrival.

Once in the bedroom, they removed what few shreds of clothing they had on until both were completely nude and they laid down on the bed. It did not take long until they were entwined in each other's arms, continuing where they left off. They made mad, passionate love until they were both exhausted. Still intertwined in each other's arms, they finally dropped off to sleep. Juan would never forget this first sexual encounter that night with Sheila. The image in his mind of the event would remain with him a lifetime. Sheila was his dream come true, the one he dreamed of forever.

When they awoke the next morning, they had another roll in the hay to start the new day. What a feeling waking up next to Sheila; she was all his dreams wrapped up in one, the only one he would ever want or need. After their quick roll in the hay, it was time to return and face the real world.

It was time to leave this magical place with fond memories still lingering in their thoughts. Their eyes met briefly; both were anticipating this cherished, intimate encounter they just shared, which they were eager to repeat many times in the future.

Sheila kissed Juan on the cheek as she rolled over him and headed to the bathroom. She told Juan as she closed the door to the bathroom, "I'm going to take a quick shower. When I finish, you can take me home, so I can change clothes for work."

"Take your time. I'll have the Irishman drop you off, and we'll wait outside for you."

CHAPTER 34

Juan and the Irishman sat in the car and waited while Sheila changed and freshened up. While waiting, the Irishman mentioned to Juan he ran into Tony last evening at a local tavern after dropping Sheila and him off at Juan's apartment. Tony told the Irishman about Carlos, the loan office's interim manager, running around town spreading gossip.

Tony told Juan, "Apparently, Carlos has become disgruntled not being appointed manager after the recent shakeup at the loan company and was spreading rumors the loan company was underwater, and in the process of going belly-up. He has the employees at the loan company upset, wondering what would happen if the loan company did sell or closed its doors."

Juan was surprised at what he heard that the loan company was on the chopping block and possibly up for sale.

The rumor Carlos was spreading could not be further from the truth. The loan company still produced the second-largest revenue for the association and still a viable, functioning business.

Carlos was upset at the way things worked out for him and bitter at Juan's decision. This was his way showing displeasure and discontentment.

After Sheila returned to the car, they proceeded to the office. Tony sitting at the table as they arrived. Juan wanted to question him further about the rumor Carlos was spreading, and if he had more information about the vile rumors being circulated by Carlos.

Juan walked to where Tony sat and asked, "Tony, who did you hear this rumor from about Carlos's bad-mouthing the loan company?"

"Oh, good morning, boss. From Roxane, who works in accounting at the loan company. She mentioned it to a friend of hers whom I met last night at one of the taverns I frequent. Her friend and I happened to be sitting next to each other at the bar talking. I happened to mention where I worked, and he said he knew Roxane who worked at the loan company. Since I knew Roxane, it piqued his interest. He wanted to know if I knew what was going on at the loan company and if it was insolvent or up for sale.

"I told him, 'This is the first I've heard about the loan company being up for sale.' I've known Roxane's friend for a long time and knew he had ties with a group in Indy, which was always looking for places to launder dirty money. I'm sure they would be highly interested in a venue in which to launder their ill-gotten money. The loan company would be a perfect front for this type of activity."

"Thanks, Tony, I appreciate your input into this matter."

Juan turned and walked back to his office, while Sheila seated herself behind her desk and preparing for the day.

Inside his office, Juan sat down, immediately picked up the phone, and called the loan company.

A clerk answered and said, "Good morning. My name is Lucy. How may I help you?"

"Yes, good morning, Lucy. I'd like to speak with Carlos."

"I'm sorry, sir, he's busy right now with a client. I'll put you on hold, or you can call back later if you wish."

"That will not be necessary, Lucy. My name is Juan Grajales. I'm CEO of the organization you work for. I need to speak with Carlos now, so please get him for me."

"Yes, Mr. Grajales. I will inform him immediately."

Soon, another voice came over the phone, "Hello, this is Carlos. What can I do for you?"

"This is Juan Grajales. Get your sorry ass over to my office immediately. I want a word with you about a rumor circulating around town about the loan company being insolvent and up for sale. You are aware of the rumor, correct? It has your name written all over it. You get over here on the double. Did I make myself clear?"

"Yes, Mr. Grajales, I'm on my way."

Juan hung up the phone and started working on other matters requiring his undivided attention until Carlos arrived. It was not long before Carlos entered the lobby, told Sheila who he was and that Mr. Grajales was expecting him. Sheila hit the intercom on her desk and informed Juan, "A gentleman by the name of Carlos was in the lobby, said he had an appointment to see you."

Juan told her, "Escort him to my office."

Sheila quickly walked Carlos to Juan's office. Juan looked up as they entered and saw Carlos. He immediately told Sheila to return to her desk.

Carlos spoke first, saying, "Good morning…Mr. Grajales?"

Juan, still looking at Carlos, said, "Sit your sorry ass down. I want to know what this I hear about a rumor the loan company being insolvent and up for sale?"

"This morning Tony, my security person sitting outside in the lobby, told me he talked to a fellow by the name of Earl last night who knew Roxane. He said Roxane had informed Earl a few days before that you mentioned the loan company was in turmoil and possibly up for grabs. I want to know why you told her that."

"I have no idea what you're talking about or why Roxane would say such a thing to this Earl. I have not said anything like that to her. The loan company, as you and I both know, is doing well."

"I'm going to ask you once again, why you are spreading this rumor?"

"Really…I don't know how this rumor got started, but it was not me, trust me, Mr. Grajales."

"I'll find out sooner or later, and if you are lying to me, it's not only your ass but your job, understood?"

"Yes…Mr. Grajales, but… I…yes, I understand."

"Get the hell out of my face. Don't let me hear anything else out of you until I get to the bottom of this matter. Understood? Get out of here and get back to work."

After Carlos left his office, Juan again picked up the phone and dialed the loan company, and asked to speak to Roxane.

Roxane answered the phone, "Whom am I speaking with?"

"This is Juan Grajales. Do you know who I am?"

"Yes, Carlos mentioned your name before he left to see you this morning."

"I need you to come to my office now. We need to talk."

"Yes, Mr. Grajales, I'll be there as soon as I can." Roxane arrived a short time later and explained to Sheila who she was and why she was there.

"Mr. Grajales phoned me earlier and wanted to meet me in his office. He had something he wanted to talk to me about."

Sheila pushed the button down on the intercom and announced, "A Roxane from the loan company is here to see you."

"Yes, Sheila, I'm expecting her, send her in."

Sheila turned to Roxane, "Mr. Grajales is expecting you." Pointing to his office, she told her to go right in.

Roxane thanked Sheila and proceeded to the rear of the building, where Juan's office was located. As she entered, Juan looked up from his desk.

Roxane said, "Good morning, Mr. Grajales. I hurried as fast as I could. What is it you wanted to speak to me about?"

"Have a seat please. It's about a rumor Carlos told you about. Did he mention to you lately the loan company was in financial trouble and possibly for sale? Did you by any chance tell a friend of yours by the name of Earl the same rumor?"

"No, of course not. Why would I do something like that?"

"I have a witness who talked to Earl last night. Earl told him you mentioned to him the loan company was in dire straits and was up for sale. So don't bullshit me, Roxane. This is not my first rodeo. I'll have Tony come in and tell you exactly what Earl told him about your conversation. I know it's you who told this Earl. I need to get to the bottom of this rumor and stop this shit in its tracks. It's not in the best interest of the organization to go around spreading rumors like this. Are we on the same page yet?"

"Yes, but I have no idea what you are talking about."

"I want you to come clean and tell me why you passed on the rumor to Earl?"

"Okay, Mr. Grajales, I did mention the rumor to Earl. It was because after dating Carlos on and off for the past year I was fed up with his promises of marriage. He kept me dangling with his promises, but when I confronted him last week, he dropped me like a hot potato.

"The other evening, I drinking with one of the local gin mills and was upset at Carlos. That's when I ran into an old friend of mine Earl, whom I dated prior to Carlos. During our conversation, he asked me if I knew of some place where he could launder some dirty money. I told him I heard through the grapevine the loan company where I work was floundering and could possibly be on the market soon. I only mentioned it out of contempt for Carlos. I made it sound like the loan company was in disarray and could possibly be bought. I told Earl it would be a great place to launder money. I really meant nothing by it, but yes, it was me who told Earl."

"I thank you for your honesty, but I'm afraid I'm going to have to let you go, Roxane. I cannot have people working for the organization who are not loyal. Do you understand my situation?"

"Yes, I'm sorry if I caused you trouble, but it was my way of getting back at Carlos for all the hurt he caused me over the past year."

"I understand, but that still does not give you the right to jeopardize the organization because of your hurt feelings. Now get the hell out of my sight, and don't show your face around here again."

She left Juan's office crying and feeling as if the world had just come crashing down on her. All because of Carlos, who kept her believing they were going to marry and spend the rest of their lives together. Lesson learned. It had been her own doings, and now she must pay the price for her mistake.

After Roxane left the office, Juan immediately called Carlos back and told him, "If I hear you screwing around with another employee while employed with the organization, I will personally fire you. Do you understand the ramifications and problems you've caused the organization for your inept behavior?"

"Yes, Mr. Grajales. I promise not to get involved ever again with an employee. I swear to you on my mother's grave."

"Good, now get your sorry ass back to work. I don't want to hear of you screwing up again, understood?"

"Yes, Mr. Grajales."

Juan hung up. It was time for lunch. He got hold of the Irishman and told to bring the car around. While the Irishman was getting the car,

Juan walked out to where Sheila was and asked, "Are you caught up with your work, if so, would you like to go to lunch?"

"Yes, I have everything cleaned up for the moment, and yes, I'm starving. Lunch sounds good."

"Okay, come along."

Before leaving, he turned to Tony and said, "Stick around the office while we are at lunch. We will not be gone long. I need you to hold down the fort until we get back."

"Sure, boss. I brought my lunch today, no problem."

"See you later."

Sheila and Juan left the office and walked out to the waiting car. Today, Juan was going to visit a new restaurant—one he had not been to previously but often thought about. He told the Irishman where it was that he wanted to have lunch. The Irishman was familiar with the restaurant and drove straight to it. Upon reaching JC's Skyline, the Irishman dropped off Sheila and Juan in front while he parked the car. Sheila and Juan entered the restaurant, which was already filling up with the lunch crowd. They were met by a friendly hostess who quickly seated them and handed each a menu. The Irishman entered and headed straight to the bar where he would eat while waiting for Juan and Sheila to finish lunch.

Juan ordered the luncheon special for both Sheila and himself. When the luncheon specials arrived, Juan could not believe how well it was presented. There could not have been a better presentation of food; it was not to be consumed, but revered he thought.

Sheila was taken aback as well when she saw her meal, commenting to Juan, "I have never seen such a meal, ever."

This pleased Juan, who told her, "Only the best for you from now on."

After lunch, Juan headed back to the office where they found Tony had everything under control. He was happy to see Sheila. He was tired of answering the phone, taking messages, etc., He had a hard time eating his lunch between the calls and messages. He had a quick lesson at what Sheila did all day; it was not as cushiony as it appeared on the surface. He found it absolutely nerve-racking at times. Trying to keep things straight, answering the phone, and taking messages were by themselves challenging. Sheila was a welcome sight as she took over her position. Once Sheila was again behind the desk, Tony was relieved.

Juan thanked Tony for looking after things while they were away. Before heading to his office, Juan told Tony, "Why don't you take the rest of the day off? The Irishman can take over for you this afternoon. I'm not leaving the office as far as I know, so get out of here and enjoy the rest of the afternoon."

"Thanks, boss."

It was a treat for Tony to be off in the afternoon. There were things he could find to do around the house needing his attention. When he arrived home that afternoon, his wife was surprised to see him but pleased at the same time. They decided instead of staying around the house they would head over to the park across town, and spend time alone enjoying the sunshine and fresh air. It was still cool outside, but the sun was shining and so inviting—a perfect day in which to spread a blanket out and relax the afternoon away.

Juan went in to talk to Palmer to see how things were looking with finances and find out if he was getting caught up with the paperwork and delinquent bills. Juan was curious if Palmer had reached a point where he had a little breathing room.

As Juan entered Palmer's office, he asked, "How are things going?"

"I'm almost finished with the financial records. Things are finally beginning to fall into place, could not be better. Once I found the errors, double billing, etc., things started turning around. Nothing looks out of line now. I'm sure what few financial accounting activities or statements remaining are correct."

"That's good news. I've been wanting to hear you say that for a while now."

Juan thanked Palmer for doing such a good job cleaning up the mess, and straightening out the financial inner workings of the business.

Juan told Palmer, "When you finish today, I'm going to give you some extra time off to regroup before starting with the current workload already piling up. Would a few days off give you time to recuperate and get back on track appeal to you?'

"You bet, it'll be a relief to have time off to recover and get my act together. When I return, I should be rested and ready to start anew. I at least have a handle on what I'm doing now. It will not be as strenuous as before, that's for sure."

"Okay, after you finish today, take the next three days off along with the weekend and enjoy yourself. Just don't forget to come to work on Monday, ha ha!"

"I'll be here Monday. You can count on that."

Juan walked out of Palmer's office and back to his office where he found several notes Tony had placed on his desk while away at lunch.

One of the messages was from Roxane; he picked it up to see what she had written.

It said,

Mr. Grajales,

This is Roxane. I need to get in touch with you. I have something important I needed to tell you. It's imperative. Call me as soon as you can.

Picking up the phone, Juan called Roxane. When she answered, he could tell she had been crying and asked her, "What's so important you needed to talk to me?"

"Remember, I told you I talked to my friend Earl about the loan company?"

"Yes, so?"

"Earl mentioned what I told him to someone else in the money-laundering business. I saw him again last night and he told me, 'The sale of the loan company has piqued a lot of interest among certain elements around town.' He said, 'Several parties are now interested in taking over the loan company once it's on the market. Some of the parties are desperate enough to approach you personally with offers to buy.'

"Since I'm no longer an associate and have no ties with you or the loan company, they've decided to cause a lot of trouble for Earl and me. Earl asked me to warn you to keep an eye out for that bunch of renegades. They're nothing but trouble.

"I appreciate the heads-up and will keep a close watch out for anything unusual not only at the loan company, but here at the office."

After talking to Roxane, he called Carlos telling him about the conversation he had with Roxane.

"I want you and Jordan to be fully aware of the pending threat and keep your eyes and ears open."

"I will do whatever necessary to keep things on an even keel here at the loan company. Don't worry, boss."

After talking to Carlos, Juan hung the phone up. Carlos immediately walked over to Jordan's office giving him a heads-up what Juan had just relayed to him. The situation around the loan company and association was once again highly volatile. It was a rude awakening learning this uncouth group was so desperate to find a place to launder their money; they would not stop in their desperate attempt even apply strong-arming tactics in order to commandeer a legitimate place just to launder their ill-gotten funds.

As the next few days and weeks passed, nothing seemed to be amiss concerning the loan company or the satellite associations. It was safe to say that since no insider help was available. The money launderers had given up the idea of causing a ruckus. Another catastrophe had been averted.

CHAPTER 35

After several weeks, things slowly turned around; the association was on firmer footing with the new changes Juan had in place.

Under Bobby's guidance, things down on the farm were back on track. Adding the breeders' additional fifteen horses was a plus at enhancing the farm's bottom line. Bobby had not lost his touch since leaving the farm he grew up on in Indiana. He had a knack for running a farm this size and was self-reliant in making difficult decisions concerning the farm.

There was only one exception; he still relied too heavily on the vet's recommendations in most matters that concerned the horses. The farm had become among the top breeder farms now in Kentucky. It had gained an exemplary status under Bobby's guidance and management. The farm was now referred to as "the number 1 breeding place" in the area, which pleased both Juan and Bobby. It was on its way to becoming a first-class breeder farm.

Bobby on his own decided to hire Ted as the full-time vet who permanently resided on the farm. His job was to handle the entire breeding and veterinarian duties. When Bobby hired him full-time, he signed a separate contract along with the normal vet contract that he would be required to keep meticulous records on each animal under his supervision and care, such as lineages, medical flowcharts, complete history and health records for each animal. One copy of his monthly record was forwarded to Indy, while two copies stayed on the farm: one copy staying with the vet, the other given to Bobby.

Juan was amazed at how well the farm was doing since Bobby came aboard as foreman. Bobby took over a mediocre farm with its many problems and turning it around. It had quickly become among the best breeding farms in Kentucky. Thanks to Bobby's drive, and determination, plus help from the vet, Ted, the farm had become a force to be reckoned with.

The Oasis Watering Hole was slowly recovering on its way back from the brink of going under. It too had built a reputation as a of late as a place to drink, but first-class culinary establishment for eating. The restaurant had been a run-of-the-mill restaurant prior to Juan's intervention. By replacing the old manager with Joe, the bartender, it had gained a reputation for being "the place" for eating and drinks. Since Joe became manager, the Oasis did a complete three sixty. Joe, true to his word, had stepped up to the challenge. Joe's first step was hiring new help; running it as a business not a personal cash cow as the former manager had done. The Oasis Watering Hole was muchly improved to the delight of Juan. The monthly statements he now received from Joe proved that.

The organization was once again on firm footing, and Juan felt it was the time he started planning for his own future. He had come a long way from being homeless, with one thing on his mind, staying alive. He had become one of the more prominent businesspersons in town, with moxie among his peers. Everyone looked up to him as one of the best organizers of businesses in town. He was called on frequently for his opinion by local businessmen in and around Indianapolis, having gained a solid reputation as the go-to man. He had a knack at sorting out complex problems that cropped up from time to time by those who valued his opinion. He had succeeded where many before him failed.

Becky, also pleased with Juan and what he accomplished since Ivan's passing, often sharing her assessment of him to others.

Now the association back on solid footing heading in the right direction; allowed himself to indulge in daydreaming about the life he often fantasized for himself.

First on his bucket list, own his own condo. He decided to look around and see what was available in and around downtown Indy. It took several days looking in order to locate the right unit. It was in his price range and would not break the bank.

On the day he purchased the condo, he approached Sheila after returning to work and told her, "I've purchased a condo and would like to know if you would do me the honors in decorating it?"

"But of course, I would be honored, but with the hope when I'm finished, you are pleased."

"Great, you can start today. Have Johnny Leopold drive you, and start shopping around to see what's available. Here's some money. If you need more, here is a signed blank check."

Juan then handed her a set of keys to the condo to check it out first in order to get a feel at what type of furnishings are needed.

Before leaving the office, she spoke to Johnny about driving her about town to shop for furniture for Juan's condo. Johnny was more than happy to oblige since he was not busy. Johnny left the office to retrieve the car from the garage, drove back to the office where he found Sheila waiting outside. She got in the back seat and off they went. Johnny drove her to several furniture stores where she purchased a few pieces of high-end furniture. Before leaving each store, she made arrangements with the companies to deliver the purchases to the condo the following day. After her afternoon of shopping, Johnny drove her back to the office.

On her return to the office, Sheila entered Juan's office, telling him of her purchases. The furniture was going to be delivered around nine o'clock the following morning to the condo. Juan was pleased with her description and selection.

He told her, "I want you to meet the delivery people as the furniture arrives and have them place the items where you think each piece belongs."

She said to Juan, "If it's all right with you, I'll have Johnny drive me to the condo first thing in the morning after I receive their call. That way, I'll be there when they arrive."

"Fine, just make sure none of the furniture is damaged. If you find it's damaged, return it."

"I'll make sure it's not left at the condo if scratched or dented."

Juan, out of the blue, asked Sheila, "Would you have dinner with me again this evening?"

"Yes, what time?"

"Say, around seven thirtyish."

"I'll be ready. We can discuss more about what else is needed at the condo while we are having dinner."

"Good idea," Juan said. After the dinner date drove back to his apartment. After arriving at the apartment, Juan asked Sheila if she would like an after-dinner drink?

"Yes, Drambuie on the rocks if you don't mind."

Juan poured each a nightcap while they continued their discussion about decorating the condo. They talked about what was needed to finish up the condo before Juan moved in. After the nightcap, they proceeded into the bedroom, where they spent the remainder of the night making passionate love. It was the wildest and craziest sex ever for both. It was worth all the dynamism they put into their sexual fantasy, well worth the price paid for their romp in the hay.

At the office the following morning, Juan found himself busy with another problem. Big Sid asked for his help. Big Sid was having a dispute in settling a grievance with an ex-employee. The employee decided to sue him after being fired for a minor infraction at work. It was a small matter, but Big Sid was not savvy as to which route he should take in settling the complaint. After Big Sid's arrival that morning, the first ten minutes was a bullshit session about things in general—what was going on in their professional lives, family, business, etc. After a brief chitchat, they got to the crux of Big Sid's dilemma.

Juan's suggestion was "Hire yourself a good lawyer, explain to him the facts concerning the infraction leading to the employee's dismissal, then let the lawyer handle the rest."

Big Sid was relieved at hearing it was not such a big deal, and all he had to do was turn it over to his lawyer. When finished with their meeting, they decided to go for a cup of coffee and shoot the bull a little longer before returning to work.

Sheila received a call later that morning from one of the delivery services about the furniture she purchased. They told her a truck was on its way and should arrive at the condo by ten thirty and asked if she could be there to meet with the delivery people when they arrived. If so, she should arrive fifteen minutes earlier and inform maintenance to pad the elevator; that would hasten the delivery time. After hanging up the phone, she walked over to Palmer's office and asked him, "Can you spare Johnny again this morning? I'm to meet the delivery truck with the purchases I made yesterday. They are to arrive at the condo around ten thirty."

"Sure, I'm not going to need him anytime soon. I've too much work to do."

"Thanks, Palmer."

Walking back over to where Tony sat, told Johnny, "Johnny, I need you to take me over to the condo this morning. The delivery truck with the purchases I made yesterday will be arriving at ten thirty. I've talked to Palmer, and he gave you the okay to do so."

"Okay, when do we have to be there?"

"We still have about forty-five minutes before they arrive. I'll let you know when it's time."

She then told Tony, "Tell Juan when he returns, I'll be at the condo assisting the delivery of furniture at the condo and will be back to work after it has been delivered."

About that time, Juan walked back into the lobby. As he passed Sheila's desk, she mentioned to him about the delivery later that morning, and that she had to meet the delivery truck at ten thirty. It piqued his interest and told her he would like to tag along to see what she bought.

"When you're ready to leave, let me know," Juan said.

They arrived at the condo around ten fifteen.

When she met the maintenance supervisor, she told him, "Mr. Grajales is having some furniture delivered at ten thirty this morning and needed the elevator padded for the delivery."

"I'll get on it right away and have the elevator ready once your delivery arrives."

"Thank you," Sheila said.

Sheila and Juan walked over to the elevator, rode it up to the penthouse floor, where his unit was located. Alighting from the elevator, they walked across the small circular area separating the two penthouse units on the top floor.

The landing on the top floor was like a small vestibule the owners decorated as they saw fit. This one previously decorated with a beautiful round aqua-colored sofa in the center of the room and large multicolor plant protruding from the center, so large it touched the twelve-foot ceiling. There were several large oriental pictures hanging on the walls, along with four beautiful high-back chairs (also multicolor in design) with lovely carved wooden arms, the two chairs one on each side of the large vestibule. A beautiful round oriental rug lay on the floor, encircling the outer aspects of the round sofa, soft muted stripped wallpaper covered the walls and soft music piped in from Musack emanating from several speakers located throughout the ceiling.

Juan opened the door and entered the condo along with Sheila into a large foyer inside the front door leading off in several directions. They first stopped in the kitchen. Sheila entered and looked around.

Perfect, Sheila thought as she admired the chrome appliances adorning the kitchen.

Juan, in the meantime, walked over to the sliding glass door leading onto the wraparound balcony. He slid the glass door open; Sheila then joined him on the balcony. As they walked around the balcony, they noticed every room had access to the balcony. They proceeded to the edge of the balcony, holding onto the hand rails. Looking down, they saw a small park across the street with a pond and several ducks swimming around its pristine waters. Looking into the distance was like they could see forever; it was almost magical.

Sheila, hearing a faint knock at the entry door, hurried back inside. Opening the front door stood a delivery man in the small lobby holding an invoice. Handing her the invoice, she read the list of furniture and pointing at each item on the list and told him which room each piece was going and where it was to be placed.

Meanwhile, Juan toured the condo, walking into each room admiring his new dig. Sheila had taken control of the delivery, Juan, impressed with the way in which she delegated her authority. She conducted herself well in the midst of the pandemonium swirling around her. It was hectic to say the least as the delivery men were running in and out, shouting, becoming frustrated with the many trips from the truck, loading each piece on to the elevator and then placing each item in the unit.

After the delivery, the maintenance supervisor came by and asked, "Is there anything else being delivered today? If not, I'll remove the padding."

"No, that's all, and I appreciate your help with the delivery."

After the maintenance supervisor left, Sheila and Juan sat down on the new couch to gather their thoughts. As exhausted as Sheila was, she turned to Juan and said, "I think it is time I return to work. I have a lot of work to catch up on when I get back."

He leaned over, kissing her gently on the cheek, and told her, "Thank you for all your help getting the place in some semblance of order before I move in. By the way, I'm very pleased with your purchases."

"I'm happy you approve of my choices. I have several pieces yet to purchase, but I can do that later."

Juan made a call to Johnny at the office. "I need you to bring the car over to the condo and pick up Sheila and me. We need to get back to work," he said and hung up.

CHAPTER 36

Arriving back at the office, Juan learned Dennis had been convicted of involuntary manslaughter and had received the maximum sentence of forty years. The trial was finally over. Juan felt relieved at not having this hanging over his head. He no longer had to worry about the organization being dragged through the mud going forward. That was the last thing he needed after all he had been through lately.

Juan found out from talking to Bobby in Lexington the breeder's group in Indianapolis had been under investigation for months. Apparently, they were participating in unscrupulous dealings involving high-valued breeding horses housed by the association and certain farms associated with them. They were being accused of selling sperm from prized horses throughout their closely knit network of breeders without the owner's permission or knowledge. It was alleged the illegal sperm was being collected and sold on the black market to farms not sanctioned by the owner's association in order to maximize their profits. This illegal activity was not only occurring at the breeder's farm in Indianapolis but also in farms throughout the area. The prohibited activity had been intentionally misdirected to benefit their own best interest, beefing up their own profit at the expense of unsuspecting owners. It was a case of greed, or easy money, versus moral obligation.

So far, the Lexington farm had not been mentioned or known to be involved. It was a matter of time before the corrupt group in Indianapolis filtered down to the Lexington farm housing the fifteen valuable thoroughbreds they kept for the breeders' association back in Indy. In recent days, the breeders' association sent several people down to the farm to remove sperm from certain horses in their care. Bobby was told to by the vet they had consent from the horse's owner. Bobby checked his sign-in sheet and found several persons of interest listed in the indictment had recently visited the farm. The indictment did not come as a surprise to Bobby or Juan. First thing Juan did upon learning of the indictment was call Anthony "Tony" Stefano to find out what was going on and what he knew about the indictment.

When Tony answered his phone, Juan said, "Tony, what the hell's going on with the breeders' association? I've just learned an indictment has been handed down to you and some of the farms associated with your association?"

"Yeah, don't worry about a thing. I'll handle it. It's not the first rodeo I've participated in. The rumors are nothing new. It has happened several times in the past, but this one caught us by surprise, ha ha ha, just hang tight."

"Easy for you to say. The farm in Lexington is the lifeblood of my organization and affects all facets of the associations I'm responsible for."

"Yeah, I know but let me handle it. I'll get back to you as soon as I find out more. Don't get your feathers ruffled."

"Keep me in the loop. Don't want to lose everything I have worked so hard for because of some error in judgment on the breeders' ineptness."

"Later."

Tony hung up his phone, leaving Juan in a quandary not knowing what to do or expect if something happened with the farm in Lexington. Although several farms were listed in the indictment, there was a possibility the Lexington farm could be included at a later date.

Juan called Bobby in Lexington to talk to him about their involvement with the breeders' horses stabled there.

"Bobby, do you think those trips by representatives of the breeders' association from Indy were sent down there under false pretenses in order to remove sperm? I've talked with Tony. He indicated to me the indictment not only alleges their involvement, but possibly any farms affiliated with them."

Bobby having some knowledge of such goings-on at the farm was still stunned to learn this happened right in front of him and on his watch. He told Juan he would keep a tighter rein on events at the farm in the future. And he would keep him posted on all activities involving the breeders' association visiting the farm.

Bobby thanked Juan for calling and told him, "Don't worry, boss. I'll keep a lid on this, will only allow permission if they produce a certified letter from the owner authorizing such activity."

"Yes, call me if you hear any rumors at all that could tie us to the indictment," Juan said, then hung up the phone.

Bobby knew breeders sent couriers down occasionally with a request for Ted the vet to remove sperm from horses boarded through the breeders' association. Bobby was not aware the sperm had been obtained for illegal purposes.

After talking to Juan, he went to find Ted the vet and find out if he was aware of the illegal dealings by the breeders. If he found Ted had been part of the scam, he would be terminated on the spot.

Back in Indy, Juan told the Irishman, "Get the car ready. I need to drive to Lexington today and see Bobby."

After hanging up from talking to Juan, Bobby immediately went to locate Ted. He found Ted doing blood work, testing of one of the horses for a urinary problem. He entered the lab and confronted Ted about the black-market scheme the breeders were running.

Bobby asked him point blank, "Are you involved?"

Ted, after a long and heated argument, eventually confessed he had been working with the breeders' association, profiting along with them by selling sperm on the black market. Later that afternoon Juan arrived at the farm where he learned Bobby had fired Ted after learning of his involvement in the illegal con.

Bobby told Juan that Ted told him, "he had been manipulated by a representative from the breeders' association. They promised to include him in any profit derived from the ill-gotten and illegal sale of the sperm, and not to worry. It was a foolproof operation. They had been doing it for years.

Bobby warned Juan, "Ted told me before he left, he was unaware of blackmailing the organization through me and eventually taking over the farm. But the breeders' association somehow was backdoored, caught red-handed in their own con job along the way."

Juan and Bobby decided they would notify each individual owner of the horses they boarded for the breeders' association, letting them know of the situation on the farm. They needed to know what avenue the owners wanted to take, whether to continue keeping their animals there or move them to a new location. If they choose to keep their animals there, they had to terminate their contract with the breeders' association in Indy and sign a new contract with the farm in Lexington.

Juan and Bobby spent the rest of the day and evening drafting personal letters to each of the owner, with an explanation as to the dire situation concerning the breeders' and the recent indictment handed down. After the letters were written, signed, and sealed, Bobby was to drop the letters off at the local post office the following morning.

Juan and the Irishman returned to Indy the following morning, arriving back in Indy in the afternoon, tired and hungry indulging in a late lunch. After lunch, the Irishman drove Juan to the hotel, dropped him off, then took the car back to the garage, where he parked the car and called it a day.

Juan had had a busy two days and looked forward to a good night's rest before returning to work.

Juan returned to work the following morning and met by Sheila on his way in.

She handed him a message she received by phone late yesterday before leaving. It read as follows:

The breeders' association is scheduled for a hearing in two weeks to hear the charges brought against them and possibly anyone associated with the breeders' group.

This was the first steps in the judicial system—giving the breeders' and their lawyers time to meet and discuss the ramifications of the case and make a plea. The court would determine at that time if it deemed it necessary or not in setting a trial date if the lawyers could not agree in settling the case out of court.

Juan contacted the association's lawyer giving him a heads-up to be ready to represent their side along with other lawyers representing the beleaguered horse owners and multiple farms listed in the indictment. There were a lot of Ts to cross and Is to dot before the prosecution, and defense attorneys would be ready to plead their cases. The lawyers had tons of work to do in the interim preparing for the upcoming hearing. Something always seemed to keep the organization from reaching its fill potential, but Juan was not deterred; he had come this far not to finish the journey.

Before leaving work that evening, Juan approached Sheila and asked, "Would you join me for dinner this evening?"

"Yes, I've been looking forward to being together with you all day. I missed you the last couple of evenings but understood your situation. Yes, dinner tonight would be fine."

"Okay, I'll be at your place around seven. We'll have dinner, then we'll go back to my place afterward for a nightcap and spend the evening together if that is okay with you?"

"But of course, it is okay with me. I'm looking forward to another wonderful evening with just the two of us." "That's settled. See you at seven."

After closing the shop, Juan dropped Sheila off at her apartment, then had the Irishman drive him to the hotel for a quick shower and dressed for dinner. He too looked forward to a nice, quiet dinner, and an evening alone with Sheila. He found himself preoccupied thinking of her recently; she had become an obsession. He'd never had such feelings for anyone as he had for Sheila. She was on his mind always ever since the first time being with her. She was everything that's right, making his life come full circle and complete.

What was it about her that was so different from the other women he had known and dated? He seemed at peace with himself when around her. She was all he ever wanted or needed and more.

Why was she so magnetic?

Her looks?

Her demeanor?

Her character?

She had all the attributes he fantasized in a soul mate.

They arrived at dinner a little after seven thirty. When they were seated, out of the corner of his eye, he spotted Becky. She was having dinner with Tony Stefano, wondering to himself, What does those two have in common? Why were they together? He'd call tomorrow. This was beyond his wildest imagination, something he'd never dreamed of. Was something going on that he had not been aware of? It did not add up. The more he questioned seeing them together, the more confused he became.

After Tony and Becky finished dinner, they left together. Luckily, they had not seen him with Sheila. He was glad; it would have been an awkward situation for all concerned.

He'd get to the bottom of this tomorrow after arriving at work. Juan and Sheila finished dinner, then had the Irishman drive them to Juan's apartment where they were dropped off.

Once inside the apartment, Juan offered Sheila a drink, where she immediately said, "You bet, I need a drink after that delicious meal. I want to thank you for a lovely dinner, I owe you a big tip, which I'll give you later. That is, if you think you can handle it?"

That small innuendo got Juan excited and aroused immediately. Juan looked forward to the tip Shelia promised once they entered the bedroom. What was it she could do to make him more stimulated or aroused than he was already? Whatever she had in mind, how could he go above number 10 on the anticipation chart?

He was to the point of premature ejaculation already without the sex. Still in control, but just barely. It was becoming more difficult with each passing minute; it was extremely painful and exhausting trying to hold back.

In a heated exchange of fondling again on the uncomfortable couch. Somehow, they were able to finish their drinks, eventually making their way into the bedroom, where they finished undressing and crawled in between the cool, clean white sheets of the kingsize bed. Beginning another night of ecstasy and absolute euphoria, which came into play rather quickly. The joy of lovemaking began the moment they were in the bed. Suddenly Sheila reached down and slowly began massaging his private area. Closing his eyes, clenching his teeth, trying to block out what she was doing to him. It was impossible to think of anything else; what she was doing sent him into orbit.

Soon her hot, moist mouth replaced her hand, and slowly she introduced his stiff shaft to the warm and moist cavity of her mouth as she moved up and down it, stimulating him even more. The exhilaration of the warmth, the movements of her tongue was more than he could stand.

Suddenly, no longer able to control his embarrassment as he prematurely ejaculated due to his feeling of euphoria. Once reaching this point along with his throbbing shaft, she continued her methodical movements until he finished. After removing herself from his now diminishing soft shaft, she looked up at him and asked, "Was the tip sufficient?"

"Oh, yes, if you had given me a larger tip, I would not be able to reciprocate, ha ha."

While looking up at Juan, she smiled and said, "Clue, all you have to do is make love to me the same way, that will validate the tip."

"You. got. it."

She shifted up from between his legs and lying next to him, she spread eagle. He rolled over on top of her, slowly begin working his way down her now perspiring soft, hot body. Lowering his head as he moved south, he kissed her firm breasts as he inched farther down her body. Both bodies were moving in unison as he kissed her feverishly on his descent south of the border. As he moved slowly down her firm, tense body, her eyes now closed, breathing was becoming heavier. Gently, she reached down encasing his head in her hands, positioning it between her legs where it was most appreciated.

Once in position, he slowly spread open the moist, soft, flexible labia or lips of her vaginal opening surrounding the clitoris with his fingers as he slowly inserted his hot moist tongue. Moving his head up and down along the inner and outer walls with his tongue extended to its full capacity. She guided his head, coaching him to all the right places. Once positioned correctly, she released her hold. She now began gyrating, contorting her body to receive the most pleasure. Breathing uncontrollably, she raised and arched her back, moaning as she held a pillow wrapped around her head to keep from screaming. Soon she let go of the pillow, reached down and aggressively pulled his head harder against her. She felt the same frenzy and exhilaration he experienced only a short time before. After what seemed like hours, she reached down, lifting his head up off her now-throbbing body, directing him back where they once again embraced and continued making love. After having sex a couple more times that evening, they called it a night, still embracing as they slowly drifted off to sleep.

CHAPTER 37

The next morning, as they awoke, they looked at each other in an entirely different light. At that moment in time as their eyes met, they knew they were one, inseparable, partners for life.

Once they were up and dressed, they met the Irishman in the lobby and followed him outside to the waiting car. The feeling they had for each other that morning was a silent bond or covenant sealed for all eternity.

Arriving at work, Sheila stopped at her desk as Juan continued walking over to say hello to Tony and Johnny, who arrived earlier and was sitting at the table talking. Speaking briefly to them, he continued to Palmer's office to find out how he was coming along with the accounting fiasco, and if he discovered new problems that he should be made aware of.

Palmer said as Juan entered his office, "Things seem to be shaping up. I think I have found most of the glitches and ninety-nine percent of the accounts are up to date. I can see light at the end of the tunnel, although it's been a long week looking for mismanaged funds along with the clerical errors, finally I have a handle on it."

"I'm glad to hear that. You've done a terrific job, and I intend on rewarding you for a job well done. The organization needs more dedicated people like you. I hope this did not sway you into leaving. I need you to stay and help me keep the organization on the straight and narrow."

"You don't have to worry about me leaving. I have no intentions of leaving anytime soon. Just glad I could be of service. If there is anything else I can do, just let me know."

"I appreciate your accomplishment in the short time you've been here. We as an organization could not have done it without you."

Juan left Palmer and gravitated into his office where he closed the door. He walked over to his desk, sat down, and reached for the phone to call Becky.

"Hello, Cohens' residence, Becky speaking."

"Good morning, Becky, Juan here. I wanted to touch base with you this morning to ask you if there was anything going on that we need to discuss. I was having dinner last evening when I happened to spot you and Tony Stefano in the restaurant. Is there something going on we need to talk about?"

"No, nothing's going. It happened purely by accident meeting at the restaurant so we decided to have dinner together."

"Well, you know the situation caused by him and his group accused of illegally collecting sperm from horses they house not only in Indy but the farm in Lexington and selling it? I don't think it's a good idea to be seen socially with him, especially at this time. I'm sure you understand what I'm saying and how it might be perceived to an outsider?"

"Yes, I'm well aware of the indictment but did not give it a second thought as we met upon entering the restaurant. It was a spur of the moment thing."

"Is this the first time meeting him since Ivan's passing or have you two seen each other on other occasions I'm not aware of?"

"We've kept in touch, that's all."

"If there is something between the two of you that's your business, but we do not need attention directed our way because of familiarity you have with Tony. Do you catch my drift?"

"I'll watch myself more closely after this."

"Good, have a nice day. I'll talk to you later."

Juan hung up the phone and immediately called Tony to confront him at seeing the two of them together last evening.

Tony answered his phone.

"Good morning, Tony. I'll get to the point. I'm calling about seeing you and Becky having dinner last evening. Did you meet her casually or unexpectantly at the restaurant? Or is there some deeper, underlying reason why you two were together? What's the story?"

"First off, I don't think it is any of your damn business what we do in private. I suggest in the future you keep your nose out of my business, capisce?"

"I see, so I can assume you two are more than acquaintances. I would appreciate if you stopped seeing her while this indictment is looming over our heads, the one you so conveniently had us drawn into."

"I'll see who I want and do what I want, so back off and go peddle your concerns elsewhere and hung up."

This did not bode well with Juan; he was caught between a rock and hard place once again. On one hand, he and Becky were business partners, and Tony the menace was becoming a determent to their business.

Somehow, Juan had to persuade Becky to stop meeting with Tony, who could cause major roadblocks ahead if the breeders went to trial and were found guilty.

More than likely she would be called to testify at trial since she was somehow involved with Tony. Juan saw them more than just friends. He was sure they would present a moral dilemma for the association if she testified. No matter what happened as this debacle plays out, it would cause Juan great concern over the future of the organization.

What was he to do now?

Juan had to find out what this extracurricular activity between Becky and Tony was before it blew up in his face, and the organization became trapped in a no-win situation. He called Jimmy Kapos, the foreman at the breeder' farm.

"Hello, Jimmy Kapos."

"Yes, good morning, Jimmy. This is Juan."

"Hi, Juan, how are you this morning? Long time since I've heard from you."

"Yes, it's been a while. The reason for my call this morning is to ask you if you have any information you could tell me concerning Becky and Tony's relationship? I need to know if they were more than acquaintances or is there more to their relationship that I'm aware of? Was hoping you could fill me in if there was more or if you're aware of something going on between those two?"

"I know personally they've been seeing each more since Ivan's passing, more so now than when Ivan was alive."

"You mean they were seeing each other while Ivan was alive?"

"Yes, they've been seeing each other privately for some time. Never understood why Ivan never caught on. Guess, he was too busy running his organization."

"Do you know of or have you heard of them discussing combining the two farms?"

"As a matter of fact, yes. I overheard Tony and one of his partners discussing something about him and Becky removing you from the partnership, so they could combine the two farms. I never knew how they were going to pull it off, but have a better understanding since Ivan's passing, and Becky now has a controlling interest in the business. If I were you, I would tread lightly around her and watch those two closely. She is not the docile person she projects herself to be. She can be very vindictive when push comes to shove. Believe me, I know. I've seen her in action. She is smarter than anyone gives her credit, even Tony better watch his step around her. She may turn on him, who knows? Once she has her claws in you, it is just a matter of time before dragging you into her lair and finishes you off."

"Thanks, Jimmy, you've been a real help. If there is anything I can do for you, you can always count on me, but I don't have to tell you that do I?"

Juan hung up and called Becky back, asking her if they could meet for lunch and discuss some troubling issues he felt should be aired out between them before it got out of hand. He left it there and said no more.

His intentions were to find out about her and Tony's relationship and her future plans concerning the association.

She had a sneaking suspicion what Juan was really after, but she reluctantly agreed to meet him at the Italian Villa that same afternoon to discuss their differences.

Juan arrived a little early in order to find a table where they could talk privately over lunch. When Becky arrived, she was shown to the table where Juan waited patiently.

As she approached, Juan stood up and said, "Good afternoon, Becky, please sit down."

"Thank you. I'm happy you decided on this place. I have not been here since Ivan's passing. It was one of his favorite places. Now what is it you wanted to talk to me about?"

"Since the farm hypothetically could be included in the indictment concerning the breeders' association. I think it would be wise that you stop seeing Tony until this accusation with his organization is over. If his group is found guilty of the charges stated in the indictment, Tony and his entire association will be out of business. If for some reason, Tony cuts a deal with the prosecution and it backfires, you may be brought up on charges as well. I think you should cut all ties with him, protecting yourself and your children from further embarrassment, and possibly the loss of the farm. I'm telling you this for your own good. Take my advice or leave it, it's your decision. I will abide by whatever you decide."

"I think I know what I'm doing, and if you don't stop meddling in my private affairs, I'll have no choice but replace you. Is that understood?"

"Yes, I understand what you are saying, but it doesn't work like that. If you remember I still own forty-nine percent of the business. You cannot just up and fire me like that. If I were you, I would think long and hard about what you are doing to yourself, your family, and the association Ivan worked so hard to build for you and the family. There are a lot of people depending on your decision, just hope you make the right one."

"I think our discussion is over. I'm leaving now. You can go back to work. I will give some serious thought to what you said, and when I reach my decision, I'll call you."

Becky got up from the table without saying another word, turned and walked out, leaving Juan perplexed and confused at what the future held not only for himself but the organization.

This came as a complete surprise to Juan that Becky was such a bitch. After she left, he ordered lunch and afterward returned to work.

When he returned to his office, he called Steven Wasserman, the association's attorney.

"Good afternoon, Steven, this is Juan. I need some legal advice concerning my contract with Becky. I need to know what legal options I have maintaining my status as a partner running the business. Am I within my rights as an equal partner in rebuffing any accusation thrown my way interfering with her and Tony's arrangement combining the two farms?"

"I can't give you an answer right now. I'll need to read over the original contract signed by Ivan and the breeders' association. Also, the partnership agreement you signed with Mrs. Cohen after Ivan's demise I need to look at it and see if she has any legal authority terminating the contract on such trivial grounds. It would surprise me she had any legal authority at all to do that. Give me a week or so to read over the contract. If there's anything besides death of an individual partner, consensual agreement to end the partnership between parties, or buy-out. Those are the basic things written in a silent partnership if I remember correctly. Just to tell you, if she was going to somehow get rid of you, no court in the country would consider such a threat. Let me get to work on it, and I'll contact you as soon as I have something substantial to report back. Until then, don't worry. I think she is just blowing smoke up her ass."

"Thanks, Steven, I'll be waiting for your assessment concerning legal ramifications I'm faced with. Can't believe she's threatening me. After all I've done for her and her family since Ivan's passing. Guess you never know people until push comes to shove, do you?"

"No, you hit the nail on the head. That's when you see the true colors surface. I've seen it a thousand times, and it's never a pretty sight," Steven told Juan.

Weeks passed, the hearing was drawing closer. Everyone was getting edgy, anxiously awaiting to learn what charges were being considered against the breeders' association. Juan talked to Attorney.

Steven Wasserman occasionally during the interim, and all he could tell Juan was, "You have no reason to worry, looking over the organization's records, I find nothing out of line or suspicious, as far as the farm in Lexington handled its business. Everything seemed to be on the up-and-up down there.

"Things should work out in your favor, but Becky and Tony, that's another story. There is too much evidence linking those two with collusion. I'm afraid they may both go down. We will have to wait and let the facts speak for themselves."

The day finally arrived for the preliminary hearing; the prosecution and defense attorneys presented their briefs to the judge. The judge, aware of all the facts presented by the two opposing attorneys representing this case, asked both sides after hearing their arguments if they would be injecting new exculpatory evidence or motions later. If so, they should declare it now before continuing.

The prosecution and defense attorneys both answered in the negative, "No, Your Honor, no future evidence or motions."

The judge set the hearing for the following Monday, telling the attorneys present, "If there are no further evidence or motions in this case, this hearing is adjourned until Monday morning at nine o'clock, at which time, we'll begin with jury selection. I have a list of potential jurors to be considered. That will be the first thing on my docket when we reconvene Monday morning."

The judge rose from his seat and exited the courtroom.

On Monday morning at nine o'clock, the prosecution and defense attorneys were each given a list of potential jurors to be interviewed by both judge and/or attorneys to determine the competency and suitability of potential jurors to serve in this case.

It took three days in which to select the jurors along with extra jurors, in case a juror was removed for reasons the judge deemed necessary. Once the jury was empaneled, the judge set the trial date for the following Tuesday at nine o'clock.

At which time, he told the court, "This court is in recess until Tuesday morning at nine o'clock."

This was being touted as one of the biggest court cases in Indianapolis for years. The case had all the attributes of drama, intrigue, mob affiliation, dark secrets, everything required in a high-profile case; something of interest for everyone.

The day the trial began, the courtroom was filled to capacity with reporters and spectators. As the hours and days passed, the jurors, reporters, and onlookers learned more about corruption, vice, exploitation, manipulation, and sleaze than they were able to assimilate. It showed just how the underworld coexisted under the radar while conducting business as usual within the real world.

As the list of witnesses narrowed, Becky was eventually called as a witness for the defense. She was sworn in and took the witness stand. The defense's opening statement painted her as a saint, telling a heartrending story about her loving husband Ivan, his trials and tribulations in running a mediocre business with little or no assistance.

She herself was portrayed as living a lonely, secluded life as a homemaker and mother of two while her beloved husband, Ivan, worked twenty-four seven just to make ends meet.

Once the prosecution began cross-examination of Becky, it became apparent she was not the sweet, innocent person as portrayed by the defense. The prosecution poked holes in every answers she gave the defense, they not only reflected back in her unbelievable answers but also pointed out to the jury her secret life with Tony Stefano. The jury was not swayed by anything she said at this point in the trial; they, too, saw the evil in her heart and eyes. It showed with her malcontent at the prosecution's questions, and it showed through her facial expressions when confronted.

She had a problem from the get-go, getting her story straight as she sat in the witness's chair being questioned by the prosecutor. She constantly denied questions by the prosecuting attorney or fabricated answers to justify her statement or blatantly lied. She began digging herself a hole the minute she began testifying. She was unbelievable as a witness from the onset. Coming across as belligerent, self-centered, and argumentative, the jury was stunned by her ragtag testimony and behavior on the witness stand. After the prosecution finished with their cross examination, the judge excused her telling her not to leave town she may be asked to return for further questioning. As she left the courtroom, she turned to face Tony and winked as if she had done well with her testimony.

The defense next called Tony Stefano to the witness stand. He was sworn in and seated.

The defense attorney began by saying, "Good afternoon, Mr. Stefano. I would like to begin by asking you a few questions about where it is you work and what it is you do. Would you describe your duties and responsibilities to the jury?"

"Yes, I'm the CEO of the Breeders' Association Farm, located north of Indianapolis. I run the entire operation with the help of two assistants, Tom Lawry and Mack McDavitt, whom you questioned previously."

"What is your main concern or objective as you run the day-today business at the farm?"

"Making sure request of owners of the animals in my care are strictly adhered to."

"What do you mean by that statement?"

"I make sure whatever the owners want or needs are provided as per our charter governing the association."

"So as CEO of the breeder association, it is your job running the farm according to a charter which holds you and the association to the highest standards of a breeding farm, is that fair to say?"

"Yes, more or less. I do much more, but it comes with the job description and territory. I schedule and conduct meetings for the horse owners, investors, hire and fire individuals. I occasionally have to dismiss unscrupulous purveyors when brought to my attention. I keep meticulous records of each transaction and most importantly a detailed genealogy record between horses used for studding. I'm involved on occasions in scheduling sperm collection, making arrangements for delivery to recipients at other farms in our network. My plate is full as you can see by the many hats I wear."

"One last question, Mr. Stefano, before I finish. Do you have knowledge of any employee/employees selling or distributing sperm under the table or under false pretenses? Or have you personally been not to leave town she may be asked to return for further questioning. As she left the courtroom, she turned to face Tony and winked as if she had done well with her testimony. The defense next called Tony Stefano to the witness stand. He was sworn in and seated. The defense attorney began by saying, "Good afternoon, Mr. Stefano. I would like to begin by asking you a few questions about where it is you work and what it is you do. Would you describe your duties and responsibilities to the jury?" "Yes, I'm the CEO of the Breeders' Association Farm, located north of Indianapolis. I run the entire operation with the help of two assistants, Tom Lawry and Mack McDavitt, whom you questioned previously." "What is your main concern or objective as you run the day-today business at the farm?" "Making sure request of owners of the animals in my care are strictly adhered to." "What do you mean by that statement?" "I make sure whatever the owners want or needs are provided as per our charter governing the association." "So as CEO of the breeder association, it is your job running the farm according to a charter which holds you and the association to the highest standards of a breeding farm, is that fair to say?" "Yes, more or less. I do much more, but it comes with the job description and territory. I schedule and conduct meetings for the horse owners, investors, hire and fire individuals. I occasionally have to dismiss unscrupulous purveyors when brought to my attention. I keep meticulous records of each transaction and most importantly a detailed genealogy record between horses used for studding. I'm involved on occasions in scheduling sperm collection, making arrangements for delivery to recipients at other farms in our network. My plate is full as you can see by the many hats I wear." "One last question, Mr. Stefano, before I finish. Do you have knowledge of any employee/employees selling or distributing sperm under the table or under false pretenses? Or have you personally been

involved in collecting or distributed for your own personal profit or gain sperm without the knowledge or consent of owners?"

"Absolutely not, I run a tight organization. I would be aware of any such transaction on my watch."

"That's all the questions I have for Mr. Stefano at this time, Your Honor. I may want to recall Mr. Stefano to the witness stand later, Your Honor."

The judge turned to the prosecution, "Do you wish to question Mr. Stefano at this time?"

"Yes, Your Honor."

"Proceed."

As the prosecutor approached Mr. Stefano on the witness stand, he started by saying, "Good morning, Mr. Stefano."

"Good morning, sir."

"Mr. Stefano, I would like to start by asking, How long have you been employed by the breeder' association?"

"A little over five years if memory serves me correctly."

"Have you or any the breeders' association been accused of selling or profiteering from dispensing or selling illegally obtained sperm of animals left in your care, without knowledge or consent of the owner?"

"No, absolutely not."

"Is it not true you have been cited within the last two years for a similar violation?"

"Uh, I don't remember. I may have received such a notice, but don't recall receiving a violation concerning such an incident, Counselor. I receive a lot of correspondence and mails daily. I may have possibly received such a document but does not ring a bell at this time. The document could possibly have slipped through the cracks, who knows?"

"Mr. Stefano, I would like to reference the charter the breeder association is doing business under. Does it not clearly state the association is to abide by all rules and regulations stated within?"

"Yes, I believe it does." "Then why have you and the association been accused of violating that charter?"

"There have been allegations in the past, but after a thorough investigation, we were found not guilty of any such violation."

"Was it because the violations were somehow dropped?"

"Yes, that's correct."

"But in this case, more mitigating evidence has come to light, in which several witnesses have stepped forward to testify. What happened in the past was just a prelude to what you and your association have been practicing all along. Isn't that right, Mr. Stefano?

"It's only hearsay, Counselor. I know nothing about this accusation you're referring to."

"Okay, Mr. Stefano, you stated earlier your job was making sure the owners and their animals under your care were your first priority or major concern, correct?"

"Yes, absolutely."

"Okay, give us an example of what services you consider would be a priority request, let's say, from an owner."

"Yes, if an owner requested transfer of sperm from the breeders' farm to a farm outside our boundaries to another location, I make sure it is done in a timely manner, according to the owner's wishes and in complete compliance with other charters and laws governing such transfers. But if a local owner requests transfer of sperm from a donor to a recipient within our network, I personally witness the removal of the sperm from the donor horse. This way, making sure it's done right, then I send the owner/owners the results of the transfer."

"I see, Mr. Stefano. Is there any chance while doing such a process, when you or someone else possibly retrieve extra sperm from the particular donor animal, then sell it on the black market unbeknownst to the owner?"

"I guess, anything is possible, but certainly not ethical, that's not how I conduct business."

"So, Mr. Stefano, you are admitting to the court there is a possibility of collecting extra sperm and the extra sperm could be set aside and dispensed illegally later?"

"I'm sure, it's a reasonable assumption, but I personally would never do that."

"Okay, Mr. Stefano, let me move on to my next question. Do you know a Mrs. Becky Cohen?"

"Yes, I've had the privilege of knowing her and her husband, Ivan Cohen, for several years."

"Was there a time before her husband's passing, she had a reason to visit the farm you oversee, alone? To see you or talk to you? Let's say, about certain aspects of running a breeding farm or social visit?"

"I can't recall if she ever came alone to the farm without her husband's knowledge, or of her inquiring about how I ran a breeding farm."

"Then are you saying your recollection of her being at the farm alone without her husband is unclear in your mind at this time? As you remember, she was always accompanied by her husband when she came to the farm."

"Yes, I think that's accurate. I saw her and Ivan on several occasions when they visited the farm on business."

"When they visited the farm, was it always business?"

"Strictly business, Ivan and I were fierce competitors in the business. We were always competing to get the upper hand on business dealings that interested us."

"So you're saying your relationship with the Cohens was strictly business, never social, is that correct?"

"Correct, Counselor."

"After Mr. Cohen's demise, was there ever a time Mrs. Cohen came calling for any other reason than business, say, a social visit?"

"Not to my recollection."

"Was there ever a time you discussed with Mrs. Cohen about the selling of sperm without the knowledge of the owners of horses in your care?"

"No, why would I jeopardize my integrity and position by doing such a thing? I run a tight ship and no way would I risk losing the charter. It's my obligation to abide by the rules and regulations stated within that document.

"Then, you're saying [under oath] you or your association is not guilty of the charges listed against you in this indictment?"

"Absolutely."

At this point the judge decided it was time to stop the hearings, telling the jury and attorneys, "Before proceeding further, I think this is a good place to stop and break for lunch. We'll continue with Mr. Stefano's testimony when court convenes after lunch."

Returning from lunch, the judge called the court to order, and the questioning by the prosecution continued.

"Good afternoon again, Mr. Stefano."

"Afternoon, Counselor."

"Mr. Stefano, I want to refresh your memory by asking a few questions we discussed prior to breaking for lunch. I was about to ask you, Do you recall the last time you met with Mrs. Cohen? Was it a social or business meeting? Have you talked to any of your staff or business associates about trying to take over the farm in Lexington owned by the association Mrs. Cohen is the major shareholder? And last, has your association been accused in the past selling sperm without permission of the owner/owners?"

"Uh, I don't recall. Hold on! Yes, I vaguely remember a couple of years back a horse owner in southern Indiana accused the association of removing sperm from one of his prized horses left in our care."

"Is it not true your association was caught red-handed selling it to a farm adjacent the farm in southern Indiana? Does that ring a bell, Mr. Stefano?"

"Yes, sort of, I recall a request from an owner living in the southern Indiana who asked for sperm from one of the horses on the farm here in Indianapolis. If memory serves me correctly, we did the extraction which I was sure was sanctioned by the owner. Don't remember much else about the transfer, after all, that's what we do."

"Yes, I understand that's the nature of your business, but only with the owner's permission, correct?"

"Well, yes."

"Let me ask you one more time if you ever willingly sold sperm from horses in your care for your own profit or profit to enhance the bottom line of your association?"

"No, why would I risk my integrity or the association's reputation by doing such a thing?"

(He, too, was as unbelievable as Becky as witness.)

"Lastly, Mr. Stafano, let me ask you, once again for the record, Have you ever been a willing participant in selling sperm to benefit your own needs or suspected of wrongdoings during the time you've been employed by the Breeders' Association?"

"No."

Once again perjuring himself. The jury keenly aware of his persona, once again grimaced at his responses.

"Before finishing, Your Honor, I have a couple more questions I would like to ask Mr. Stefano."

"Continue, Counselor."

"Thank you, Your Honor."

"Mr. Stefano, since you and Mrs. Cohen are basically in the same business, have you ever approached her about joining forces combining the two farms?"

"Not that I remember."

"It has been brought to the attention of the court, Mr. Stefano, on several occasions in the past, you and Mrs. Becky Cohen have been seen together discussing certain aspects of your businesses. Is this true?"

"No, we may have been seen together talking business, but not about merging the farms."

"We've acquired a letter recently sent from Mrs. Cohen to you that she was ready to proceed with your suggestion accusing Bobby Baker and Juan Grajales, along with their accountant Jim Logan of altering the books at the farm for their own benefit. If Mrs. Cohen follows through with her allegations, it would give her ample reason for breaking her contract with Mr. Juan Grajales, is that correct?"

"Yes, it would be sufficient evidence breaking any contract I believe."

"Of course, allegations of mismanagement would only hold up in court if Mrs. Cohen could prove maladministration on the part of the accountant and collusion with Mr. Baker and Mr. Grajales, is that not also true, Mr. Stefano?"

"Yes, I believe so, Counselor."

"If successful, Mrs. Cohen's accusation of mismanagement, she would become sole proprietor of the farm in Lexington, is that not correct?"

"I'm not familiar with the letter in question, but if what you say is true, Mrs. Cohen could possibly become sole owner of the farm in question."

"Mr. Stefano, I think if you wish not to perjure yourself, you may want to rethink some of your answers to my questions."

"Again, Counselor, I'm not aware of the letter you are referring to."

"Okay, Mr. Stefano, let me move on. Since Mrs. Cohen wrote a letter to you of her intentions to accuse Mr. Grajales, Mr. Baker, and Jim Logan of collusion, would this not give you and her free rein to draw up the necessary paperwork and combine forces. This would eliminate any future worries about who owned the farm in Lexington, correct? You and Mrs. Cohen would be home free to do as you please with the farms no longer needing to hide your ongoing relationship. Is that correct, Mr. Stefano? I'll ask one more time, Mr. Stefano, so we are crystal clear on the subject of the letter. Did you receive such a letter from Mrs. Becky Cohen, Mr. Stefano?"

"As I stated earlier, Counselor, I receive a lot of correspondence daily from owners, breeders, and business associates. I deal with lots of people every day. Do you expect me to remember every note, letter, or correspondence or meeting I've had in the past?"

"No, Mr. Stefano, but I would expect you to remember this particular piece of correspondence since it concerned such important information. And especially since it came from Mrs. Cohen whom you both had big ideas about what you two were going to do when she became sole owner of the farm in Lexington."

"Well, I don't keep close company with her as you have alleged. We've never discussed combining the farms. It's just she and I are good friends, that is the extent of the relationship."

"No more questions at this time, Your Honor."

"The witness may step down," the judge said. Tony stepped down from the witness stand, and as he turned to the jury, he smiled as if to say, "You are all a bunch of idiots to think I would admit to anything the defense counselor asked me on the witness stand. I'm smarter than that, don't you know that by now?" thinking to himself he showed them with his superficial commentary while on the witness stand how smart he really was. Or at least thought he so.

He turned from the jury as he swaggered slowly back to his seat next to his attorney, who patted him on the back and whispered, "Good job, Tony."

The jury saw his smugness before, during, and after his testimony, and the attaboy look from his attorney and the congratulatory pat on the back. All this showmanship by Tony and his attorney was now deeply implanted in the jury's minds. They would remember his arrogance and transparency once inside the deliberating room.

He was under the impression he outsmarted them all, but they saw through his thin armor as he tried portraying himself as the good guy. He had not fooled anyone with his egotism or conceit, only enhanced it. He did not realize how shallow his appearance had been in the eyes of the jury, the judge, and gallery. It was evident in his actions and persona he was a cocky, overrated thug. He was totally out of his element in the courtroom among his peers. He was not this dynamic character with charisma, just a superficial con man with big brass kahunas. A real nobody who would sell his mother to the devil if it meant making a profit.

The judge stated it was getting late and he was going to adjourn court for the day. Looking over at both the prosecutor and defense attorneys, he reminded them, "Now, the evidence has been presented to the jury, you should be prepared to deliver your final arguments tomorrow morning to the jury at nine o'clock."

The judge asked both the prosecution and defense if they had any unfinished business pertaining to this case that they needed to take care of before adjournment. Both indicated they had no more witnesses and were finished.

With that, the judge announced, "I would like to see the attorneys in my office after court, to go over a few things before tomorrow's closing arguments. Court is adjourned until nine tomorrow morning."

The judge stood up and walked out of the courtroom, heading to his chambers in order to get ready for closing arguments briefing. The judge would pass on to each lawyer instructions as to what he intended on giving the jury and inform the lawyers to relate to the jury only issues used in the case, not issues outside the case or evidence not presented during trial.

Once final arguments were given and final briefing by the judge to the lawyers was done, the next procedure by the judge was to sequester the jury and for them to render their verdict.

As far as Juan was concerned, the defense had hastily prepared their witnesses and case; it had been a joke. The witnesses they called to testify were unbelievable, untrustworthy, and definitely unscrupulous. The jury along with the judge saw through their thinly veiled defense. The witnesses the defense attorneys assembled were a ragtag of unbelievable characters, a fiasco from the beginning to the end.

Tony, with the evidence stacked against him and the sloppy way the defense delivered their case, had finally come to an end. Tony had tainted the breeders' charter, which was coveted by the breeders was all but destroyed. All because of his own obvious thirst for money and power. Running the breeders' business, he eroded the base on which it was built.

He had absolutely no understanding of consequences of his actions when he began his deceitful undertaking of selling the product he was in charge of or accountable for. He could not see far enough ahead to visualize the consequences of his own actions and greed. It seemed innocent enough in the beginning, but complex and highly volatile at the end. Tony's greed had become so controlling over the years; the desire for wealth and power was overwhelming, eventually leading to his downfall.

CHAPTER 38

It did not take the jury long after entering the deliberation room to determine Tony's innocent or guilty verdict. Only three hours into the deliberation, the jury found him guilty on all charges. The jury returned to the courtroom where the jury foreman handed the bailiff the verdict, who handed it to the judge. The judge read the verdict silently to himself and handed it back to the bailiff, who returned it to the jury foreman. The judge asked the foreman to read aloud the verdict to the court.

"We, the jury, find the accused Mr. Tony Stefano, guilty on all charges."

There was a momentary outburst in the courtroom, but the judge quelled it quickly as he hammered his gavel on the desk. After the court settled back down, the judge thanked the jury for their attentiveness and veracity in the case. Without further fanfare, he released the jury and told them he would render his decision on the sentencing phase within the next two weeks.

At the end of the two weeks, the judge would return to court. Once court resumed, the judge would rendered his decision. He gave Mr. Tony Stefano seven years in prison and a hundred thousand dollars fine to compensate those horse owners for their losses.

After the sentencing phase of Mr. Tony Stefano, the judge then turned to the attorneys, asking, "Does the defense or prosecution team have other information or business relating to this case? If not, court's adjourned."

Juan and Bobby learned of the verdict and were elated the court found Tony Stefano and breeders' association guilty on all counts. They could now continue business as usual without this dirty cloud hanging over them.

It was a time for celebration.

Back at the office, Juan gathered his staff together and invited them over to the Oasis Watering Hole to celebrate the guilty verdict. That afternoon was followed by eating, drinking, and celebrating now the eight-hundred-pound gorilla had been lifted from their backs. And life as they knew it returned.

The next morning, Bobby met Juan in his office before returning to Lexington. He and Juan had a long and constructive conversation concerning the farm, and now it was time to get back to work. Juan phoned Becky to talk about what type of arrangement they could make concerning the business relationships both were invested in.

Becky answered, "Hello, this is Becky Cohen. Who is calling?"

"Becky, this is Juan. I've called to discuss a very touchy subject. We need to talk about some sort of amicable arrangement as to our shared partnership in the organization. I want to begin by saying I'm sorry what happened, but I think it turned out better than either of us expected. Sorry you had to be dragged into it, but you were warned it could happen.

"So, with that said, I personally think you should step aside. As you know, I have been running this business without your help since Ivan died. You have been sitting on the sidelines reaping the benefits of my endeavor, and I've been up front and honest with you throughout this whole ordeal. I'm asking you, partner to partner, to sign over your share of the business to me, so I can run it unencumbered going forward.

"I will still pay you your fair share of the profits as in the past, but without you having any invested interest in the businesses itself. If you agree to my terms, I'll have the attorney draw up the necessary documents signing everything over to me. I will then have him draw a separate document providing ample money to take care of you and your children in the lifestyle you have grown accustomed. I will include a college fund be set aside in their names, but once they graduate, they will cease to be compensated. That's my one and only offer, if you accept it, I will get it started today."

"I don't like what I'm hearing, but at this point, I really have no choice, do I?"

"No, if you want to continue to live your life as you have in the past, I suggest we get this done as soon as possible. I know how you must feel toward me giving you such an ultimatum, but I think it is best for all concerned. You were not looking to the future as this calamity unfolded in front of you. You were relishing only in the moment. If you agree, I'll call the attorney once we hang up and begin the process of getting this settled once and for all. I'll have the attorney's office send you the papers to sign, if you agree to my terms."

"Okay, that will be fine, Juan. I'll sign the documents and send them back as quickly as possible."

"Sorry it had to end this way, but guess things don't always turn out like we anticipate, do they? Accept my apology for going this route, but as we both know, we have no choice."

Juan hung up, then called the attorney to cancel the old contract with Becky, and prepare a new document giving him full and absolute control of the organization. Juan explained he had talked to Becky, and she was agreeable to his ultimatum.

Once Becky received and signed the documents, she relinquished all rights and control concerning the association. It was a difficult decision on Becky's part, but she chose her destiny in this matter with no backup or way out.

After Tony Stefano's incarceration, the breeders' association immediately elected a new CEO from outside of the organization, who quickly made application for the cherished charter to be reinstated. It was a monumental set of hoops to jump through, but the powers in charge decided to reinstate the charter with several new addendums attached.

One morning, as guards, making their rounds at the prison where Tony was incarcerated, checked his cell and found him lying in a pool of his own blood on his cell floor. Tony Stefano had been murdered after serving only two years of his sentence. It was determined he had been stabbed to death with a homemade shank, which eventually was found stuck in one of the sink's drain lines inside his cell. It was never revealed who murdered him or why, and still remained unresolved to this day.

Both Becky's children graduated from Indiana University with honors, and both became successful in their own rights. One now lives in California in Silicon Valley working as a computer analyst; while the other lives in New York as a freelance journalist. Neither married or had children. Becky spent the last remaining years of her life as a recluse and died at the early age of sixty from heart failure, more of a broken heart, if the truth be known. She was buried alongside her husband, Ivan, in Memorial Park Cemetery in Indianapolis.

CHAPTER 39

Juan literally brought the organization he inherited from Ivan from the brink of disaster to become one of the most profitable organizations in the state. Juan's determination and foresight in the business world showed what could be done if one had the drive and fortitude to be the best they could be. He exhibited strength and fortitude from the get-go succeeding in whatever goal or endeavor he put his mind to. It had been a long and painful road, but in the end, he delivered with flying colors.

He and Sheila married soon after the trial. She bore him three children all of which were the spitting images of Sheila. They had none of Juan's features, but each had his drive to succeed.

Juan eventually contacted his parents and invited them to the condo to meet their daughter-in-law and their three grandchildren. After meeting his family, they were delighted and pleased with the turnaround in Juan's life and achievements after his banishment from home.

His parents enjoyed spending time with the grandchildren at their house or the condo. Occasionally driving them down to Disney World in Florida. The children appreciate the time spent with Grandma and Grandpa, cherishing every minute.

Juan's parents passed away a few years later. He grieved at their passing but enjoyed reconnecting and becoming reacquainted after the years of being separated. His life had come full circle, especially having his family around. Time seemed to heal all wounds; Juan and his family were a fine example of that quote.

Juan and Sheila had a long and successful marriage, along with three great kids. Both Sheila and Juan were proud parents; they seemed to have the perfect family, if there is such a thing. All three graduated from college, each becoming successful in their own field of endeavor.

As time passed, Sheila became ill and died of pancreatic cancer. She showed no symptoms until one day she became deathly ill and taken to the hospital for observation. While in the hospital, a series of test was performed; that's when Juan learned how ill she was. Sheila's stay in the hospital was short-lived. She had waited too long; there was nothing they could do except send her home. Not long after arriving back at the condo, she passed peacefully one night in her sleep. It came as a heavy blow to both Juan and their three children; they were going to miss her. A few years later, Juan passed.

In the meantime, the three children fully grown by now and working with their dad in the business they would eventually inherit. After Juan's death, each inherited one-third of their father's thriving business where they still work today.

The horse farm in Lexington became the showcase of the breeding circuit. Bobby Baker still worked there when he passed at the age of seventy-two. Juan's youngest son working on the farm took over the responsibility of managing the everyday operations and became a very successful horse breeder in his own rights.

The middle son inherited the loan company after earning his degree in accounting from Princeton. He was the only one who had knowledge in accounting and finance and the expertise in running a successful loan business. He was the obvious choice. He still runs the loan company and has since expanded into several larger cities throughout the Hoosier state.

The oldest, the daughter, took over managing the Oasis Watering Hole. She's the one with a bubbly attitude, a knack for communicating while being a force to reckon with when push comes to shove. She still works every day at the Oasis and has become a very successful businessperson in her own right.

The three works as one, running each individual entity to its fullest potential. They still try to get together for holidays and special occasions when time permits.

They are all married and have children of their own. They were the apple of their parents' eyes growing up. Juan and Sheila could not have been prouder of each in their own rights. It seemed only natural they follow in their father's footsteps after he passed. They assumed the responsibilities in running the association's businesses daily and strive to improve each business to its full potential, same as Daddy Juan.

ABOUT THE AUTHOR

William Wilson moved from Indiana to Florida in 1976, and retired in 2004. Mr. Wilson wore many hats during his long and colorful career. Served four years in the military during the early sixties. Became a bartender and bar owner several years after his stint in the military. He had the privilege traveling to several countries throughout Europe while stationed in Greece. Also, cruised extensively throughout the Caribbean after moving to Florida. Since retirement, Mr. Wilson has taken up a new vocation, that of writing.

His first novel *"The Ravenous Undertaker"* took several years to complete. Since that time, he's written three more novels. Writing has evolved into his number one passion, second only to reading. He has become not only an avid reader but writer. This is his published works.

CPSIA information can be obtained
at www.ICGtesting.com
Printed in the USA
LVHW112059191222
735554LV00004B/62

9 781959 450818